Georgette got up and put her empty glass on the table. Longarm raised his head. Georgette bent down a bit further and sought his lips with hers. Her tongue parted his lips and darted inside his mouth. Georgette slid down into his lap.

"Is this one of the times you didn't feel like telling me about a while ago?" he asked when they broke the kiss.

"You know it is. Now, please don't ask any more questions, Longarm. You're not any stranger to women. You know what I want you to do. Just go ahead and do it. . . ."

TABOR EVANS

LONGARM

AND THE
OUTLAW LAWMAN

A JOVE BOOK

LONGARM AND THE OUTLAW LAWMAN

A Jove Book/published by arrangement with
the author

PRINTING HISTORY
Jove edition/June 1983

ISBN: 0-515-06257-X

Jove books are published by Jove Publications, Inc.,
200 Madison Avenue, New York, N.Y. 10016. The words
"A JOVE BOOK" and the "J" with sunburst are trademarks
belonging to Jove Publications, Inc.

PRINTED IN THE UNITED STATES OF AMERICA

Chapter 1

Half a mile ahead the thread-thin line of the seldom-used trail zigzagged up a sharp rise. Dawn had brought a fitful wind whistling over the raw crests of the Continental Divide, but it was dying now as the sun moved toward noon.

Longarm twitched the reins lightly and the cavalry horse he'd requisitioned at Fort Russell stopped obediently. The paired hoofprints Longarm had been following were still fresh, their edges sharply defined in the light soil that covered the creamy limestone below it in a thin brown layer.

Easing himself to one side in the saddle, Longarm took a slim cheroot from his vest pocket and flicked a steely thumbnail over the head of a match. He studied the hoofprints while he puffed the cheroot into life.

Old son, he told himself thoughtfully through the cloud of blue-grey smoke that wreathed his bronzed face, *there ain't but one place that fellow can be headed for. Big Bitter Creek's the only water between here and Green River, and it's a silver dollar against a scrag hunk of cut-plug that he's riding one hell of a lot drier than you are.*

Since he had crossed the summer-shrunken headwaters of the North Platte three days earlier as he followed his quarry west into the arid Great Divide Basin of central Wyoming, Longarm had found no fresh water. Along the trail there had been only two brackish puddles, inches deep, their contents more mud than liquid. The horse had managed to snuffle up enough to keep it from suffering, and Longarm had nursed the contents of his canteen as he followed the trail he'd picked up at the saloon in Medicine Bow.

Clamping his teeth on the half-smoked cheroot, Longarm toed the roan into motion again. The hoofprints wound up the

1

trail to the crest of the ridge. The noon-high sun outlined their shallow depressions as thin crescents of shadow against the earth. As the horse carried him higher up the steep slope, still more ridges came into sight beyond the one he was mounting. Each one was a bit higher than the last, and the farther was outlined against the ever-present shimmer of heat haze that blurred the air and hid the western horizon.

Longarm didn't expect the shot that greeted him as he topped the ridge. The whistle of the rifle slug cut the air inches from his head, the sharp bark of the weapon coming a fraction of a second later. The second shot met only thin air as its menacing whine sang above the roan's empty saddle.

Even before the first report had begun echoing, Longarm had rolled from his saddle on the roan's off side. His sharply honed reflexes sent his hand back to grab the butt of his Winchester as soon as he started rolling to his left. He had swept the rifle out of its scabbard even before he began dropping to the ground.

Holding the Winchester in his right hand, Longarm broke his fall by planting his left hand flat on the rocky soil. The instant his toes hit the dirt he lowered himself to his knees, then stretched out flat on his belly. A third slug from the hidden sniper's rifle scored the front bow of Longarm's McClellan saddle and glanced off the sturdy birch bow beneath the leather. The scar left by the slug was only a short distance above the almost-empty canteen that hung from the saddlestrings.

Longarm realized that the bushwhacker was now making the horse a target. He scrabbled forward far enough to grab the reins and yank. The cavalry mount knew what it was expected to do, and dropped to the ground without even a protesting whinny.

Longarm sighed with relief. In the late summer heat of the Great Divide Basin a man on foot without a full canteen was as good as dead. He'd seen enough dried, shrunken bodies in the basin's arid expanse to prove that.

An almost inaudible crunch of boot soles on the thin soil beyond the crest of the ridge reached Longarm's keen ears. Moving noiselessly, he brought the Winchester's butt to his shoulder and waited quietly, certain that he had come to the end of the trail he'd been following.

It had not been a tremendously hard trail, once Longarm had made clear that he intended to follow it alone. He'd been set on the chase from Denver, not quite two weeks earlier, when Billy Vail had walked into the Windsor Hotel and found Longarm at his usual poker game in the private room off the bar.

"Cash in," Vail had told him curtly.

"Now, damn it, Billy!" Longarm had protested. "I'm just about to bust a losing streak that's been plaguing me for more'n an hour! Wait'll I finish out this hand." Without giving his chief time to repeat his command, Longarm had tossed a half eagle into the sizable pot that lay in the center of the table. "I'll boost it another five this time," he had said.

Vail opened his mouth to say something, changed his mind, and stood watching quietly while the betting went around the trio of players left with cards in their hands. The third man called. Longarm leaned back in his chair and laid his cards on the green felt tabletop, one by one: a deuce, another deuce, then two aces. He prolonged the suspense as long as possible by holding his fifth card shielded.

Finally, the player who had called said impatiently, "Damn it, if it's another deuce, I got you beat! If it's another ace—"

"Which it is," Longarm announced, laying down the card he'd been holding back. It was the ace of spades.

"It's your pot, then." The impatient player nodded, tossing his own hand on the discard stack.

"You aim to argue, Bob?" Longarm asked another player.

"Nope. He said it. Your pot."

Longarm raked the money from the center of the table into his hand. "I hate to leave you fellows so early but, as you can see, I ain't got much choice, with my boss here."

Vail indicated a hackney carriage waiting in front of the hotel as they reached the street. Longarm waited for his chief to get in and settled down beside him. The carriage started down Larimer Street.

"I guess you'll tell me when you get around to it what's got you prowling around so late, Billy," Longarm said after a few moments. "Not that I minded you getting me out of that game. At least I came away a winner this time. But it must be something important to bring you out after office hours."

"It is," Vail replied. "It's a case I've got no right to send you on, but there's no way I can dodge it."

"Well, go ahead," Longarm invited when Vail fell silent.

"Somebody's kidnapped Commissioner Mason's daughter," Vail replied. "And he's—"

"Wait a minute, Billy," Longarm broke in. "You mean

3

Mason, the federal land commissioner up in Wyoming Territory?"

Vail nodded. "It's not really our case, because no federal law's been broken. But Mason's come down from Cheyenne and got hold of Senator Pitkin, and Pitkin's been driving the Attorney General crazy, sending wires to Washington. So the long and the short of it is, we've got orders to find the kidnapper and the girl—whether it's our job or not."

"I got the idea that when you say we, you mean me," Longarm said thoughtfully.

Vail nodded. "That's about the size of it. I know you're due for a few days' leave, but you can make that up later."

"I'll just add it to what I'm still waiting to make up from last year," Longarm said philosophically. "Sooner or later, me and Uncle Sam will be even, I guess." He sat quietly while the hackney turned off Larimer Street into Broadway. "Well, go ahead and tell me about it, Billy. Now's as good a time as any for me to find out what I'm up against."

What he was facing had seemed simpler in listening to Vail than it had turned out to be in reality. The commissioner's daughter, Betty Mason, had been abducted when she started from home to downtown Cheyenne in response to a faked message from her father. A note signed "John Smith," demanding $20,000 ransom, had been delivered to the commissioner an hour after the girl disappeared. Two-Chin Smothers, the sheriff of Laramie County, had mishandled the case and Betty Mason's abductor had fled, taking his captive with him.

A week had passed since the kidnapping when Longarm arrived in Cheyenne. He'd listened to the story of confused sheriff's deputies and vain efforts to trace the kidnapper, then had laid down his plan to work alone on the case, and resisted all efforts to change his mind. The argument had wasted a day, but Longarm started out the next morning after getting the cavalry roan from Fort Russell.

For the next several days he'd prowled in widening circles around the capital city until at last he'd uncovered the trail fifty miles from Cheyenne in Medicine Bow. Whoever was using the alias "John Smith" hadn't bothered to hide his trail very effectively when he'd led his captive out of the little cow town and started southwest across the basin. Longarm had only to follow the hoofprints left by the mounts of "Smith" and the kidnapped girl until they mounted the ridge where he now lay, waiting for the abductor to show himself over the crest.

A rock sailed over the rim of the ridge and landed a yard from Longarm's head. Longarm did not move out of the position he'd taken, but brought his Winchester to his armpit, ready to shoulder the gun in one swift move. Again the sound of feet scuffling over dry earth reached his ears. Longarm slid the butt of the Winchester to his shoulder, his eyes fixed on the spot where the stone had come from.

Suddenly, a dozen feet to the left of the spot at which he was aiming, the kidnapper's head and shoulders burst over the rim. "Smith" had his rifle cradled ready to fire, and before Longarm could switch the muzzle of his own gun, the kidnapper let off a shot. But Longarm had moved the instant his adversary's head appeared. The slug plowed into the ground where he had been stretched out waiting.

Longarm triggered his own rifle before "Smith" could let off a second shot, but the movement he'd just finished threw off his usually accurate eye. The bullet from the Winchester chipped a boulder only inches away from the kidnapper, but by the time Longarm could get off a follow-up shot, the man had dropped out of sight again behind the ridge-crest.

Swearing at his own carelessness, Longarm uncoiled. Bent over to keep from silhouetting himself, he began running toward the spot where he'd seen the abductor. Grating footsteps from the opposite slope told him that "Smith" was running, too, on the far slope, taking a course roughly parallel to the one Longarm was following.

Suddenly the noise of running footsteps stopped. Longarm halted abruptly when he no longer heard the kidnapper's boots grating on the ground. Dropping to one knee, he inched upslope until he could look down the opposite side of the formation. Squinting into the glare of the early afternoon sun, he surveyed the terrain ahead. There was no one in sight, only the barren, boulder-strewn ground slanting down to a shallow valley that lay between the ridges.

Longarm knew that "Smith" had taken cover behind one of the big stones, but he had no clue as to which one the kidnapper had chosen. "Smith" himself solved the problem. To Longarm's right, he popped up from the cover he'd chosen and snapshot. Longarm was turning as "Smith" fired, and the slug went wild.

Longarm's quick reflexes brought him around, Winchester ready, and he fired without aiming. The slug hit the rock inches from the outlaw's face. Letting his rifle fall to the ground,

5

"Smith" brought his arm up over his eyes, but it was too late to shield them. Rock dust and chips spattered in the fugitive's face. With a scream of pain, he dropped out of sight behind the big boulder.

Levering a fresh shell into the rifle's chamber, Longarm started running toward the huge stone. He rounded its side and could see the kidnapper. "Smith" was on his knees, rubbing his face with both hands.

"Get your hands up!" Longarm called. "You ain't got a chance, and you know it!"

"Smith" did not obey. He clawed for his holstered Colt and had the gun out before Longarm could bring up his Winchester. He sent a slug from the pistol in the general direction of Longarm's voice. The bullet went wide by fifty feet. Longarm had the Winchester up by now, and "Smith" in its sights. He hesitated for a second as his finger tightened on the trigger. It wasn't his custom to gun down a helpless man.

"Smith" began swinging the muzzle of the revolver toward the sound of Longarm's voice again. Longarm reached a quick decision. "Smith" was still kneeling, his face contorted, his eyes slitted, but the muzzle of his gun was on Longarm now, and Longarm knew the danger of a lucky, unaimed shot finding him.

Longarm fired first. The Winchester's bullet was true. It caught the kneeling outlaw in the chest. "Smith" stiffened, then held himself erect for a single, frozen instant as he tried to lift the revolver. Then the impact of the rifle slug took effect and he toppled over backward, the Colt dropping to the ground.

Longarm walked up to where "Smith" lay. The wounded man's face was turned up, and his wide-brimmed Stetson had come off his head when he fell. Longarm recognized him at once in spite of the week's growth of beard.

"Hell," he said, "I knew your real name wasn't Smith, but I didn't get a clear look at you till now. You're Little Al Manning, if I recall correctly."

"That's right. You sent me up for that mail-coach job me and Dude Klemer pulled." Manning tried to grin, but the effort was not successful. "Looks like I won't be going up this time, don't it?"

Longarm nodded. "Looks like. Damn it, you oughtn't've made me shoot you."

"Wasn't you, it'd been somebody else, down the road a ways."

6

"Who was with you on this job, Al?" Longarm asked.

"Nobody. Figured it out and—pulled it—all by myself." The wounded man's breathing was labored now. "Knew that lard-ass sheriff—in Cheyenne—couldn't catch me." Manning gasped and squeezed his eyes shut with pain. After a moment he opened them and went on, "If I'd knowed they was going to send you after me, I ain't so sure I'd've took that girl."

"Where is she?" Longarm asked.

"Over the next ridge. I set out to backtrack. Didn't know you was so—so close." Manning shut his eyes again.

Longarm stood quietly for a moment, waiting for him to open them. Then he realized that the kidnapper was dead. Picking up Manning's guns, he went back to the spot where he'd left the roan. The horse had gotten to its feet, but still stood as though anchored in place. Mounting, Longarm toed the animal over the crest and to the top of the next ridge.

Just as Manning had told him, there were two horses there, and Betty Mason was in the saddle of one of them. Her ankles were bound with a rope that passed under her mount's belly and her hands were tied together and lashed to the saddlehorn. A none-too-clean bandanna gagged her mouth. Wide frightened eyes peered over the edge of the bandanna. They grew wider when she saw Longarm.

"Don't worry, Miss Mason," Longarm said quietly. "I'm a deputy U.S. marshal. It's all over now. We'll be starting back to Cheyenne soon as I clean things up here." He reined in beside the tethered horses and dismounted. Reaching up, he took the bandanna from the bound girl's face.

"Was that you shooting, Marshal?" she asked.

Longarm nodded and began unknotting the rope that bound her wrists. "I had to kill the man who kidnapped you."

"He deserved killing," she said, rubbing the rope burns on her wrists. "Why'd he have to pick me out to kidnap?"

"For the same reason most men go wrong, I'd say," Longarm replied as he worked at the rope that held her ankles. "Money." He freed her feet and helped her out of the saddle. "Now, are you all right?"

"Why, of course I am. That man—the one who kidnapped me—he threatened me with a lot of bad things, but he didn't do anything. Except I'm real thirsty right now." She looked around at the barren landscape. "And I'm going to have to—to go to the bathroom pretty soon."

"There's water in my canteen." Longarm handed it to her.

7

While she drank, he added, "I'm going to leave you here by yourself for a few minutes, while I pile some rocks on that dead man." He added quickly, "It's not something you'd want to watch. Unless you're afraid to stay here by yourself for a little while."

"You go on. I know what you have to do, and I don't want to watch. And don't worry about me being scared. I wasn't afraid of that outlaw, not after a while."

When she stood beside him, Betty Mason's head did not quite reach Longarm's shoulder. She looked up at him and smiled. "Well, my goodness! You're a real big man, Marshal—"

"Long's my name, Miss Mason. Custis Long."

"Oh, I've heard about you!" she said. "I've heard Daddy speak of you. Only he didn't always call you by your name. Sometimes he'd call you Longarm."

"That's a sort of nickname my friends use," Longarm said.

"Do you mind if I—"

"Not a bit, Miss Mason. I answer to it better'n I do to my right name."

"Then you'd better call me Betty. Or Bett. That's what my friends call me sometimes."

"That strikes me as a real fair swap, Betty. Now you just stay here, close to the horses. I'll go do my chores and be back in a few minutes."

Longarm wasted little time on Little Al Manning's sepulcher. The soil was too hard for him to dig without a pick and too thin to stay in place when piled on the corpse. Stones were plentiful, however, and it was the work of less than an hour to cover the outlaw's body with a heap thick enough to discourage the occasional coyote that might pass the deserted spot. He rode back to where Betty was waiting.

Her first words as he dismounted were, "Can we start back to Cheyenne right away, Longarm?"

"Not till we've filled the canteens. It's a three-day ride to the first water east of here. We've got to push ahead to Big Bitter Creek."

"But that's taking us the wrong way," she protested.

"You're right. But it's the closest good water to where we are right now. If we move along pretty good, we can make it there before it gets too dark to see."

Betty frowned, gazing across the barren ridge-tops that rose ahead of them. Then she shrugged, a surprisingly mature gesture. "Well, you were smart enough to find me, so I guess you'll be smart enough to get me home."

They rode west across the ridges, climbing higher as they penetrated the foothills of the Rockies. As the slow miles dropped behind them, the declining sun shone first on their chins, then flooded their faces. Longarm studied his companion. He'd been told her age was nineteen, but with her unblemished skin and clear blue eyes, Betty Mason could have passed for sixteen.

Like all those who lived close to the land in the West, she was tanned, but only to a light golden color that made her face glow in the light of the waning afternoon. Her hair was tawny, with bright, sun-bleached streaks, and was caught up in a loose knot at the nape of her neck. Her face was an imperfect oval— imperfect only because her jaw was a bit too square and jutting.

Below a high forehead, Betty's eyebrows were symmetrical, thick and unplucked, and shaded long lashes. Her cheekbones were round and high, her nose uptilted saucily. Her lips were a bit too full and red; they were a woman's lips in a girl's face. If she was conscious of Longarm's scrutiny, she did not show it.

They reached the top of an unusually high ridge and the ground fell away from them to the west, still bathed in sunlight. Longarm reined in and looked around. Downslope, a few yards off the trail, in a small patch of fresh green shrubbery, his eyes caught a glint of silver.

Longarm shook his head. "That's funny. Sure looks like a spring down there, but there wasn't one the last time I rode this trail. Maybe we won't have to ride all the way to Big Bitter Creek tonight, after all."

"Do you think the water would be good?"

"Likely it will, this high up. We'll ride over and find out. If it is, we can camp right by it and save about three hours of riding tonight and in the morning, too."

Walking their horses over, they reined in at the bubbling spring. Longarm swung out of his saddle and cupped his hand to bring a swallow of water to his mouth. It was cold and tasted sweet. "It's good water," he told Betty. "Dismount and we'll make camp."

Chapter 2

When the horses had been unsaddled and tethered at the edge of the patch of green that surrounded the spring, Longarm began exploring Manning's saddlebags. Ignoring the dead outlaw's few spare garments, he unwrapped the few thin packages that were done up in butcher's paper and shook his head.

"That Manning was about as careless in figuring out the grub he needed as he was in watching his backtrail," he told Betty.

"You mean there's nothing to eat?"

"Mighty little. You see what's laying there. A scrap of bacon end and that little stub of summer sausage and a few crackers."

"Surely you brought food with you?"

"Some, not much. Jerky and parched corn's about all I ever take with me when I'm on a trail this way. I wasn't figuring I'd have to scratch grub for anybody but myself."

Betty smiled. "I'm so hungry I'll eat whatever we've got. At least there's plenty of good, cool water." She looked at the little spring which bubbled from a cleft in a huge boulder that surfaced from the thin soil. The spring had formed a pool in a small depression a yard from its source. "Where did the spring come from, Longarm? You said that it wasn't here the last time you were along this trail."

"It wasn't, but it's been three or four years since I passed this way. I'd imagine the water's been down under the ground all the time, and that rock was sorta like a cork in a bottle. Maybe the rock just got old and split; maybe a lightning bolt hit it and cracked it. But, whatever happened, once the rock busted, the water just began bubbling out."

"Well, that little pool looks awfully good to me." Betty hesitated for a moment, then said, "I'd like nothing better than to get in it and bathe. I haven't had a bath since that terrible man grabbed me and started hauling me all over the Territory."

"It'll be dark in a little while. We'd better eat supper, such as it is, and soon as it's dark you can have your bath. I'll turn my back while you're in the water."

"That'll be wonderful. I know I'll feel better after I get all the dust and dirt off."

They ate the sausage and crackers, and were still hungry. Longarm got his travel rations out of his saddlebag and, after chewing on the dry victuals and drinking from the spring, their hunger was almost satisfied. While they ate, the sun made its slide down the western sky, and when they'd finished only a thin, luminous arc of its rim was visible. The low ground of the huge saucer they overlooked from the high ridge was invisible, shrouded in deep shadows.

"Once the sun's gone, it'll get dark right sudden," Longarm told Betty. "I'll fix up our beds while there's still light enough to see by."

"My blankets are on the cantle of my saddle," she said.

"You mean Manning didn't make you sleep with him?"

"He tried to attack me the second night out from Cheyenne. But when he untied my ankles, I kicked him where it hurts the most. After that he left me alone."

Longarm nodded. "That was smart." He started toward the saddles, turned back, and said, "Go on and have your bath, Betty. I'll walk off a ways and enjoy a cigar after I spread out our bedrolls."

Longarm selected the smoothest spot he could find on the rough, broken ground and spread their bedrolls a yard apart. He walked a few paces away, sat down on a convenient boulder, and lighted one of his long slim cheroots, wishing that he had a tot of Tom Moore to go with it. Darkness came as quickly as he'd said it would after the sliver of the sun's rim vanished. The moon had not yet risen, but a glow in the sky promised it would soon appear. He finished the cigar and ground its stub under his heel, then walked slowly back to the spring.

Betty was standing in the little pool, visible only as a shimmering column of white in the shrouded darkness. She gasped with surprise when she heard Longarm's boots crunching on the ground as he came close to the spring.

"I'm sorry," Longarm said. "I didn't stop to think you might not be finished bathing. Guess I ought've said something to let you know I was coming back."

11

"It's all right," she assured him. "It's my fault, Longarm. I should've been through by now, but this water feels so cool and so good after the hot day we've had—"

"Sure it does. You go ahead and enjoy it. I'll just walk on away and smoke another cigar while you get finished."

Unexpectedly, Betty said, "Wait, Longarm. You must feel as sticky and uncomfortable as I did. Don't you want a bath, too?"

"Well, I did sorta halfway figure I'd wash off after you got through. But I can wait awhile."

"I—I wouldn't mind a bit if you joined me."

"Now, wait a minute, Betty! It wouldn't be right for me to get in there with you. Why, you're just—"

"Longarm!" she broke in, her voice sharp. "If you say I'm still just a little girl, I'll be very, very angry."

"But you're only—"

"Nineteen. And a woman. I'm grown up enough to've been married, you know."

"No, I didn't. Your daddy didn't say anything about that when we talked back in Cheyenne."

"Daddy wouldn't. He'd like to forget it ever happened. And it's his fault that I'm not *still* married."

"Maybe you better tell me about it," Longarm suggested.

"There's not much to tell. I ran away—eloped—with a boy I loved very much, or thought I did at the time. That was two years ago. We got married in Denver and went on to Colorado Springs. It took Daddy six weeks to find us. He had influence enough to get the marriage annulled, and then he persuaded Lester's folks to move away. That's all there is to it."

Thoughtfully, Longarm said, "You'd never know you'd been through something like that, Betty, just looking at you."

"I suppose you mean that as a compliment."

"Why, sure. You don't look like you're a day more'n sixteen and never even been kissed."

"Thank you, Longarm. That's a nice thing for you to say."

"I mean it, too. And here I am, more'n twice as old as you, and I wouldn't feel right about—"

"About bathing with me?"

"It ain't just bathing, Betty, and you know it as well as I do. If I was to get in that water with you—"

Betty interrupted him again. "Longarm, if I hadn't wanted to do more than just bathe with you, I wouldn't have invited

12

you. Couldn't you tell I've been thinking about you almost from the first minute I saw you, back there on the trail?"

"I guess I had too many other things on my mind to notice."

"Well, you know now. Am I going to have to invite you again?"

"No," Longarm replied thoughtfully, beginning to unbutton his grey flannel shirt. "No, I don't expect you are."

Before taking off his boots, Longarm went over to the beds he'd spread and picked up his rifle. Undressed, he laid the Winchester on top of his clothing and put his gunbelt beside the rifle. Then he stepped to the edge of the little pool.

While Longarm undressed, the moon had started rising. It hung now with half of its radiant circle above the ridge to the northeast. Betty had sat down in the pond's center while she waited. The water came almost to her waist. In the soft light Longarm could see only a blur of white shoulders and arms, the outlined swelling of full, high breasts and the dark circles of their rosettes, and the shadowed suggestion of her eyes and mouth. He waded slowly toward her in the calf-deep water.

"One thing I couldn't do myself was to rub my back good," she said as he stopped beside her. "Will you, Longarm?"

"Why, sure."

Betty bent forward, the swell of her breasts more pronounced as she inclined her torso. Longarm stood behind her. He cupped his hands and dipped water over her back, then began to rub her soft skin as gently as he could. She worked her shoulders from side to side as he rubbed, then arched her back.

"Ah, that feels good," she sighed. "There's always a place in the middle of my back that I can't quite reach. But don't treat me like I'm made of china, Longarm. Rub harder."

Longarm increased the pressure of his hands on her back, and Betty stretched her arms in front of her, bending forward as he continued to run his callused palms up and down the satin smoothness of her skin. After he'd rubbed for a few minutes, Betty spread her arms wide and looked over her shoulder at him.

"I guess that's all I needed to feel bathed," she said. "It's your turn now. Sit down and I'll rub your back for you."

Longarm was glad to sit down. Feeling Betty's warm, water-slick skin under his hands while he thought of the implicit promise of what would eventually follow had brought him half erect. He sat down as Betty was standing up. She stood beside

13

him for a brief moment, and in the brightening moonlight he had a quick glimpse of her full, high breasts, the tips of her rosettes protruding now, the soft swell of her abdomen and thighs, and of the glistening drops of water that clung to her tawny pubic brush.

Betty moved behind him. Kneeling, she splashed Longarm's back with a shower of cool water, then began to rub. Her fingers encountered the raised welt of an old scar. She stopped rubbing and traced its outline with a fingertip.

"Isn't this from a bullet wound?"

"Most likely. That or a knife."

Betty's hands continued to explore Longarm's back. She exclaimed when her fingers found another scar, then another. Her hands moved to his ribs and encountered still more reminders of battles past.

"No wonder you're not sure what caused which scar!" she exclaimed. "How did you stand so many wounds?"

"The only way I know, Betty. Grit my teeth and hang on. There's times it ain't easy, but it's worked so far."

Now Betty's hands were wandering from Longarm's torso in their exploration. She stroked his cheeks and chin, smoothed the brown moustache that curled like the horns of a longhorn steer. Her hands sought his chest and stroked the thick mat of curls on it before she fingered the bands of muscle below the curls, pressed on his taut abdomen, and moved down to his hips. Longarm had softened and shrunk when he sat down in the cold water, but her caresses were once more bringing him erect. Betty slid her hand down past his hips and reached around to encircle his shaft.

"My, you're big!" she exclaimed. "I didn't expect . . ." Her voice trailed off as she tightened her fingers around him and felt him swell as she fondled him.

Longarm stood up, pulling Betty to her feet. She did not release him even when he turned to face her. She raised her face to his. Their lips met in a kiss, gentle at first, but growing in intensity as Betty's hand tightened on Longarm's swelling erection. Her lips parted and their tongues met and entwined.

Longarm broke the kiss at last, and began caressing Betty's bare shoulders with his lips and tongue. As he trailed a line of kisses down to her quivering breasts Betty's hands tightened on his erection and she tried to pull him toward her. Longarm was bending over her now, moving his lips from one to the other of her breasts. Their tips were erect and firm, jutting hard

14

from her dark pebbled rosettes. Betty moaned and her hands tightened on Longarm's shaft.

"Take me now, Longarm!" she gasped. "I can't wait until we get to the bedroll! I want you in me right this minute!"

She pulled herself close to Longarm and tried to lift her legs to bring his jutting erection between them, but he was too tall. Still grasping his shaft firmly with one hand, Betty threw her free arm around his neck and tried to lift herself up to match his height, but could not.

Longarm grasped her waist in his strong hands and lifted her. Betty clung to him with the arm she'd wrapped around his neck and with her other hand guided him between her outspread thighs. Longarm felt her wet warmth and lunged. He went into her shallowly, and Betty moaned expectantly. When Longarm made no move to go into her deeper, she wrapped her legs around his waist and locked them, and pulled herself toward him.

Soft cries of pleasure and surprise flowed from Betty's lips as she drew her hips forward until Longarm was fully buried in her. Her body tautened, she wriggled and cried out, and Longarm could feel the muscles of her stomach contracting and relaxing under his hands until at last she went through a final, frantic convulsion and relaxed.

"Oh, no!" she cried. "I didn't want to let go so soon, but I couldn't stop! Oh, Longarm, you didn't—"

"No. Not yet," he assured her. "Not for a while."

"That's good," she sighed. After a moment she looked up at him and asked, "Do I weigh too much, or can you just carry me to the bedroll? Because I feel so good with you inside me the way you are that I don't want to change a thing."

Instead of answering, Longarm waded the few steps to shore and carried her to the blankets he'd spread. They'd been out of the water for quite some time, and only Longarm's calves and feet were wet. Still holding Betty by her hips, both her arms now locked around his neck, Longarm let himself down on his knees and lowered her to the blankets, letting his body move with her, the fleshly bond connecting them still unbroken.

With a sigh of contentment, Betty lay back. She unclasped her ankles and stretched her legs high. Looking up at Longarm, she said, "Whenever you feel like it, I'm ready to start again."

Longarm did not wait for a second invitation. He began thrusting, slowly and deliberately, sinking into her full length and holding himself buried inside her for a moment before withdrawing to begin another deep penetration.

"Oh, yes," she sighed. "That's wonderful. I could stay like this forever, feeling you push into me until I'm so filled up that I can't think of anything else."

"Go on and enjoy it," Longarm told her. "I sorta like it myself."

Betty's passive enjoyment did not last long. She began to shiver into life, her inner muscles contracting each time that Longarm reached the end of one of his deliberate strokes. Though Longarm felt himself mounting to a climax, he did not hurry. He was not surprised when Betty was suddenly galvanized into motion. She began meeting Longarm's thrusts, then outpacing him.

"Now," she panted. "Now, Longarm! Faster, faster!"

Longarm speeded up. Betty was gasping, her hips twisting in wild gyrations. Longarm knew that she was near the point of no return, and began relaxing his own control. He was ready when Betty arched her back and drove up to meet his downward thrust while a stream of joyous cries flowed from her throat. He let himself go and jetted, pushing hard against her tautly quivering body until she sighed deeply and went limp. Then he let himself relax on Betty's soft, still pulsing body while he drained.

"I suppose I knew there were men like you around somewhere," Betty whispered in Longarm's ear after they'd lain quietly for a while. "I didn't know how much more of a woman I'd feel after I'd been with one, though."

"Maybe it's all part of growing up," he suggested.

"I guess. But there are still a lot of things I've got to learn about." She sighed.

They lay in silence for a few moments, then Betty said, "Longarm, you're older than I am, and I guess you've learned a lot about women. Haven't you?"

"A little bit."

"Don't treat me like a baby! I really want to know!"

"You tell me what you want to know, Betty. I'll try to answer you if I can."

"That's better." She thought for a moment and said, "Now, out there in the pond, I felt different to when we came up here and lay down. Why?"

"Because different positions make things feel different."

"Is it true that women can do it on top?"

"Sure."

16

"And does it feel different then? Better? Because Lester never would try it that way."

"I guess it depends on the woman."

"And from behind, like dogs and horses and cattle?"

"Well, that'd depend on the woman, too."

"I want to find out for myself, Longarm. You're the first grown man I've ever been with, you know."

"I sorta figured that."

"Did I do all right? Was I as good as a grown-up woman?"

"Every bit."

"Then will you show me what it's like, the other ways?"

"Tonight?"

"Of course. Unless you're too tired."

"Well, I ain't all that tired."

"Will you, then?"

"If that's what you want."

"It is. And I know how I want to start. With me on top. What do I do first?"

Before Betty's curiosity had been satisfied, the moon had set and the false dawn was showing in the east. They fell into a deep sleep and woke only when the rising sun touched their faces. In unspoken agreement, they neither kissed nor clung. Both of them were aware that the ride back to Cheyenne was a long one, and that there would be two more nights for them to share.

"I don't know enough words to thank you properly for bringing Betty safely back to us, Marshal Long," George Mason said after listening to his daughter's greatly censored story of her rescue and return.

"Why, I don't need no thanks for doing my duty, Mr. Mason," Longarm replied. "That's all part of my job."

"It may be, but I'm still grateful. And to think that you found her before that vicious criminal harmed her."

"Betty's as much responsible for that as I was," Longarm said. "You've got a mighty smart, brave girl there."

"Thank you, Marshal," Betty said demurely. "If I knew how to thank you any more than I have already, I'd do it."

"Like I said, I been thanked enough. Now, I'd better be on my way. My chief's going to be wondering what's happened to me."

"I'm afraid he already is." Mason took a sheaf of telegraph flimsies from his inner coat pocket and handed them to Longarm. "I read them, Marshal. They weren't in envelopes when the messenger delivered them, so I allowed myself the liberty."

"I don't guess there's anything secret in 'em," Longarm replied. He leafed through the flimsies quickly. They were much the same, all of them urging Longarm to wind up his case and hurry back to Denver. He told Mason, "I'll send a wire from the depot that I'm back and on my way. Billy Vail must have some new case he wants to send me out on."

"You're sure you can't stay? You'd be very welcome as our guest," Mason said.

"Thanks, Mr. Mason. I appreciate it. But when my chief says for me to get on the job, I'd better do it without wasting time. I'll catch the night train to Denver."

"Will you be back soon?" Betty asked.

"I can't say, Betty. I might be back here tomorrow, or I might not get back for a year."

"Well, when you do, remember Daddy's invitation. And thank you again for everything you did for me."

Longarm looked at Betty. Her face wore a cherubic smile. Keeping his own face expressionless, Longarm replied, "You don't need to thank me any more, Betty. I was glad to do what I did."

Chapter 3

"It sure as hell took you long enough to get here," Billy Vail commented sourly as Longarm walked into his office the next morning. He sniffed at the odor of bay rum that had come in with Longarm's entrance and added, "Wasted a lot of time stopping at the barbershop, too. Didn't you read those wires I sent you? I said to get here as fast as you could!"

"Now, simmer down, Billy!" Longarm protested. "I got on the first train out of Cheyenne, but it didn't pull into Denver until nine o'clock last night. Anyhow, look at that." He pointed to the banjo clock that hung on the wall. "At least give me that much credit. I got here on time this morning."

"Which is more than you do four or five days out of every week," Vail growled.

Longarm hooked the toe of his boot around a leg of the red morocco upholstered chair that stood against the wall and dragged it up to Vail's desk. He settled into it, saying, "All right, Billy. You won't feel good until you tell me what's gnawing at your belly button, and I can see it's going to be a long story." Fishing a slim cheroot from his pocket, he lighted it and leaned back. "Go on, now. Fire away."

Vail had exhausted his supply of impatience. He pawed through the piles of papers that littered his desk and finally dug out a printed sheet from the third stack. He passed it over to Longarm, saying, "Take a look at this."

Longarm unfolded the sheet and saw that it was one of the standard "WANTED" circulars which the office received by the dozen every week. He glanced at the sketch portrait at the top of the flyer and frowned. Then he looked up at Vail and said, "Damned if this fellow don't look enough like Gil Bright to be his twin brother."

19

"Read the description," Vail told him. "It makes me sick at my stomach to say so, but I've got a feeling that the man that flyer was put out on *is* Gil Bright."

"Oh, hell, Billy! This flyer's got nothing to do with Gil. It couldn't."

"I don't suppose you've swapped letters with him lately?"

"You know I ain't much of a hand at letter-writing. Come to that, Gil's not either. But we don't need to do a lot of writing back and forth, Billy. We know each other too well. Hell, if Gil was to walk into this office right now, we'd be talking together just like we used to when we was teamed up."

"Yes, I know how that is," Vail said. "I've got a lot of good friends from away back when, and we don't swap letters, either. And I'd say about them the same thing you've just said about Gil Bright."

"Well, you don't need to worry about Gil. He's in Fort Smith, doing his job at old Judge Parker's court."

"No. He's not."

Longarm's head snapped up and he stared with a puzzled frown across the desk. "You sure about that?"

Wordlessly, the chief marshal passed Longarm a folded telegraph flimsy. Longarm read:

DEPUTY MARSHAL GILBERT BRIGHT NOT AVAILABLE TO REPLY STOP ON EXTENDED LEAVE OF ABSENCE STOP CHIEF CLERK TOLBERT

"Well, if Gil ain't on duty, where in hell is he?" Longarm demanded.

"I'm not as interested in where he is right now as I am in where he was when that Indian agent got shot in the Nation," Vail replied. "It's all in the flyer. Read it, damn it!"

Longarm scanned the terse, matter-of-fact lines. A $500 reward was offered by the Indian Bureau for the arrest and conviction of one Shiner, first name unknown, wanted for the murder of Timothy Clark, agent of the Bureau, at the settlement of Broken Arrow, Indian Territory. The description of the wanted man followed, and when he came to the third line of the description, Longarm half rose from his chair and slapped his palm with a report like a pistol shot on Vail's desk.

"Damn it, Billy! I'm starting to think that hunch of yours is right, even if I don't want to believe it is! There ain't two men walking around that fits the same description, right down to that missing little finger of Gil Bright's."

Vail nodded slowly. "I was waiting for you to get to that."

"But why in hell would Gil want to kill an Indian agent?" Longarm frowned. "Me and Gil Bright buddied for a lot of years. You know how it is when two lawmen work together for a long time. If they ain't twin brothers to start off, they get like twins after a while. But I don't have to tell you that."

"No, you don't," Vail agreed. "I've got my own buddies, men I served with on the Texas Ranger force years ago. Some of them I haven't seen for ten years or more, but even now I'd know how they'd act in a tight spot if we got in one together."

Longarm was only half listening. As much to himself as to Vail, he said, "There was two years when me and Gil was both deputy town marshals together, and both of us trying to get appointed U. S. Marshals. Gil got his appointment first, and I was about six weeks behind him. Then we both put in a hitch training, down in New Orleans, where they start all the new men."

"Then I got you both up here in Denver." Billy nodded. "And you made a right good team. How long was Gil here? Four, five years?"

"Close to five. When Washington transferred him to Little Rock, he didn't much want to go, except that it got him close enough to where his mother lives so he could get to visit her now and again. That's the only reason he took the transfer."

"I remember," Vail said soberly. "You tried to get a transfer there, too, but there wasn't an opening. You know, I took that kind of personal at first, but I got over it after I understood why you wanted to go."

"I told you why at the time, Billy. Hell, I never did have anything against you as a boss. Still don't."

"Yes. I'm not sure I believed you at first."

"Well, even if me and you don't always see eye to eye on everything that comes along, I ain't tried to leave since then, have I?"

"No. I'll give you that. But we're getting away from Gil Bright. Maybe you'd better light up another one of those stinking stogies before I go on with it."

"You mean there's more?"

"I'm afraid so."

Vail leaned back and waited while Longarm pulled a cheroot out of his vest pocket and lighted it. He waited so long after the cigar was glowing that Longarm got nervous. "Well, Billy,

21

if you got something else to get off your chest about Gil, you might as well spit it out," he said.

Vail opened a desk drawer and took out a thin sheaf of papers. He unfolded them and said, "After I got that flyer with the description, I remembered looking at some flyers that had come in earlier."

"Not more that reminded you of Gil?"

"They didn't when I'd looked at them the first time," Vail replied soberly. "But you know how a man's mind gets after he's been in our line of work a while."

"Sure. You see something and don't give it no mind for a while. Then you see something else, and all of a sudden you connect things up, and there you've got a case."

"That's as close to being right as anybody'll ever come to describing it, I guess," Vail nodded. "And that flyer I tied up to Gil was sticking in my mind pretty tightly. So, when I remembered these, I went back to the file and dug 'em out."

Longarm extended a hand for the flyers, but Vail shook his head.

"What's the matter, Billy?" Longarm asked. "Don't you think I'm entitled to see 'em?"

"Oh, it's not that. I've already picked out the key things in them that might take you a while to get around to. It'll save time if I just hit the high spots."

"All right," Longarm said soberly. "Go on and hit."

Vail lifted the first of the flyers. "This one's almost three months old. It's a federal want for a man who bushwhacked a U.S. attorney right in Little Rock."

"An attorney from Judge Parker's court?"

"Yes. The same court Gil was assigned to. There were three witnesses to the killing. The murderer wore a mask, so nobody saw his face. But how about the description?" Vail read from the flyer. "Tall, thin, and when he ran from the scene of the killing he favored his left leg."

Longarm frowned. "One of Gil's ankles was busted when a horse bucked him off and stepped on his leg—his left leg, unless I disremember. That ankle never did knit right. You wouldn't notice anything if he was just walking around, but when he ran, Gil would limp and favor it, all right."

"That's the way I recall it, too," Vail said. "I just wanted to see if you remembered it the same way." He put the first flyer aside and picked up the second. "This one came in about six weeks ago. A guard at the federal pen in Leavenworth was murdered. Somebody gunned him down in a saloon where he'd stopped like he always did on his way home after his shift, to have a drink."

"And the description of the killer fits Gil? Limp and all?"

"There's a good description of the killer, and it fits Gil, but it doesn't mention him limping. The killer didn't run this time, though. He just turned and walked out of the saloon, cool as you please, before anybody could stop him."

"I ain't sure I'll go along with you tagging Gil for that one, Billy," Longarm said. "Why in tunket's name would he want to shoot a prison guard?"

"That's something I can't answer. The reason this flyer stuck in my mind was the way the killer was described and because the man who was killed was a federal officer connected with law enforcement."

"Well . . ." Longarm's voice showed his reluctance to accept Vail's theory. "Well, maybe. But I still won't say I'm sure."

"There's only one more." Vail unfolded the last flyer. "This one's right fresh. A deputy sheriff in North Platte was shot on a downtown street a week ago by a man who'd followed him out of the bar in a hotel there."

"Why'd you pick that one out, Billy?"

"You'll see, when I finish. First, the description of the killer mentions that the little finger of his left hand was missing. Second, the description fits Gil Bright: tall, thin, dark-haired. And, third, when the men in the saloon heard the shooting and ran out into the street, the killer began running. And he limped."

"On his left leg?"

"It doesn't say in the flyer. But it'd be a real long shot if there were two killers out murdering lawmen who fitted the same description and both limped. Wouldn't you say so?"

Longarm didn't answer, but sat silently for a long while. He'd finished his cheroot long ago and tossed the butt in the spittoon that stood at the corner of Vail's desk. Absently, he took out another of the long, slender cigars and lighted it. His face was puckered in thought and his eyes weren't really seeing the familiar details of the chief marshal's office.

Vail finally broke the silence. "Well?"

"I'm trying to decide whether I'm going to be sick to my stomach, Billy. I guess I ain't, but I sure feel like it."

"You've got the same feeling I've had ever since I began putting all these odd pieces together."

Longarm's voice had a foreign note of pleading when he

asked Vail, "You sure there ain't some way we could be wrong? When you come right down to it, all we been doing's guessing."

"Not guessing. Deducing. Damn it, Longarm, we've both been lawmen long enough to know the difference."

"Oh, sure. But that's sorta like stirring sugar into honey. It don't make it taste no sweeter."

"Do you think we're wrong?" Vail asked.

For several moments the ticking of the banjo clock was the only sound that broke the room's silence. Then Longarm shook his head. "No, Billy. I don't."

"We've both seen lawmen go bad," Vail said quietly. "It's not something that happens often, but it does happen. You know that as well as I do. And when a lawman goes wrong, it's just like having one bad apple in a barrel. If somebody doesn't take the bad one out and get rid of it, pretty soon the rot spreads to the whole barrel."

"I got me a hunch about what you're easing up to," Longarm told Vail. "You ain't come right out and said so yet, but I can see it's coming." He stopped, his eyes slitted as he searched his chief's face. When Vail said nothing, Longarm went on. "You're about to tell me that I'm going to be the fellow that reaches into the barrel and gets the bad apple out. Am I right?"

Vail nodded. "You worked with Gil Bright for a long time. You know how he thinks better than anybody else would. You know how he'll act, given a situation."

"But, damn it, Billy, Gil's my friend! Hell, we've backed each other up in more shootouts than I like to think about. We've drunk out of the same bottle and split our last grains of parched corn. We've been through bad times and good ones side by side. You can't order me to go bring him in—because you and me both know that he'll be stretching a rope."

"I'm not ordering you to bring Gil in," Vail said, in what was for him a gentle tone of voice. "I'm asking."

Longarm thought for a moment. "What if I was to say no?"

"Are you?"

"Not right yet. I'm just asking what you'd do."

"I'll tell you that when you give me your answer."

Now it was Vail's turn to sit quietly and wait. When Longarm showed no sign of replying to the question, Vail went on, "I don't think I need to waste time explaining what the man who goes after Gil Bright will be up against."

"I don't guess you do. Gil's been wearing a badge for a

24

long time. He's seen all the tricks crooks use when they're on the dodge, and I don't imagine he's forgotten a one."

"You've seen all of them, too," Vail pointed out. "And your memory's as good as Gil's."

"Oh, I don't argue that, Billy. I likely wouldn't be here right now if I hadn't learned a lot of lessons from some of the snakey sons of bitches I've gone out after."

"Whoever goes out to find Gil Bright and bring him in needs to be able to think the same way Gil will be thinking," Vail said thoughtfully. He was not looking at Longarm, but at the big map that covered most of the wall on one side of the office. "He has to keep his mind one jump ahead, though. Gil's going to be doubling back, changing his clothes, and doing everything he can to stay free, once he realizes somebody's after him."

"That's something else I won't argue about," Longarm agreed, quietly and thoughtfully.

"There's nobody who fits into the job like you do."

"Granted you're right, Billy—I still ain't sure I got the stomach for it."

"I could order you to take it, you know."

"A minute ago you said you wouldn't do that. Have you changed your mind so quick?"

"No. I'm still asking."

Longarm repeated the question he'd asked earlier. "What if I was to say no?"

"I'd send somebody else. There's nobody who'd handle the case as well as you, though. Or I might decide to go myself."

"Billy, you've been riding that damn desk so many years I misdoubt you'd be able to stay in a saddle on a horse."

Longarm's smile was strained, but it was a smile, the first that Vail had seen on his face since Gil Bright's name had been mentioned as a wanted killer.

"Don't underestimate me," Vail said. He smiled, too, while he waited for Longarm to reply. Before the silence grew too strained, the chief marshal asked, "Well? Are you going to give me an answer? Yes or no?"

"Damn it, Billy, you know it's gotta be yes. Was I to say no, you'd send somebody else, and they might wind up getting killed. Or killing Gil without him ever having a fair trial. I can't sit by and let that happen."

"It took you long enough to figure that out."

"Oh, I saw it real clearly, right from the first. But I just

25

couldn't talk myself into taking on the job, not until right now. And it still turns my stomach, thinking about what I'll be going out to do."

"I want Gil brought in alive, you know."

"Sure. So do I."

"And I want you alive to bring him in."

"Don't worry, Billy. I ain't starting out to get myself killed, even if Gil Bright's one of the best friends I ever had."

"He'll be unpredictable," Vail warned.

"I know that. Like you said, I got to think ahead of him."

"As long as you've made up your mind, there's no use wasting any more time." Vail opened his desk drawer again and took out a fat envelope. He handed it to Longarm.

Longarm took the envelope and hefted it. He asked Vail, "What's this, Billy? You giving me orders to follow because you can't go along yourself to tell me how to handle the case?"

"You know better than that," Vail replied.

"Well, it's got too much in it just to be a travel and expense voucher."

"It's a little bit more than that. You know that fellow down in the district building superintendent's office? The one that draws pictures?" Longarm nodded, and Vail went on, "I had him make up a copy of Gil's picture from that flyer. And since you're likely starting a long chase, I had the clerk make up a dozen blank travel vouchers and ten blank express vouchers. Use them whatever way you need to, Long. You won't be asked any questions about anything you do this time."

Longarm whistled. "I never saw you hand out a package like this one before."

"It's not likely you ever will again. But I'm not making the mistake of underestimating Gil Bright. You're going to be on a long, tough chase. You won't have time to stop and wire the office here for expenses or new travel authorization."

"You were sure from the start that I'd take this case on, weren't you, Billy?"

"No. Knowing you, I wasn't, and I damn sure wasn't going to order you to, knowing the way things stand between you and Gil. I'm not sure I'd have taken it, if I was wearing your boots. But I thought I might as well have everything ready, if you did."

Longarm stood up. "As long as I'm going, there ain't much use wasting time. That last killing, Billy, up in North Platte. How long's it been since it happened?"

"A week. Closer to two, now, counting the time it took you to close the case you were on up in Cheyenne."

"It's still the only trail that ain't stone cold." Longarm took his watch from his vest pocket. "The special cars the UP runs up to the main line to connect with the Limited will be pulling out of here at noon. I'll be on one of 'em."

"I thought you might be." Vail got to his feet. "One more thing. Forget about reports. Wire if you need anything, but let the paperwork wait until you're back here with Gil Bright."

"I wasn't figuring on doing a lot of writing, Billy. And don't wish me luck. I ain't rightly sure yet how I feel about this damn case."

In his rooming house on the unfashionable side of Cherry Creek, Longarm moved with swift efficiency to prepare for what he knew might be a long trip. After cleaning his Winchester, he took the cylinder out of his Army Model Colt .44. He swabbed it with powder solvent and ran a solvent-soaked rag through the barrel before renewing the thin film of oil on the revolver's ratchet and taking off the sideplate and butt-plates to clean and oil the already spotless action. His derringer got the same care before he snapped it back on his watch chain. He put a full box of fresh cartridges for each gun in his saddlebags.

His other preparations took less time. He rolled his blankets and ground cloth, including a spare pair of long johns and a fresh grey flannel shirt in the roll. Then he took a quick look at the fittings on his McClellan saddle, regretting that he didn't have time to stop for repairs to the torn leather of the pommel where Manning's slug had cut a groove. Nor did he have time to replenish his depleted emergency rations. That could be done when he got to North Platte.

Saddle in one hand, rifle in the other, bedroll balanced on one shoulder, Longarm walked from the rooming house across the Cherry Creek bridge to Colfax Avenue, where he knew he could flag a hackney cab that would get him to the depot. He tried not to think about the case he was starting on. He knew it might well be the toughest one he'd faced since pinning on his badge.

Chapter 4

Just before sunset, Longarm swung off the UP Limited when it braked to a stop at the North Platte depot and hurried along the platform to the baggage car. He got there just in time to grab his saddle from the baggagemaster before the bag smasher had a chance to throw it from the car to the platform. Longarm waited for the Limited to pull out before shouldering his saddlebags and bedroll and starting across the tracks to the Pawnee Hotel.

"I guess you still got that little livery stable behind the hotel, for somebody like me who needs a horse?" he asked the clerk as he signed the register.

"Of course, Mr.—" The clerk read Longarm's signature without turning the fat registery ledger around and quickly amended himself. "Marshal Long. Do you need the horse at once?"

"I ain't right sure. Have the boy take my saddle out there, and if it don't put you out too much, save me a good horse in case I need one later on."

"Be glad to, Marshal. If there's anything else you need, just let us know."

"Sheriff's office is still in the same place, I guess?"

"Sure is. You'd know where the courthouse is, since I take it you've been here before."

Longarm wasted little time in his room, staying just long enough to wash the cinders and ash off his hands and face. He rubbed his chin experimentally, decided he could do without a shave until later, and started for the courthouse.

Sheriff Delaney's face shriveled into a thoughtful frown when Longarm introduced himself. "Long? You wouldn't be the man they call Longarm, would you?"

28

"Some folks call me that," Longarm admitted.

"Hell, I've heard about you. Who're you after here in North Platte?"

"It's more'n likely the fellow I'm after's not even around here any longer, Sheriff. And I misdoubt you ever found out his name, but he's the man who killed your deputy a few weeks back."

"That son of a bitch!" Delaney exploded. "I'd give a lot to get my hands on him, Long! Pure damn cold-blooded murder's what it was!"

"Maybe you'd better tell me about it," Longarm suggested.

"There's not much to tell, but sit down and take a load off of your feet. I'll give you what I can."

Longarm nodded and settled back into the chair Delaney indicated while he listened to the sheriff's story.

Ed Samuels, who had just gone off duty, was standing next to his son-in-law at the Roundhouse Saloon. They paid no attention to the man who walked up to the bar and stood behind Ed. Samuels and his son-in-law were talking about family matters when the newcomer tapped Samuels on the shoulder.

"Excuse me," he said. "Didn't we get acquainted in Dodge City a year or so ago?"

Samuels shook his head. "It's been a good ten years since I seen Dodge, mister. Never stayed there long, either."

"Maybe it was somewhere else. Coffeyville? Independence?"

"Nope," Samuels had replied. "I've been here in North Platte three years. Before that I was a railroad detective for the Kansas Pacific."

"I guess you worked the army spur that ran from Wichita to Fort Dodge?" the stranger said.

"Sometimes. Why?" Samuels was getting irritated and it showed in his voice. "Listen, if you're trying to find some old friend of yours, mister, it sure ain't me. As far as I recall, I never saw your face before."

"Oh, you're right, I'm sure. Sorry I bothered you."

Samuels turned back to his interrupted conversation. The inquisitive newcomer finished his drink and put his glass on the bar. Then, unnoticed by anyone, he drew a revolver from his belt, pushed the muzzle into the base of Samuels's skull, and pulled the trigger. The shot and Samuels crumpling to the floor drew the attention of the half-dozen men in the saloon.

At first, no one realized that Samuels had been shot from behind. The bullet had smashed through his spinal cord and plowed through his brain, coming out of his forehead; the men who'd run to cluster around him assumed that the blood on the dead man's face had come from the bullet's entry wound.

In the confusion, the stranger quietly made his way to the door and pushed through the batwings. By the time the men in the bar connected the shooting and the stranger, the killer was a hundred yards away. Three or four of the men from the bar started to chase the murderer, yelling to the few people on the street to stop him. The killer began running, and that was when the pursuers noticed his limp.

Before the pedestrians ahead of him on the street understood that they were being asked to stop the running man, the fugitive had ducked between two buildings and disappeared. As far as the sheriff knew, nobody had seen him after that.

"And I don't know where he came from or where he disappeared to, any more than I know his name," the sheriff concluded. "I got out all the men I could rouse and made up a posse. We went through North Platte like a dose of salts, but there wasn't any trace of him by that time."

"You got a good description of him, though. At least, you described him pretty good on the 'WANTED' flyer you put out."

"Is that what's brought you to North Platte? You're looking for that killer, too?"

"That's about the size of it, Sheriff. Any help you can give me—"

"Not a hell of a lot," Delaney confessed. "If you know his name, you know more about him than I do. But there's one thing that didn't go on that flyer because we didn't know about it until after the thing was all printed up. The killer had a bushy black moustache. Not trained, like yours—just straggly."

"Are you sure about that?"

"Real sure."

"How'd you come to miss a thing like that when you wrote up your flyer, Sheriff?"

"Why, Ed's son-in-law—Buddy Cane's his name—was so busy tending to getting Ed's body to the undertaker and then soothing down the family that I didn't get to talk to him but a minute or two before I wrote out that flyer. Aside from Ed,

Buddy was the only one that got a good look at the killer's face."

"And that's why the moustache got left off, then." Longarm nodded. "You haven't put out another flyer?"

"There didn't seem to be much use. Tell me something, Marshal Long. If you'd just killed a man in cold blood and was running away, what would you do with that moustache of yours?"

"I'd shave it off." Longarm nodded. "I see your point." He took out a cheroot and lighted it before asking, "What about the gun the killer used? Did Cane see it?"

"He said he just got a glimpse of it. As far as I could tell from his description, it was a pocket pistol. You'd know the kind. Stub barrel, nickel-plated. Gambler's gun, whore's gun. Probably .32 caliber."

"You didn't find the bullet? You said it went through Samuels's head and came out his forehead."

Delaney cleared his throat. "To tell you the truth, Marshal Long, I didn't look for it. There wasn't time right after Ed got shot. We were all busy trying to run down the bastard that did it. And—well, after we finally gave over looking and Ed was put away, it seemed to me like it'd be nothing but a waste of time. Hell, Ed was buried, the killer'd disappeared, and I don't mind saying right now, I don't think you nor anybody else is going to find him."

"That's as might be. You said you searched the town right away. Didn't you find any kind of trace of him?"

"Oh, we found out where he'd been holed up, after it was too late. There wasn't a thing left in the room he stayed in but a bunch of dirty handkerchiefs."

"That don't make much sense, does it?" Longarm frowned.

"No. It didn't to us. But there was a big pile of 'em in one corner of the room. That was the only trace he'd left."

"Handkerchiefs," Longarm repeated, the frown still on his face. "What kind of handkerchiefs?"

"No special kind, just like you'd buy at any general store anyplace, the kind that sells six for a nickel. We showed 'em to the stores here in town, but nobody could say for sure whether they'd sold 'em or not. Just plain white handkerchiefs, that's all they were. All snotted up, though. As close as I could tell, they'd been used but never washed."

Longarm made a mental note to find out more about the

handkerchiefs later if he could. He asked Delaney, "Ed Samuels's son-in-law's somewhere around town, I guess?"

"Sure. Lives over on G Street. It's just a step or two from here. You want me to take you over there and introduce you?"

"I'd take it right kindly, Sheriff Delaney."

Buddy Cane was an agreeable young man, still somewhat shaken over his father-in-law's murder. His story was a virtual repetition of the sheriff's until Longarm began asking questions.

"You didn't see the killer's gun until he fired, then?" Longarm asked.

Young Cane shook his head. "No. When Ed started toppling over, I saw the man's hand holding the gun. A little shiny one."

"I don't guess you'd know the make?"

"Marshal, I don't carry a gun. Never have. I don't know one from another."

"You did see the killer before he shot, though?" Longarm persisted. "While he was talking to your father-in-law?"

"Why, sure. Ed had turned around away from me to talk to the fellow. I got a pretty good look at him."

"Did he have a coat on?"

"No. Just a vest. He wore a white shirt under it. A high collar shirt with a little necktie like yours." The young man nodded to indicate Longarm's string bow.

"Since he wasn't wearing a coat, you ought to've noticed if he wore a pistol belt, with a gun in a holster," Longarm suggested.

"Now, come to think of it, I would've. And I'll swear he didn't have on a heavy belt or a gun on his hip, Marshal."

"Or a coat that'd have a pocket big enough for a gun." Longarm nodded. "Now tell me about the gun. Was it little and flat, or did it have a cylinder?" Longarm saw Cane's frown and took his own Colt out of its holster. "This is the cylinder. Don't you think you'd have noticed it, the way it bulges out?"

"Why, sure I did! I remember now! I thought it was a kind of gun I hadn't seen before, all shiny, with that little short barrel and the big bulge in front of the handle," Cane said.

"It sounds to me like a .32 New Line Colt," Delaney said.

"Or a Remington-Smoot .31," Longarm suggested. "Even if there's not too many of them around any more. But it'd be easy for somebody who didn't know pistols to take one for the other; they look so much alike."

32

Delaney nodded and turned back to Cane. He asked, "Why didn't you tell me about the gun and that the killer didn't have on a gunbelt, Buddy?"

"I don't know, Sheriff." Young Cane shook his head. "I guess I was still too worked up when you was asking me about how it all happened to remember what I'd seen. But I do remember now about the man wearing a vest and not having a holster on and how the pistol looked."

Longarm took out the copy of Gil Bright's picture sketched from the Fort Smith flyer. He asked Cane, "Would you say that this is the man who shot your father-in-law?"

"It sure looks a lot like him," Cane said after studying the drawing for a moment. "Except the man that shot Ed had a big black moustache." He shook his head. "I just can't say for sure."

Longarm spread his big thumb over the mouth and chin of the sketch. "How about now?"

"That looks like him, all right," Cane nodded. "But if there was a moustache on the picture, I'd be a lot more sure."

"I'd draw a moustache on this picture to help you make up your mind, except it's the only copy I got," Longarm said. "And all a man that wears a moustache or a beard has to do to make hisself look different is to go into a barbershop and get shaved. But you've been a real big help, Buddy. I do thank you."

As Longarm and Delaney walked back toward the courthouse, the sheriff said, "There's a lot of things I'd like to know about this case, Marshal Long. Why you're here looking into it is just one of them. Do you intend to tell me the whole story?"

"I wasn't aiming to be mysterious, Delaney. Sure, I'll tell you all about it, but not on an empty belly. Where's the best place in town to get a good steak?"

"I'd say the Headlight Café."

"If you feel like eating supper with me, I'll tell you the whole story. But before we eat, I want a swallow or two of Maryland rye whiskey. It's your town, so you lead the way."

"You know, Long, I'm glad to find you're a man that has good taste," Delaney grinned. "It just happens that the saloon next door to the Headlight keeps a few bottles of Maryland rye on hand just to accommodate me. And the drinks and dinner are on me."

Seated in a quiet corner of the saloon, a bottle of Tom Moore between them, their glasses having been emptied once and refilled, Delaney asked Longarm, "You mind telling me something?"

"Ask away."

"Did you get any help from what Buddy Cane told you?"

"Some. I'm pretty sure the man who killed his daddy-in-law is the one I'm looking for. I know the fellow I'm after has got a habit of tucking a .31 Remington-Smoot in his belt when he's wearing a vest and no coat."

"Why in hell didn't Buddy tell me all those things he told you, Long?"

"I'd imagine it's about like he said. When you questioned him right after the murder, he was so upset and had so much on his mind he just forgot. He's had time to remember by now."

"You believed him, I guess?"

"Seems to me he told a pretty straight story."

"How can you be sure he didn't imagine part of what he told you tonight, though? It's been three weeks since Ed was killed."

"You know Cane better'n I do, Delaney. Did his story strike you as being made up?"

"Well—no, I can't say it did," the sheriff conceded.

"Me, neither." Longarm drained his glass. "I don't aim to hurry you, if you want another drink, but I'm so hungry right now that I'm about ready to take a bite out of this tabletop."

"And I want to hear why a federal marshal's come all the way from Denver to North Platte looking into a murder case that ought to be handled under my jurisdiction. Come along—we'll go next door and eat."

When Delaney had heard Longarm's abbreviated explanation of the reason for his visit, he shook his head soberly. "I don't envy what you've got to do, Long. I'm not so sure that if this fellow Bright was an old friend of mine, I'd want to take on the job of bringing him in."

"If you got the idea I like it, you're wrong."

"You don't think he's still hanging around North Platte, do you? That he might've shaved his moustache off and found himself a place to hide?"

"No. I had to have a place to start, and this was the last town I knew he'd been in."

"My boys and me have turned the place inside out and upside

down, looking for the man who killed Ed Samuels. I'll swear he's not here any longer."

"I didn't expect him to be."

"Where do you think he'd be likely to go from here?"

"I've been asking myself that ever since I got on the train out of Denver. I wish I knew the answer."

"For what it's worth, you might try Fairview." Delaney shook his head. "No, wait a minute. They call it McCook, now, just changed its name. But right now the town's booming, and boom towns are easy places to get lost in."

"Which way is this McCook?"

"About seventy miles south. Just a little way above the Kansas border. Word's got out that the Katy's building a new line up to St. Louis that'll go through McCook, and from what I hear, people are so thick there that you can't stir 'em with a spoon."

"Sounds like the kinda place I'd head for, if I was on the run. I sorta figured Bright might backtrack. His mother lives in Missouri, and I got a hunch he's going to sneak back to pay her a visit sooner or later."

"Well, I wish you luck, Long. I know it's like you told your chief—one bad apple spoils a barrel—but I'm still glad it's you and not me that's trying to find this one."

Mounted on a chestnut mare that he'd gotten from the Pawnee Hotel's livery stable, Longarm was ten miles south on his way to McCook the next morning when the deputy sent by Delaney caught up with him.

"Sheriff Delaney said you'd sure want to get this telegram before you got too far," the deputy told him, handing over a pink flimsy.

Longarm unfolded the thin paper and read:

BAD APPLE LIKELY IN DODGE CITY STOP MAN HIS
DESCRIPTION KILLED TOWN MARSHAL THERE STOP
VAIL

Stuffing the flimsy in his pocket, Longarm said, "Glad you caught up with me. Now I'll have company to ride with on the way back to North Platte. That is, if you don't mind riding as hard on the way back as you did coming after me. Because on this trip, I haven't got any time to spare."

Chapter 5

For a day and a night Longarm juggled railroad schedules in his head as he crisscrossed the flat, fertile prairie. Thanks to his own encyclopedic memory, and aided by the railroads' telegraph systems, he covered a great deal of space in a very short time. He left North Platte on an eastbound Union Pacific freight, which got him to Omaha in time to race across town and swing aboard a work train just leaving the Kansas Pacific repair shops for an emergency job. The bobtailed work train, a fast six-car drag, pulled into Topeka a bare quarter of an hour before the departure of a westbound Santa Fe passenger haul.

Less than twenty-four hours after he'd been overtaken by the deputy sheriff on the road to McCook, Longarm stepped off the Santa Fe day coach at the Dodge City depot. He was grimy with coal smoke, his eyes were red-rimmed from the cinders that had blown into the open windows of the coaches and the work train's caboose, and he had a two-day growth of bristles on his cheeks and chin.

Dodge City was bustling. Though the buffalo hunters no longer used it as a shipping point for hides, the town was still a combination of frontier settlement, trading post, and a railhead's hell on wheels. Between railroad construction gangs, cowhands in town with trail herds, and settlers on their way to newly opened homestead areas, the town boiled like a disturbed anthill across the calendar and around the clock.

Longarm waited beside the baggage car to collect his saddle, picked it up, and started across the platform toward Railroad Street. The sign on the depot restaurant caught his eye and his stomach reminded him that, since breakfast at the Pawnee Hotel the day before, he'd had nothing but a hard-boiled egg from the lunch box of a brakeman on the KP work train and two sandwiches of stale bread and paper-thin ham from the butcher boy on the Santa Fe. He headed for the café.

Half an hour later, still grimy but no longer hungry, Longarm stepped into Dodge City's police headquarters. The uniformed man at the desk inside the door looked up and inspected Longarm's unshaven, soot-spotted face without interest.

"What's your trouble, mister?" he asked. "Get cleaned in a poker game or rolled in one of the whorehouses?" Without giving Longarm time to reply, he went on, "If you got a complaint like that, we can't help you. Anybody goes into the joints has himself to blame for whatever trouble he gets into."

Irked by the man's insolent attitude, Longarm replied, "I stopped in to talk to your chief. I ain't sure who's got the job right now. Dodge City changes police chiefs faster'n a boardinghouse landlady changes bedsheets."

"Well, Jim Masterson's chief town marshal. He ain't around now, though."

"That'd be Bat's little brother." Longarm nodded. "Long's my name. Tell Jim I want to see him. I'll be at the Dodge House getting cleaned up." He turned to leave.

"Wait a minute, now!" the man said. "How'm I going to tell Jim who wants to see him if I don't know who you are?"

"You got my name," Longarm replied curtly. "Jim knows who I am."

"You mind telling me, so I'll know, too?"

"Not a bit. Deputy U. S. marshal, out of the Denver office. And I didn't drop in for a social call. I'm on business."

"Long," the desk man repeated. "Gawdamighty! If you're from Denver, you'd be the one they call Longarm!"

"My friends call me that," Longarm nodded. "You just be sure Jim gets my message."

"Yes, sir, Marshal Long! I sure will!"

A bath and a shave in the barbershop off the lobby of the Dodge House improved Longarm's appearance as well as his disposition. It was mid-morning now, and because of his haste to get rid of the travel grime Longarm had passed up his eye-opener. He strolled through the hotel lobby and into the saloon across the street.

He'd downed one tot of Tom Moore and was lighting a cheroot before refilling his glass when the batwings were pushed open. Looking up, Longarm recognized Jim Masterson and waved him over with a smile. His smile faded when he saw the man who was following the town's chief marshal through the swinging doors.

Longarm saw that a few lines had appeared on Jim Masterson's face. He was no longer the somewhat callow young man he'd been when Longarm had last seen him. Part of the change was due to the thin, neatly trimmed moustache he'd let grow, but most of it was in Masterson's eyes, baby blue, but set deeply into their sockets now. The chubbiness of his cheeks and chin that had amplified his resemblance to his older brother was gone. His jaw muscles protruded below high cheekbones, his cheeks were a bit sunken, and his chin jutted out below his thin mouth.

Masterson stopped at Longarm's table and stuck out his hand. He said, "I won't say welcome to Dodge, Longarm, because you're not all that much of a stranger here."

"It's been a while, though," Longarm replied. He took Jim Masterson's hand, shook it quickly, and picked up his glass before Masterson's companion reached the table.

"I guess you remember Wyatt," Masterson said.

Longarm was settling back into his chair. His voice was expressionless as he replied. "Yep. I remember him, all right." Instead of offering his hand he nodded and raised his glass in a salute as he asked, "How are you, Earp?"

"About the same as always." Earp pulled out a chair and started to sit down. He looked at Tom Moore's smiling face on the liquor bottle and shook his head. "I'll just step over to the bar and get a bottle of bourbon."

Wyatt Earp had changed much less than Jim Masterson had, Longarm thought. Even as a younger man he'd had deeply sunken eyes and thin brows that grew on a jut of bone that protruded from his straight, high forehead. His slightly over-long, aquiline nose was a bit longer and more sharply pointed than Longarm recalled, but the big change was in Earp's moustache.

A thin pencil line when Longarm had seen him last, the moustache had now been encouraged to grow. It was two or three times the size of Longarm's neatly trained steerhorn sweep. Earp's moustache drooped over his lips, overshadowed his chin, and hid the unpleasantly thin lines of his lips, then swooped back along his jaws halfway to his ears.

"What's he doing back in Dodge?" Longarm asked as Jim Masterson sat down across the table from him. "Last I heard,

38

all the Earp bunch had moved farther west, after they wore out their welcome here in Dodge."

"Arizona—place called Tombstone," Masterson said. "I can't say what Wyatt's come back for, because he ain't told me yet. As far as that goes, I'm curious to know what's brought you down here from Denver. Ain't Dodge a little bit outa your territory?"

"Well, it is and it ain't," Longarm answered. He looked across the saloon and saw Earp returning, carrying a bottle and glasses. Longarm knew that the Masterson brothers and the Earps were long-time friends, and he had no desire to irritate Jim Masterson by showing openly his dislike for Wyatt Earp. He'd learned long ago that Earp was a blow-hard, a liar who boasted of gunfights that had never taken place and of cutting down men he'd never faced across gunsights. He said, "I'll tell you about it soon as I get a chance to."

"Why not go ahead and tell me now?" Masterson suggested as Earp came up, placed the bottle and glasses on the table, and sat. "The duty officer at headquarters said you acted like you were in a hurry to find me."

"It'll wait a little while," Longarm replied. "I got to find out about that brother of yours. I never could figure out why he pulled that fool stunt that got him beat when he was running to get reelected sheriff. He ought've known the folks in town wouldn't overlook him walking off the job to work for the Santa Fe when they were having that fuss over Raton Pass."

"It was a jackass play, all right," Jim agreed. "But Bat had his reasons. He told me he needed the money the railroad was ready to pay him, and he figured the people here would have forgot about it by the next election," Jim said. "I'm just lucky they didn't judge me by what he done."

Almost before Masterson had stopped talking, Wyatt Earp broke in quickly. "What happened to Bat could've happened to you and me, Jim, when we had that shootout with them cowhands."

"I guess we did get off light that time." Masterson nodded. "But, anyhow, Bat got his feelings hurt so bad when the vote went against him that he pulled up stakes. Swears he won't ever come back to Dodge."

"Where's he at now?" Earp asked. "I had it in mind to talk to him while I was back here."

"As far as I know, he's to hell and gone someplace over in New Mexico or Colorado. Us Mastersons ain't much for writing letters, and I just sorta lost track of him when I got so busy here, after they appointed me chief marshal," Jim said. He turned back to Longarm. "You was about to tell me what kind of case you're here on. If you want me or my boys to give you a hand on a case, I'd best tell you we're busy as the devil right now. I guess you heard one of my deputies got gunned down last week?"

Longarm still didn't relish talking to Masterson with Earp listening in. Privately, he considered Wyatt and his brothers as prime candidates to become the same kind of bad apple Gil Bright had turned into. With Masterson pressing him, though, Longarm felt he had no choice. He said, "Matter of fact, Jim, that's why I'm here. I got a hunch the fellow that shot your deputy is the same one I'm after for some other killings."

Masterson frowned. "The hell you say! You think you know who he is, then?"

Longarm nodded. He took out his wallet and removed the sketch copied from the North Platte "WANTED" flyer. Unfolding it, he handed it to Masterson. "Does he look like the descriptions you got of the man that killed your deputy?"

"It fits him pretty good," Masterson said after he'd studied the drawing for a moment.

Earp had been craning his neck to look at the sketch. He said, "Damned if that don't look like somebody I know, Long. Who is it, anyhow?"

Stifling a sigh, Longarm replied, "Gil Bright." Then a thought struck him and he said to Earp, "You might've run into Gil at that, Wyatt. Don't I recall that your folks settled in Missouri when the family moved West?"

"Yes. This man's from Missouri, too?"

"His mother still lives there, down around Lamar."

"Well, damn it, I got my first job as a lawman in Lamar!" Earp exclaimed. "Had my first gunfight there, by God. Me and my brothers against a bunch that was trying to hurrah the town." He shook his head. "That was a while ago, though— ten, twelve years. Was the man you're after in Lamar then, Long?"

"For all I know now, he could've been."

"I'm sure I know that face from somewhere," Masterson said, smoothing the folded paper on the tabletop. "Gil Bright's his name, you say?"

Longarm nodded and said, "It wouldn't surprise me if both of you had run into him. He's been down at Fort Smith lately, with Judge Parker's court. But me and Gil go way back. We partnered for the first time when we was appointed U. S. Marshals. Both of us trained together down in New Orleans."

"A lawman?" Earp's face showed his surprise.

"And used to be a good one," Longarm replied. "It makes me sick to have to hunt him down, but he's gone bad now, and it's a job that's got to be done."

"You got another one of these pictures?" Masterson asked. "If you have, I'd like to show it to some of my men. A couple of them was in the office when Jimmy Bob got killed. They'd know quicker than me if this is the man that done it."

Longarm was almost as surprised as Earp had been, but he kept his face straight, his voice level. He said to Masterson, "You don't mean to tell me that Gil—I just got to figure it was him, even if I ain't certain yet—you don't mean he walked right into your headquarters and gunned down one of your deputies and got out with a whole skin?"

"That's about the size of it," Masterson admitted. "Don't expect me to tell you how it could happen that way, but it did."

"By God, Jim, you're making the same mistake Bat did!" Earp exclaimed. "He let his men have too much rope when he was sheriff here, and that's one reason he lost that election. Now, if you want to have an A-number-one force, me and Luke Short—"

Longarm frowned as he interrupted Wyatt. "Luke Short? Is he still in Dodge? I thought he'd got run out a long time ago."

"Oh, Luke left town," Earp said. "Matter of fact, he made us a visit in Tombstone. But he's back now, dealing poker at the Long Branch again. And while he was out staying with us, me and him got to talking about what Dodge needs. Why, if you was to let us take charge, Jim—"

"Not now, Wyatt," Masterson interrupted. "I've told you once what I think about that half-assed idea you and Luke got, and I'll tell you again, if you want me to. Right now, I'm more interested in giving Longarm what help I can in running this fellow Bright to earth."

While Earp and Masterson talked, Longarm had poured himself half a glass of Tom Moore. He tossed off the swallow of sharp, smooth Maryland rye now and pushed his chair back from the table.

"If you and Earp are done arguing, let's get on over to your headquarters and find out if I'm on the right trail or not," he told Jim Masterson. "Because, if I ain't, I'm wasting one hell

41

of a lot of time here that I oughta be putting to better use."

"Ah, hell, Long!" Earp said. "Even if it was your old friend that shot Jim's deputy, he'd be long gone by now. I'll bet a good solid silver dollar to a plugged dime that this fellow Bright's a hundred miles from Dodge and still running. I'd say he's headed west, where nobody knows him. He could drop out of sight in a big place like Texas, or he might not stop running until he got to New Mexico—maybe even Arizona Territory."

"I don't recall asking your advice, Earp," Longarm said, keeping his voice low and even. He turned away from Wyatt and went on, "Jim, if you're ready, let's move on."

Masterson had already gotten to his feet. "I'm ready if you are," he told Longarm.

Left sitting alone at the table, Earp said sullenly, "You two go on about your business. I'll finish my drink and walk over to the Long Branch. I'll be there when you're ready to talk about that scheme me and Luke have worked up, Jim."

As they walked toward police headquarters, Longarm asked, "What's this idea Earp's got, Jim?"

"Oh, he wants to get some sort of bunch together to stand back of my deputies when they get in trouble with the selectmen. Wants to call it the Peace Commission, or something like that. It's Luke Short's idea, I guess, but it's a harebrained scheme, and nothing's going to come of it."

Masterson led the way into the headquarters. The desk man who'd been on duty when Longarm had stopped there earlier in the day had been relieved, and from an open door at the back of the room Longarm heard a jumble of voices.

"Men getting ready to go out on their beats," Masterson explained. "I've got four men out from noon to midnight, and four others come on at eight and work through the night, when we're busiest. Daytimes, there's three, but with Jimmy Bob gone, we're shorthanded."

When Longarm and Masterson entered the assembly room, the men fell silent. Masterson said, "Blackie and Frank, you come in my office with me and Marshal Long. The rest of you go on about your jobs."

Jim Masterson's office was small, and the four big men crowded it. Masterson explained why he'd called the two deputies in. "Now, Marshal Long's got a picture he wants to show you. I ain't saying who it is, but you men take a good look."

Longarm passed the sketch to the deputies, and they'd no sooner glanced at it than Blackie exclaimed, "By God, that's the fellow that gunned down Jimmy Bob! Ain't it, Frank?"

"Sure looks like it," Frank agreed. "Of course, he was in and out so fast—"

"Don't be in too big a hurry to make up your minds," Longarm told them. "And whether that's a picture of the killer or not, I want your story of what happened."

"I don't need to look at it again," Blackie declared. "It's like Frank said, though. It all happened real fast."

"Even if I didn't get all that good a look at him, I'm sure now that this is a picture of the man who shot Jimmy Bob," Frank agreed. "Hell, neither one of us even had our gunbelts on. It was just about this time of day. Me and Blackie and Jimmy Bob was a little bit—" He looked at Masterson and paused, then went on. "We was a little bit late getting here, so we told the others to go on, we'd catch up with 'em outside."

"Well, we wasn't all *that* late," Blackie said defensively. "Not more than a minute or two. Anyhow, this man come in, and—"

Longarm interrupted. "What was he wearing, Blackie?"

"What most of us do this time of year. Pants, a shirt, and a vest. Had on a narrow-brimmed fedora. Grey, as I recall."

"Was he wearing a gunbelt?" Longarm asked.

"No, sir," Frank answered. "I noticed that right off."

Blackie took up the story. "He asked which one of us was Jimmy Bob Blake, and me and Frank pointed to him. To Jimmy Bob, I mean. Damn it, we wasn't paying all that much attention. There ain't hardly a day goes by that somebody don't come looking for us back here."

"Jimmy Bob stepped up to see what the man wanted, and me and Blackie started for the door. We was putting on our gunbelts, not looking at them. We was still a step or two away from the door when we heard the shot," Frank said. "Both of us looked around, and there was this wild-eyed fellow heading for us. Had us covered with a stub-barreled nickel-plated pistol. Well, it'd've been like suicide for us to try to get at our guns. I just let my belt and holster drop when he waved his gun at me."

"Me, too," Blackie chimed in. "I seen men killed just as dead with a little snub-barreled thirty-two like he was waving as they'd be if they was shot with a forty-five, so I dropped my gunbelt, too."

43

"You're sure about his gun?" Longarm asked.

"Sure as can be." Blackie nodded. "I'd swear it was a .32 New Line Colt. We see a lot of 'em here in Dodge, Marshal Long. Tinhorns like 'em. They can tuck one in their belt under their vest, the way I guess this fellow did."

"That's a killer's trick, Blackie," Longarm said. "It's old, but it still works. Hereabouts, when you look at a man in shirtsleeves, or just wearing a vest, and you don't see a gunbelt, you figure he hasn't got a gun."

"That's right," Masterson nodded. "Like the whores, who don't have anyplace to carry a gun—they'll keep a thirty-two under their pillows, in case a customer gets ugly. But even a thirty-two's way too big for a dance-hall girl, so they mostly pick them little twenty-five caliber popguns they can stick in their garters."

"Dodge ain't the only place they do that," Longarm said. He turned back to Frank and Blackie. "All right. Go on."

"Well, there's not much left to go on with," Frank told him. "When that fellow run into me and Blackie after he'd shot Jimmy Bob, he damn near knocked us over. Then he slammed the door shut when he run out. Sanders was on the desk, but he didn't know what'd happened, so the man got by him. There wasn't hair nor hide of him in sight when we got outside."

Masterson said thoughtfully, "Seems like to me he's working off some kind of grudge he's got against lawmen. Funny, ain't it—when he was one hisself such a long time."

"He wouldn't be the first bad apple to turn on his own kind, Jim," Longarm pointed out. "Gil Bright's crazy, no question about that. But he's crazy like a fox, because he's used all the tricks himself."

"We've combed the town since that shooting," Masterson said earnestly. "We've opened up all the holes rats go for when they're running, and we've talked to everybody we can think of—in rooming houses, whorehouses, saloons, hotels, all like that. He's not holed up here in Dodge. I'll guarantee that."

"It figures," Longarm said. "Gil would know what you and your men would do. He'd know you'd be looking everyplace. It's not much wonder you didn't find him."

"You think he's gone, don't you?"

"Sure. What bothers me is, I can't figure out where he's gone to. He come down here after he killed that deputy up in North Platte. Now he's killed a man here. Is he going to run on south, or will he double back and go north? Or what?"

"Wyatt figures he's headed west," Masterson frowned.

"I heard Earp say that," Longarm nodded. "Which makes me pretty sure Gil's gone some other direction. Not south, toward Arkansas; he's too well known there. His mother's in Missouri, and he'd figure there'd be somebody on the lookout for him there, so I misdoubt he'd head east. What I've got a hunch Gil would do is to double back. He'd figure since he come from the north, nobody'd think of him moving that way. And I'm betting he won't run far this time. He's been on the move, and likely he's getting tired. Jim—you feel like giving me the loan of a horse so I can start up to Fort Hays?"

Chapter 6

Longarm pulled up on the south bank of Big Creek. The rain that had begun falling after he'd crossed the Smoky Hill River had diminished now to a light mist. Drops of water had collected on the edge of his hat brim; he shook his head to dislodge them, then wiped the moisture off his face with his callused palm.

Sliding a hand under his oilskins, he fumbled for the pocket where he carried his cheroots, took one out, dug for a match, and flicked his thumbnail across the head. The matches had drawn dampness, and it took three tries to get a light.

When the slender cigar was sending a trail of grey-blue smoke winding up into the thin mist, Longarm looked around. It had been a while since he'd visited Hays, and he studied his surroundings as any careful lawman will when entering a strange place.

Fort Hays was on his left, a neat array of standard Corps of Engineers buildings standing in precise geometrical alignment. There were two short rows behind the flagstaff that marked the parade ground, the administrative offices flanking the barracks and officer's quarters on one side, the stables and storehouses on the other.

In contrast, the town's houses and stores straggled in disorderly array along the opposite bank of Big Creek. A line of beaten earth, more trail than road, wound in and out between the structures. The town was imprisoned between the edge of the water and the raised gravel grade of the Kansas Pacific tracks that swept in a shallow arc beyond the settlement.

Old son, Longarm told himself, *there ain't no way a man on the run can get lost in an army post the size that one is. If he don't have a place to fit into, somebody's going to ask him who in hell he is, even if he's got a uniform on. And in a little bitty town like Hays, a stranger's going to stick out like a sore thumb. If Gil Bright did come this way and he ain't been smart enough to move on, this here's the best place you've hit yet where you got a chance to catch up to him.*

Prodding his borrowed horse with his boot toe, Longarm let the animal pick its way across the ford and toward the town.

Hays was a mixture of leftovers. A handful of its buildings were left over from the days soon after the fort was established. These housed the purveyors to the needs of lonely, isolated troops, the saloon keepers and whorehouse madams who trailed the army as it expanded its outposts to the West.

North of the Smoky Hill River, as the Cheyennes and Pawnees were pushed off their tribal hunting grounds, a few farmers took up land, homesteaded as much as they could, and always planted fields far beyond the boundaries of their homestead claims. The first stores came to Hays following the farmers. So did a livery stable, a blacksmith shop, and a dozen or so dwellings.

These became leftovers when the Kansas Pacific track-laying crews arrived. The railheads of the KP leapfrogging across the prairie attracted the usual group of mobile followers hauling their own buildings or setting up tents to form what the railroaders called hell on wheels. Most of these operators of cheapjack shops, peddlers' carts, gambling joints, saloons, and brothels moved on with the work crews when the railhead advanced. A few became leftovers, staying on in anticipation of the boom that usually began when the trains started to run.

For Hays, the boom had come and gone. There were a few new stores on the main and only street, and some new houses set away from the older ones. But to Longarm's eyes, as he held his horse to a slow walk into the town, Hays had a look of weather-beaten uniformity. A few freshly painted homes and storefronts made bright spots along the irregular road, but the general tone was one of pine boards left to weather to deep brown.

Longarm saw ahead a narrow false-front building that bore a sign: CAFÉ. He pulled up the horse, looped the reins around the hitch rail, and went in.

The restaurant was empty except for a pot-bellied man wearing a grease-splotched apron who sat at one of the back corner tables. He got up when Longarm came in and moved to the center of the room.

"You're too late for dinner and too early for supper, mister," he announced. "Best I can do for you is eggs and ham or bacon and heated-up biscuits."

Longarm was taking off his slicker. He draped it over a chair and took off his hat, shook it free of moisture, and put it on the chair seat before replying. He said, "Ham with the eggs, then. And I don't want no spuds."

Within a few minutes the sizzling of eggs in hot fat sounded from the kitchen and the aroma of ham being heated wafted into the café. Longarm sat patiently until his food arrived. The pot-bellied man deposited a platter in front of him, went back to get coffee, and stood by the table while Longarm picked up his knife and fork.

"That'll be two bits, mister. No offense, but in my place you pay before you eat."

Longarm fished a twenty-five-cent piece out of his pocket and laid it on the table. The pot-bellied man picked up the coin and dropped it into his pocket, then returned to his chair.

Keeping his voice casual, Longarm said, "Not much going on in Hays these days, I'd imagine."

"Damn little. Weather's been cold; wheat's going to be cut late. No redskins left much to stir up trouble, and the army keeps pulling men outa the fort. Town's sorta dead. You staying awhile, or just passing through?"

"That depends." With his habitual dislike for lying, Longarm stuck to the literal truth. "I swung by here looking for a fellow I used to travel with. Sorta lost track of him lately, but I figured he might be around Hays somewhere."

"Your friend's got a name, I guess?"

Longarm avoided answering by taking a bite of ham. While he chewed and swallowed, he took out the sketch copied from the flyer and held it up. "This is a right good likeness. I don't suppose you've run into him?"

"Hell, I see a lotta men come and go, mister." The pot-bellied man flicked a finger at the picture Longarm held and went on, "There's a half-dozen men comes in here off and on that looks about like that picture. This fellow work at anything special?"

"Odd jobs, I'd say. He used to get around a lot, but I guess he might've slowed down some since I seen him last."

"Well, I'd say your best bet's to ask around town. There's a lot of coming and going since the railroad started running. Try the saloons. If your friend's a gambling man, the Star runs poker tables every night. And you might ask at the hotel and Miz Anson's rooming house."

Longarm nodded and tucked the picture of Gil Bright back into his wallet. He finished his meal in silence, the proprietor being obviously not interested in asking questions or continuing their conversation. He drained his coffee cup and stood up.

"I guess that'll hold me till supper," he said, putting on his hat and reaching for his slicker.

"Stew'll be done at six," the pot-bellied man said. "It's good and thick, lots of meat in it. Or I can fry you a steak if you'd rather. Stew's thirty cents, steak's a half-dollar."

"Thanks. I'll remember."

Longarm let the horse set its own slow pace as he rode on into town. The drizzle had stopped, but the sky was still cloudy. As he looked at Hays, he tried again to put himself in Gil Bright's situation, to see the town through a fugitive's eyes.

A man's on the run, he don't want to hole up in a place this size, he told himself, scanning the buildings he was passing. *In towns like Hays, folks talk a lot, like that fat-bellied cook in the café. Some stranger shows up outa nowhere and ducks into a hidey-hole, don't come out and mix around, people are gonna start asking why he's afraid to stir out.*

Longarm reached the last of the houses and reined in. He took out a cheroot and touched a match to it, then turned to ride back. His thoughts ran on: *Gil knows that, just like you do, so he'd be smart enough to act like he didn't have nothing on his mind. He'd've found him a way to be where there's other people, so he wouldn't stick out like a sore thumb. He'd get him a room, go out and eat, maybe have a drink at a saloon now and again, might even set in a poker game.*

He was passing the center of Hays now. There was a saloon on each side of the street, another restaurant, three stores, and the hotel. Set back off the street he saw a sign, ROOMS, on the front of one of the town's few two-story houses. It was still too early for him to check the saloons. He twitched the reins and started the horse toward the rooming house. Reining in, he wrapped the reins around the hitch rail and knocked. A woman, well past middle age, opened the door.

Longarm touched his hatbrim. "You'd be Mrs. Anson?"

"I am. And if you're looking for a room, I've got two nice ones vacant. Come on in, I'll be glad to show you."

She opened the door wider, and Longarm stepped inside. She started down the long, narrow hall. He called, "Just a minute, Mrs. Anson. I ain't sure I'll be staying in Hays. Fact is, I'm looking for a fellow I used to travel with, and somebody told me he might be renting a room from you."

"Is that a fact? Well, I can tell you soon enough if he's one of my roomers. What's his name?"

Longarm had anticipated her question, and was already taking the sketch of Gil Bright out of his wallet. He handed it to her, saying, "This here's a good likeness of him. You'd know if he's renting a room from you."

"Well, I should hope I would!" Mrs. Anson snapped. She took a pair of gold-rimmed spectacles from her apron pocket and set them on her nose before taking the sketch. One glance and she exclaimed, "Why, that's Mr. Peterson! Harvey, he said his first name was."

"You're sure?" Longarm repressed the surge of excitement he felt at having hit a hot trail so unexpectedly.

"Of course I'm sure! Except that his face is a little thinner than it shows in this drawing. He was letting his beard grow out, too, he said. And you're not looking for him any harder than I am, mister! He sneaked away owing me just over half a week's room rent. And I want my money—or I want to take it out of his hide!"

"He ain't been gone long, then?" Longarm asked.

"Night before last was the first night his bed wasn't slept in," she replied. "I got suspicious right off, but then I said to myself, well, maybe he went out to one of the farms, like he'd said he was going to do, looking for a job. But when he didn't show up all day yesterday, and his bed wasn't slept in last night, I knew good and well he'd sneaked off."

"What about his luggage?" Longarm asked her. "He'd've had a suitcase or something."

"No," she said. "All he left behind him was a dirty handkerchief. Looked like he'd been using it a week, it was so stiff and soiled."

Longarm frowned. This was the second time used handkerchiefs had been mentioned in connection with a room occupied by Bright. He asked Mrs. Anson, "Don't you expect a stranger who's looking for a room to rent to have some kind of baggage?"

"Well, of course I do!" she snorted. "And I ought've known something was wrong when he didn't have one, but he told me he'd checked his bag on the train and they hadn't put it off at the depot. Said the baggageman here had wired ahead, that they'd put it off next stop and send it back. But when it didn't get here, and didn't get here, and he kept saying it was the railroad's fault, I ought've known then he was lying!"

"How long did—" Longarm hesitated momentarily while he recalled the name Bright was using—"did Mr. Peterson rent a room from you?"

"A week and— Let's see; it was four—no, five days." Mrs. Anson pursed her lips and her eyes narrowed as she looked up at Longarm. "You're some kind of lawman, aren't you? And this man Peterson is a crook you're trying to catch." When Longarm did not reply at once, she added, "Now, don't *you* start lying to me! I've got no respect for anybody who's untruthful."

"No more have I," he replied. "I won't lie to you. I'm a lawman, and I'm looking for this man to arrest him."

"I guess you've got a badge to prove you're who you say you are?" she demanded.

Longarm was still holding his wallet. He flipped it open to show her his badge.

"Oh, my! A United States marshal!" she gasped. "This must be a real bad man you're after, then. What'd he do?"

"I'm afraid I can't tell you that, Mrs. Anson. Not just yet, anyhow. But it was bad enough. And I'd be grateful to you if you'd answer a few questions for me."

"Well, my laws, come on into my parlor," she said. "If it's going to take a while, we might as well be comfortable."

Settled down in the trim, spotless parlor, Longarm reached for a cheroot, thought better of it, and asked, "What about the clothes this Peterson was wearing?"

"Why, they were just clothes. A white shirt and collar and a vest and pants—blue serge, both of them. And shoes."

"If he didn't have anything else to wear, he must've looked pretty shabby. Did he buy anything new while he was here?"

"Not a thing. But I told him it'd be all right if he washed his collar in the bathroom. Usually I don't let roomers do that, but if the ladies do a little bit of hand laundry on the sly, I don't say anything. Women who have to live in furnished rooms have a hard enough time. I feel sorry for most of them."

"Did Peterson spend most of his time away from his room?"

"Not for the first two or three days. I just guessed he was tired from traveling when he didn't go out at all the first day. He went out for supper the next day, but later he'd go out a little while—looking for work, I thought then—and going out to eat. I didn't find out till later he was sick."

"Sick? What'd he have?"

"He said he had a bad cough, which wasn't any news, because his room was right over mine and I could hear him cough in the night. He asked me about a doctor, and I told him there wasn't any but Dr. Simmons, except for the army doctors at the fort."

"Did he see Dr. Simmons, then?"

"I guess. I don't rightly know, because he didn't ask about a doctor till the day before he ran off."

"I don't guess I'll have any trouble finding the doctor?"

"His office door's got his name on it. It's just a few doors up from that terrible Star Saloon."

"You said a while ago that all he left behind was a handkerchief. I don't suppose you kept it?"

"Laws, no, Marshal! It was so stiff and dirty I threw it in the cookstove."

"And you're sure that handkerchief was all he left?"

"When I clean a room after it's been vacated, I *clean* it!" Mrs. Anson said tartly. "He didn't leave anything else."

"How about your other roomers? Did he get acquainted with any of them?"

"Not a bit. I'd have known if he did. And they've all been with me a long time. If you're thinking about bothering them with a lot of questions, I guess I can't stop you, but I'd as soon you didn't. Something like this gives a rooming house a bad reputation if it gets talked about, you know."

Longarm nodded. "I'll keep it just between the two of us, and ask you to do the same." He stood up. "And I do thank you, Mrs. Anson."

Riding the short distance to Hays's only street, Longarm had no trouble finding the doctor's office. Dr. Simmons was a sober man well past middle age, going bald, but compensating for the nakedness of his scalp with a well tended cavalry beard.

"Of course I remember the man you're looking for, Marshal," he told Longarm after hearing the reason for his visit and looking at Bright's portrait. "Though he wasn't clean-shaven; I'd say he had about a week's growth of beard. And I have good reason to remember him. He stole about thirty dollars from my wallet."

Longarm wasn't surprised. After hearing Mrs. Anson's story he'd deduced that Bright was broke, and the theft explained his sudden disappearance.

"How'd he manage to do that?" he asked Simmons. "Seems to me, if he'd come for you to treat him, you'd've been with him all the time he was in your office."

"Normally, that would be the case, Marshal. As it happened, I had another patient in my surgery. That's in the next room, and after I'd asked the man what was wrong with him, I left him sitting here in the office while I finished my treatment. When I came out, he'd disappeared. I thought he'd simply gotten tired of waiting. My coat was on the clothes tree, right where it is now. It wasn't until I took my wallet out to buy myself a drink after I'd closed the office that I found it was empty."

"There wasn't anybody else in here that could've done it?"

Simmons shook his head. "I had two other patients during the rest of that day, and neither of them was alone for a minute. No, it was your man Peterson who rifled my wallet."

"Did he tell you what was wrong with him?"

"Yes. He'd been diagnosed somewhere—I can't recall that he mentioned exactly where—as being tubercular."

"That's a real bad disease, from what I hear."

"Very. There's no known cure except rest in a climate of thin, pure air. Even then, the patients rarely recover. After the disease reaches a certain stage, it accelerates and is fatal."

"How far gone was—" Longarm caught himself before mentioning Bright's real name—"was this Peterson fellow?"

"You understand, Marshal, I didn't examine the man—"

"Sure, I know that. But you did get a good look at him, didn't you?"

"Good enough for a snap judgment, which I try to avoid. In this case, though, from the man's appearance, I'd have agreed with the diagnosis, even without examining him."

"You don't object to telling me why, do you, Doctor?"

Simmons thought for a moment, then shook his head. "No. I see no reason why I shouldn't tell you. You're a duly appointed law officer pursuing a fugitive. I suppose it's my duty."

"Thanks. I got good reasons for needing to know."

"I'm sure you have. Well, the man was emaciated to an advanced degree, and appeared listless. He coughed frequently, with sputum discharge which he caught by holding a handkerchief to his mouth. I got an impression that he'd already formed a habit of preparing to catch the sputum when he coughed. That indicated to me that the disease could be in an advanced stage."

"Now, I'll be obliged if you'd tell me how much longer you think he can keep going, running like he is."

"That's a somewhat complicated problem, Marshal Long. Without adequate rest and proper food, the disease accelerates. The degree of acceleration is impossible to forecast without a very thorough examination."

"Couldn't you just guess?" Longarm asked.

Again Simmons shook his head, then thought for a moment and said, "I suppose a guess is justified, under the circumstances. But you understand, I'm telling you this in confidence."

"I won't let out a word of what you say, doctor."

"Very well. My best prognosis is that, given the proper rest and treatment, the man could live a year at most. As a fugitive, under constant strain and forced to move and act under adverse conditions, he might last as long as four to six months, but it's likely to be a much shorter time."

"How much shorter?"

"Two months—three at most."

"Thank you, Doctor. Now, there's one more thing I want to ask you. Did you report him stealing your money?"

Simmons smiled and shook his head. "It wouldn't have done any good. The thief was gone. I'm sure he left Hays at once. Even if the sheriff had been able to catch him, my money would most probably have been spent. The man's doomed anyhow. To have caused him to be sent to jail would have been vindictive."

Thanking Simmons again, Longarm left the office. As he swung into the saddle and rode down the street in the direction of the Star Saloon, his face was wrinkled with worried thought.

Chapter 7

The ground ahead undulated in a descending series of wide, shallow valleys that lay between low ridges and stretched as far as Longarm's gunmetal-blue eyes could see through the heat haze. The valleys ran roughly from east to west. They were not deeply sculptured, roughly scratched and fissured. Rather, their sides sloped gently upward to softly rounded ridges. Longarm had counted the valleys once, the second time he'd covered the country between the Arkansas and the Cimarron Rivers on horseback, but that had been a long time ago, and he'd forgotten the exact number, even though he still recognized the features that distinguished the valleys themselves.

Longarm had acted on nothing more than a hunch when he decided to double back south after a long night of sitting and thinking in the Star Saloon at Hays.

Paying off old grudges before he cashes in his chips, that's what that damn fool Gil's doing, he'd told himself. *And no way to know who he's after or where they're at. Only thing for sure is, he's going from Hays without killing nobody here. He likely figures somebody's after him by now, and doubled back up here to throw 'em off. Now, was I in Gil's boots, I'd figure whoever was after me would think I had a reason for heading north, and was going to keep on moving that way. Then I'd double back south again to get to where I really wanted to go.*

Longarm had considered his idea through half a dozen drinks and several cheroots. The more he thought about it, the better he liked it. The next morning, waiting only long enough to go to Fort Hays and requisition a cavalry horse, he started back for Dodge, still riding the horse he'd borrowed from Jim Masterson and leading the cavalry mount to keep it fresh.

Wyatt Earp had left Dodge, heading back to Arizona, by the time Longarm reached the town. Jim Masterson had listened to Longarm with a thoughtful frown when he explained his hunch that Bright had doubled back on his trail again and was moving south once more. Then Jim had offered to ride along on the search.

Longarm had been firm in rejecting the offer. "It ain't that I don't appreciate it, Jim," he told Masterson. "But if you leave your job and go skittering off like Bat did before you, these folks in Dodge are going to turn you out, too."

"I always heard two heads was better than one," Masterson argued. "Seems to me if there was two of us, we'd stand twice the chance of finding Bright."

"It's a lot more likely he'd see two pursuers easier than he would one. No. There's just one of him and one of me, and the best thing I see to do is to keep it that way."

"You act like you got a pretty good idea where he's going."

Longarm had smiled grimly. "I wish I had. All I really got is a hunch that Gil's making tracks for one of two places."

"I guess you're going on more than a hunch," Masterson said. "You'd know Gil better than anybody else."

"I guess. But it don't make my job any easier. He's most likely going into the Indian Nation or back to Fort Smith."

"How do you figure that?"

"Gil was broke in Hays, Jim. Had to steal money to travel on. Fort Smith's the place he's been living. He'd have ways of getting money there. From friends, if he don't have some put by in a bank, which I figure he does."

Masterson nodded. "It makes sense. More than the Indian Nation does."

"Not much. The Indian Nation's in the Fort Smith marshal's jurisdiction. Gil must've learned a lot about it. He'd know men there, crooks he could blackmail, things like that. And there's another reason. If Gil's settling old grudges, he'd've had more run-ins close to his home office than anyplace else."

"You're talking about a whole lot of territory, Longarm."

"Oh, it ain't such a much, Jim. The Indian police do a pretty good job of handling their own people. You know what's left for us federal marshals to worry about."

"Sure. That little strip of No Man's Land up to the northwest and a dinky little corner down by the Red River that Texas claims. But that's still a lot."

"Well, I'll just have to cover it the way the little boy ate the apple. One bite at a time, till I get down to the core."

A full day's ride from Dodge brought Longarm to Crooked Creek, where he camped overnight. Starting before dawn and pushing the cavalry mount as much as he dared, he crossed the Cimarron River a little more than an hour before sunset and pushed on into No Man's Land. The little strip of territory, only sixty miles wide and twice as long, had somehow been overlooked by surveyors and mapmakers when the borders for Kansas, Colorado, Texas, and New Mexico were officially established.

None of the four states was anxious to claim jurisdiction over what had come to be called No Man's Land. As a result, the embarrassing little monument to the Federal government's inefficiency provided a safe haven for wanted men whom the states and New Mexico Territory would rather see outside their borders than in them. Semi-officially, the strip was included in Indian Territory, where its eastern edge butted on the Cherokee Outlet, but the Cherokees disclaimed jurisdiction, too.

Everything in No Man's Land was subject to debate. The stream that Longarm reached as the after-sunset sky darkened was called Palo Duro Creek in Texas, identified on army maps as the North Canadian, and known to the Indians as Beaver Creek. When he got to the creek, Longarm was less concerned with its name than he was with finding a place to camp for the night. He'd left the gently rolling grassy valleys behind when he crossed the Cimarron, and no matter whether he looked upstream or down, all he could see was precipitous, rocky banks and hard, barren soil.

With darkness settling fast, Longarm was not inclined to waste time debating. He twitched the reins to start the horse moving east, and let the animal pick its way along the low bluff that rose steeply from the streambed. The night was moonless, and Longarm was just about ready to stop at the first level spot and spread his blankets when he saw the unexpected: a gleam of light breaking the darkness ahead.

As he drew closer to the light, the single gleam divided. The formless blobs took shape and Longarm could identify their sources: the large rectangles of open doors, and smaller squares that outlined windows. One light-blob, apart from the others, was the dancing blaze of a small cooking fire.

Longarm reined in. No Man's Land was not a place where a man rode up to a strange camp with the assurance that he'd be welcome. At some camps, all strangers were suspected of being lawmen, and anyone failing to stop at a safe distance might very well get a greeting of hot lead. In No Man's Land, as he remembered it, there'd been no settlements, and not even any fixed camps.

Things change, old son, he told himself. *A few years back, nobody'd ever have nailed two boards together here in No Man's Land. But damned if that place don't look like a whiskey ranch.*

In the Indian Nation itself, liquor was prohibited by Federal edict. But there were dozens of places scattered through all the reservations, little clumps of two or three shacks, where illicit alcohol was sold to the Indians.

Longarm studied the pattern made by the lights for a few minutes, but darkness and distance made real observation almost impossible. Thoughtfully, Longarm rubbed his hand over his chin and cheeks, felt of the three-day stubble that covered them.

Looking like you do, old son, you'll pass for a man on the run without no trouble. And sitting here stewing ain't going to get you noplace. So you might as well get it over with and have a look at what you found.

Walking his horse, Longarm approached the buildings. He could see movement inside two of them, but still was unable to make out any details. The campfire seemed deserted, but the dark shapes of spread blankets were visible at one side of it. A dozen yards from the nearest of the buildings, he reined in.

"Hello in there!" he called. "Anybody home?"

A dark shape blotted out the door of the biggest house and Longarm caught the glint of light from a rifle barrel as a man came out. He squinted at Longarm, who sat his horse at the edge of the light, and said, "Step up closer, where I can see you."

Longarm nudged the horse into the light glowing from the door. The man said nothing more until he'd finished a quick but thorough inspection. Then he asked, "Anybody riding with you?"

"No. You can see I'm by myself."

"What's your business here, mister?"

"I ain't got any business in particular right now," Longarm replied. "Just looking for a place where I can spread my bedroll for the night. Didn't know there was any whiskey ranches here in No Man's Land, or I'd've made a beeline for this one soon as I spotted the lights."

"Sounds like you've been in the Nation before."

"Yep. But I been away for a while. You got any objections to a new customer? Like I said, I wanta spread my bedroll someplace and grab some shuteye."

"Plenty of space all around here," the man told him. "How come you picked this place out?"

"I didn't. I just seen the lights and rode up for a look-see. Fact is, I'm short of grub, and I figured I might be able to buy me some supper. I ain't short of the money to pay for it."

"Who told you about this place?"

"Nobody." Longarm had smelled out the character of what he'd stumbled onto by now. This whiskey ranch was also a hideout for outlaws, where strangers were greeted with suspicion. He gave the proper reply in terms that were universally used by those on the wrong side of the law. "I just come down from Kansas in a sorta hurry. The weather got too hot for me up there, and I figured I'd better be moving on."

"I suppose you got a name?"

Longarm stuck to the literal truth. "Sure I got a name. I imagine you've heard it. You can call me Smith."

Slowly, the man in the door lowered his rifle. "You come from a hell of a big family, Smith." He chuckled. "I guess it's good enough for now. Mine's Reeder, if you give a damn. We was just getting ready to turn in for the night, but I guess we can fix you up." He gestured toward the hitch rack that stood at one side of the big building. "Your horse and gear'll be safe out here. Light and come inside."

Longarm followed the big man through the door. The room was a little more elaborate than the whiskey ranches he'd seen deep in the Indian Nation. They were simply dirt-floored hovels, bare of furnishings. This one had a floor, but the wide planks from which the floor was made had obviously been laid on the bare ground and had cracks almost an inch wide between the boards.

Its scanty furnishings made it a crude, scaled-down version of a saloon. There were three small tables with homemade pegged-stump stools instead of chairs. The bar was a pair of planks stretched across two hogsheads. In back of the bar, another plank between two barrels held half a dozen bottles.

"Come on out, girls!" Reeder called. "This fellow's all right. He says to call him Smith. He's just hungry and thirsty and I guess he wouldn't mind a little cheering up."

A door in the end of the room opposite the bar opened and two women came out. One had dark hair, the other was a streaked blonde. They were about of a size, the brunette being just a trifle taller than her companion. Both wore knee-length taffeta dresses, stained and grimy, with tight, low-cut bodices that emphasized their full breasts. Longarm tried to guess their ages, but the heavy coating of rouge and powder that caked their faces and the generous application of lip cream that covered their mouths made even guessing impossible.

"Netta's the blonde one, the other one's Laurie," Reeder told Longarm. "They'll pour your drinks and rustle up some grub for you. And if you're interested, they'll listen when you clink a couple of cartwheels in your pocket."

"You ladies are right tempting," Longarm told the women. "Only right now, I'm so hungry and tired all I got any interest in is some grub and a drink before I bed down for the night. But if it turns out I don't have to hightail it outa here before I rest up a day or so, we'll sure get better acquainted later on."

Reeder started for the door. He stopped short, turned back, and told Longarm, "If you want a roof over you tonight, one of the cabins back of the place here's vacant."

Keeping to the front he was putting up, Longarm asked, "You lending or renting, Reeder?"

"I'll lend it to you tonight, seeing you're new around here. If you stay on, we'll dicker about the rent."

"Fair enough." Reeder disappeared through the door and Longarm returned his attention to the women. "Now, then. What kind of grub can you dish up for a hungry man that's rode longer than he ought've today?"

"All we got tonight is some rabbit stew," Laurie replied. "There'll be fresh beef coming in tomorrow, but we're scraping bottom right now."

"Rabbit stew'll taste real good," Longarm said, sitting down at one of the tables. "And I hope one of them bottles back of the bar there's got rye whiskey in it."

"Sure has," Netta said. "Laurie, you bring in a bowl of stew from the kitchen and I'll pour Smith's drink."

Laurie disappeared through a crude, doorless archway that apparently led to the kitchen, while Netta moved to the bar, selected one of the bottles, and filled a tumbler.

While he was alone at the table and unobserved, Longarm examined his surroundings and began trying to form a plan of action. He had little time to think, though, for Netta quickly returned to the table, bringing the glass she'd filled. She set it in front of Longarm. At such close range, the aroma of her perfume drowned the smell of the liquor.

"Don't I remember you from someplace else, Smith?" she asked. "I'm sure I've run into you before."

"Well, now, I been a lot of places," Longarm answered. "And if I'd seen somebody as pretty as you before now, I'd sure remember her."

"Just like I'd remember a man as big and good-looking as you are," she replied archly, thrusting out her breasts and smoothing her skirt. She smiled knowingly. "I remember meeting a lot of Smiths at one place or another. You don't mind if I call you Smitty, do you?"

Longarm returned her smile. "Lady, I don't mind a bit what you call me, as long as you don't forget to call me when you want something."

"After you've had that drink and ate your supper, maybe you'll change your mind about not wanting to do anything but sleep tonight," she suggested.

"We'll just have to see, won't we?" Longarm asked her.

He sipped the whiskey. It was bitingly harsh, a raw-edged liquor that had obviously never been inside an aging cask. He swallowed what he'd taken into his mouth and put the glass on the table. Laurie came in from kitchen carrying a bowl and a plate of biscuits. She put the bowl and plate on the table.

"Did you collect?" she asked Netta.

"Not yet." Netta faced Longarm. "That'll be three dollars, Smitty. Two for the stew and a dollar for the drink."

Since a bowl of stew cost only twenty to twenty-five cents at most restaurants, Longarm opened his mouth to protest, but thought better of it before he'd said anything. There was something about this whiskey ranch that tickled his well-honed hunter's instinct, but he couldn't yet put a finger on it. He decided that he'd better buy some time.

Sliding his hand into the pocket of his pants, he fumbled for a moment, then pulled out the handful of mixed gold and silver that he'd gotten when he cashed one of the government expense vouchers in Dodge. He cupped his palm and held his hand close to his chest as though trying to avoid showing Netta and Laurie how much he was carrying, but he made sure that they got a glimpse of the coins.

"Looks like I'm a little bit short of cartwheels," Longarm said at last. He brought out a twenty-dollar gold piece. "I guess you'll just have to take what I owe you outa this double eagle."

Netta's hand closed on the coin with an eagerness she barely bothered to conceal. "I'll have to get change from Reeder. It won't take but a minute."

Longarm picked up the tumbler and brought it to his lips as Netta went to the door through which Reeder had made his exit. The smell of the raw liquor depressed him. He said to Laurie, "Seems like I'd oughta get a cup of coffee to go with my supper. I guess you got some in the kitchen, ain't you? This whiskey's fine to rouse my appetite, but I like coffee while I'm eating."

"Why, sure. I'll go get a cup for you."

As soon as Laurie's back was turned, Longarm bent down and emptied the glass under the table, pouring the raw liquor into one of the wide cracks between the boards. By the time Laurie had come back carrying a thick mug filled with coffee, he'd put the empty glass on the table and was spooning up the stew. It might not have been bad if it had been hot, he thought, but the food was barely lukewarm.

Netta came back into the room just as Laurie was putting the coffee cup down beside the bowl of stew. She put seven silver dollars on the table in a neat stack and topped it with a ten-dollar gold piece. Seeing the empty tumbler, she picked it up.

"I'll just bring you another drink," she said. "This one's on the house."

"Well, now. That's right nice of you," Longarm said as soon as he'd swallowed the mouthful of stew he'd been chewing. "And since I ain't going to be out the price of a nightcap, you and Laurie might as well have what it'd've cost me." He gave each of them a dollar from the stack on the table before dropping the rest of the money in his pocket.

"Thanks, Smitty," Netta smiled. "Now I'll get that nightcap you'll be wanting in a minute."

Laurie followed Netta to the bar, and the pair stood close together, whispering. Longarm watched them covertly while he finished the stew. He was lighting a cheroot when Netta came back with his drink. Laurie had gone into the kitchen.

"Here you are, Smitty," Netta said. She put the tumbler on the table, leaning over to allow Longarm to look down her dress into the cleft between her full breasts. "Have you changed your mind about not wanting to do anything but sleep tonight?"

"Like I told you, Netta, I been in the saddle a long spell, and I'm right tired. But if I can make a dicker with Reeder to put me up and feed me, I figure to stay here awhile and rest up. There ain't anyplace I got to go in a hurry." Longarm picked up his empty coffee cup. "I like a sip of coffee, sorta like a chaser, with my nightcap. Think you could get Laurie to fill this up about halfway?"

"No need to bother Laurie. I'll get it for you myself," Netta replied.

She took the cup and started for the kitchen. As soon as she went through the door, Longarm quickly dumped the whiskey into the same crack where he'd poured the first glass. By the time Netta came back with the coffee he was holding the tumbler with his big hand wrapped around it to conceal that it was empty. She handed Longarm the coffee cup, and he went through the motions of tossing off a drink, gulping hard, then drinking the coffee. He lighted a fresh cheroot and stood up.

"If you'll just point me toward that cabin Reeder told me I could use, I'm going to turn in," he told Netta. "That's all I'm fit for doing tonight."

Netta smiled and nodded. "Sure. I know how it is when a man gets tired. I'll take this lantern and hold it for you while you're spreading your bedroll."

Leading his horse, Longarm followed Netta between two dark cabins to a third one that stood a bit apart from the others. The campfire he'd seen from a distance had died away, but the dark shape of a wagon loomed beyond the fire's last glimmering coals.

Longarm asked no questions. He made quick work of unsaddling, carried his saddle and bags and bedroll into the cabin, and spread the bedroll on the ground beside one of the end walls. Netta watched in silence during the few minutes required for him to complete his preparations.

"I guess I'll say good night, Smitty," she said when he'd pulled the wrinkles out of the blankets and stepped back.

"Good night, Netta." Longarm yawned, even if he wasn't all that sleepy. "We'll talk some more tomorrow."

Longarm was sleepier than he'd thought, and almost as

sleepy as he'd pretended to be. After he'd finished his usual bedtime preparations, Colt in its holster where it would be within easy reach of his hand, derringer in the pocket of his vest, folded with the pocket up beside his head, he levered out of his boots and turned in.

He lay awake for only a few minutes before he drifted into slumber. It seemed to him that he'd just closed his eyes when a faint scraping sound on the hard ground outside brought him instantly awake and fully alert. His hand closed on the butt of his Colt as he slid out of the blankets and stepped away from the bedroll. His eyes were fixed on the faint rectangle that marked the door, and he was not prepared when the two shots came through the window.

Longarm's eyes were blinded for a moment by the two bright streaks of muzzle blast. He could see nothing, but he heard the weapon's barks, so light that they were little louder than the popping of a cork. His reflexes were already responding before the second shot sounded. Before its echoes had died away, he'd swiveled the Colt and triggered it. Its boom echoed in the confines of the ramshackle little cabin as he fired a shot through the window.

Working along the wall, he moved to the window and looked out. His ears caught the faint whisper of retreating footsteps, but there was no sign of movement in the night's deep gloom.

Chapter 8

Longarm waited, peering out the glassless window, trying to penetrate the night's blackness. The faint scratching of footsteps that had roused him originally had not sounded since his shot, and the first noise to reach him was that of voices coming from the direction of the saloon. Both cabins between the one where he'd been sleeping and the whiskey ranch's main building remained dark, but a dim, flickering glow came from the spot where he'd seen the wagon by the dying fire. Then the windows of the saloon suddenly shone with the yellowish light of a lantern.

For a moment, the light flickered, then it brightened suddenly, and as suddenly dimmed, though the windows remained bright. Reeder appeared at the corner of the building, holding a lantern above his head. By its light Longarm could see that he'd pulled on a pair of trousers over his suit of knit underwear and held an Old Model Navy Colt in his other hand.

Reeder's harsh voice broke the quiet. "Netta? Laurie? Zara? Smith?" he called. "Which one of you let off that shot?"

Wondering who Zara might be, Longarm left the window and moved to the door of the cabin. He did not reply immediately to Reeder's question, but stood holding his Colt, watching.

Reeder started toward the shack Longarm occupied. He'd taken only a few steps when Netta and Laurie emerged from the saloon building and followed him. A few steps short of Longarm's cabin, Reeder stopped and raised his voice again.

"Zara? You all right?" he asked.

To Longarm's surprise, it was a woman who replied. Her voice was deep-toned, with an accent he could not identify.

"Yes," she said. "You are not to worry for me, Reeder.

And the zhot, it was not me who fired."

Before the unseen woman had finished speaking, Longarm had stepped up to the door of the cabin. He had time to locate her position. She was in or near the wagon.

Reeder started forward again. Netta and Laurie had caught up with him when he stopped, and followed him as he made for Longarm's cabin.

"That was me shooting, Reeder," Longarm said as the trio came up. He did not emerge from the cabin. For all he knew, the sniper was still around, and in the lantern's light he'd be an easy target. Staying just inside the doorway, he went on, "I was just shooting back."

"Shooting back at who?" Reeder asked. He stopped a yard or two from the door, the women still following him.

"Damned if I know. I was sound asleep and didn't get a look at whoever it was. But somebody shoved a gun in through the window and took a couple of potshots at me."

"One shot was all I heard, Smith." Reeder's voice was heavy with doubt and suspicion.

"It ain't likely you'd've heard the first two. I damn near couldn't hear 'em myself. They sounded like them little strings of Chinese firecrackers, except there was only two of 'em."

"You girls hear more'n one shot?" Reeder asked Netta and Laurie. Both of them said no.

"Well, damn it, bring that lantern inside," Longarm said. "Maybe you'll believe me when you see some bullet holes."

Reeder and the two women followed Longarm to the wall where he'd spread his blankets. Longarm dropped to one knee and carefully smoothed the rumpled bedclothes, disturbing their position as little as possible. He could see the two bullet holes. They were about in the center of the blanket, at the approximate spot where his chest would have been when he was lying down.

"There's your proof," he told Reeder.

"Hell, they could be moth holes for all I can tell," Reeder snorted.

"Just wait. I ain't finished yet," Longarm said.

He slid his folded vest from the corner of the blanket, moving it carefully so the derringer in the pocket would not fall out. He laid the vest a few inches from the top of the blankets, where he could reach the derringer easily if he needed it. Then he flipped the blankets back, exposing two tiny, almost invisible dents in the hard-packed earth of the cabin floor.

Taking out his clasp knife, Longarm opened the blade and slid it into the dirt beside one of the dents. He levered the knife blade up, bringing a chunk of soil with it. Emptying the clod into his hand, Longarm broke it and rubbed the dry dirt to powder. He blew away the loose earth, exposing two small, cone-nosed lead pellets lying in his palm.

"You want any more proof than that?" he asked Reeder.

"They look like bullets, all right," the big man agreed, his voice reluctant. "Got the same shape and all. But they didn't come outa no .32, or not even a .31. They're too little."

"You're right about that," Longarm told him. "They'd kill a man just as dead, though, if they hit the right spot."

"All I heard was one shot," Reeder said stubbornly. "If there'd been more, they'd have roused me. I'm a light sleeper."

"You wouldn't've heard 'em, as far as it is from here to where you was. Them two shots wasn't hardly louder than a cough."

"There's not a gun made that don't go off loud enough to wake me up!" Reeder insisted.

"This one don't. I know what kind it was." Longarm turned to Netta and Laurie. "You'd know, too, I guess. It had to be one of them garter guns. A little .25 caliber five-shot that ain't much longer or bigger around than a finger."

"I've seen them," Laurie said. "But I never owned one."

"Me, either," Netta chimed in.

"I wasn't suggesting you did," Longarm told them. "You both come outside right after Reeder did. There wasn't hardly time for you to've let off them shots and get back that fast to where I seen you right after Reeder come out."

"Who was shooting, then?" Reeder demanded. "There ain't nobody here but you and me and the girls and Zara. You heard what Zara said when I asked her about the shots."

"I heard somebody over in that wagon yonder say they wasn't hurt," Longarm retorted. "Besides, who in hell's Zara? I never heard nobody say a word about her before now."

"We don't talk about whoever might be staying here," Reeder said curtly. "You, Zara—whoever it might be. Now let's get back to this shooting business. How come they missed you?"

"Because I heard 'em poking around outside, coming up to the window. I got outa my blankets right quick. You and me's

67

both been around long enough to know that anybody sneaking up on you at night ain't doing it just to give you a friendly handshake."

"I won't argue that," Reeder nodded. He looked at Longarm, who'd taken off only his coat, vest, and boots before going to bed. "Looks to me like you might've been expecting somebody to come calling. Or maybe you had in mind just sneaking off and being on your way after you'd caught a little shuteye."

Before Longarm could reply, the big man raised the muzzle of the rifle. Holding the weapon like a pistol, his finger curled on the trigger, Reeder went on, "I don't like to pry into anybody's business, but I don't want trouble here, Smith. It's time for you to do a lot more talking than you've done so far."

"Hold on, Reeder!" Longarm protested. "Since when did a man stopping at a whiskey ranch have to explain anything?"

"Like I said, it's not my way to ask questions. But I don't want the law poking around here, because lately the possemen have been tearing down any of the ranches where they find somebody they want hiding out."

"Damn it, why'd anybody come to a place like this if it wasn't to hide out?" Longarm demanded.

"Hiding out for an old job is one thing. It ain't quite the same as hightailing from a job you've just pulled. If there's a posse riding after you, I don't aim for this to be the place where they catch up with you."

Longarm's eyes flicked down to his Colt, which he'd left lying on the turned-back blanket.

"Don't try it, Smith," Reeder said coldly.

"Don't worry," Longarm replied. "I ain't a damn fool."

He knew that he had to talk, to give some credible explanation of his presence, but he knew also that if he revealed his true identity and purpose, Reeder would have no compunction about pulling the rifle's trigger. Nor could he afford to stall until the big man thought of searching him or the bedding. Before turning in, he'd placed his wallet containing his badge and the Federal travel and expense-money vouchers in the folds of the vest that now lay at one edge of the turned-back blankets.

Reeder lifted the rifle muzzle so Longarm was forced to look into its menacing black orifice. "Now, what kind of job are you on the prod from? Where'd you pull it? Who was in it with you?"

Longarm hardened his voice until it was even colder than

Reeder's and fixed his eyes on the big man's to match stares with him. "I ain't damn fool enough to answer no questions, either," he said. "I won't risk you selling me out to the law."

"So there's reward money on you." Reeder nodded. His eyes went to Longarm's saddlebags, lying against the wall. "Netta, open up them saddlebags. I wanta see what's in 'em."

Netta picked up the saddlebags. She opened one side, rummaged through it with her hand, and told Reeder, "There's not anything in here but some jerky and parched corn and a little bag of oats." She explored the other side and said, "Just a pair of longjohns, I guess. No—wait a minute. They've got something wrapped up in them." A moment later she held up Longarm's telegraph key. "Now, who'd want to carry a thing like this around?"

"A telegraph key!" Reeder grinned. "Hell, I figured the Murphy gang wore that trick out, Smith."

"I don't know what you're talking about," Longarm said.

Reeder snorted. "Like hell you don't! Zack Murphy and his boys used it until the railroads caught on to them and started making the stationmasters use a code number on their messages."

"Who's Zack Murphy?" Longarm asked, stalling for time.

"You oughta know. I'm betting you're in the same business Zack and his men was: robbing trains."

"You're stretching that telegraph key into something it ain't, Reeder," Longarm said evenly. "I never have worked for a railroad. I learned how to use that key in the army. I just lug it around as a sort of souvenir."

"Like hell you do! Maybe you think I don't know what I'm talking about, but I'll prove you're not pulling any wool over my eyes. Zack and his boys started it, near twenty years ago. They'd cut the key in on the railroad telegraph line by the track and send a message to the station down the line that there was a crew of gandy dancers working on a washout or something. They'd say the next train could get through, all right, but it'd have to take it slow. Then, when the train slowed down, they'd take it like a sitting duck."

"It's your story, Reeder," Longarm said levelly. "I don't think it's very funny."

Reeder remained unconvinced. "So you're a train robber, are you? Maybe cheated a little bit on splitting up the take? And your pards found out and taken out after you?"

"I ain't saying it, you are," Longarm replied. He hid his relief at Reeder's erroneous deduction, which had saved him a lot of explaining.

"Well, I guess that's all I need to know," Reeder said. "If some of your old pardners show up, I'll leave it to you to handle 'em. Just keep me and the girls out of it."

"Damn it, Reeder, it wasn't you or them got shot at, it was me. And, as far as I know, there ain't nobody trailing me to get even for anything."

In the familiar gesture of the day, Reeder pulled down the lower lid of one eye and squinted at Longarm. "See any green there, Smith? Hell, I don't expect you to admit anything. But I don't want you to bring no trouble here, either. I got enough of my own. You can stay out the night, but I want you on your way by noontime. You understand?"

Longarm made time to frame his reply by going over to his coat and taking out a cheroot. He lighted it, let a puff of smoke swirl around, then said evenly, "If that's how you feel, I'd about as soon saddle up and ride out right now. It'll be daylight in another two or three hours anyhow."

"Suit yourself, Smith." Reeder's voice was curt. "Stay or go, it's all the same to me. Come on, girls. Whoever was after Smith is long gone by now, and we got fresh beef coming in tomorrow."

Reeder turned to leave. Netta and Laurie hesitated for a moment, then followed him. They took the lantern with them, and Longarm stood in the dark for several moments, the glow from his cigar lighting his face, while he waited for his eyes to adjust to the darkness again.

You sure didn't play that hand like you should've old son, he told himself. *Not that you held much in the way of cards, but you got yourself backed into a corner, and neither one of them girls is going to do more'n give you the time of day now. If Gil Bright did pass this way, you sure missed your chance to find it out.*

Thinking hard, Longarm puffed his cheroot until it was down to a stub and ground the butt into the dirt with his heel. He waited again while his eyes adjusted to the complete darkness. Then, having made his decision, he rearranged his blankets and crawled into bed again. He was just drifting off to sleep when he heard a soft rustling outside. He picked up his Colt, got out of bed noiselessly, and started for the door, its opening outlined against the starshine.

Standing just inside the opening, Longarm waited. His ears caught the soft thud of a stone being kicked by a slow-moving foot as the unseen person drew closer. The noise stopped for a moment after that, and was resumed only after a moment of complete silence.

Longarm's keen ears told him when the unseen prowler reached the cabin wall. There was the brushing of a hand against the rough wood as the intruder felt along the wall toward the door. Longarm flattened himself to the inner wall at the edge of the doorframe and stood ready, his Colt poised.

A shadow darkened the door opening. Longarm whirled. His left hand swept down on the intruder's shoulder, and he pushed to turn the prowler away from him while his right brought the Colt up and shoved it into the back of the stranger's neck.

"Make a move or a sound and you're dead!" he gritted, his voice harsh and threatening.

A whispered reply came softly through the gloom. "I mean no harm to you, *gaja*. You do not need the gun."

Only then did Longarm realize that his pre-dawn visitor was a woman. He still did not ease the pressure of the Colt's muzzle against her back, in spite of her assurance.

"You'd be the one Reeder was talking to. Zara, ain't it?"

"Yes."

Longarm strained his eyes in the darkness, but could not see his unexpected visitor. Zara was nothing more than a vague form in the blackness, her features invisible. He became aware now of the faint aroma the woman had brought into the cabin with her. It was a musky fragrance, part human scent, part perfume, not objectionable, but as unidentifiable as was her face to his eyes. Zara stood totally motionless, seemingly unconcerned by the continued firm pressure of his gun in her back.

"You're some kind of Indian, I guess," Longarm said. "Only I can't figure from what tribe. You ain't Comanche or Cheyenne or Kiowa, by the way you talk. One of the northern tribes, maybe? Shoshoni or Cree?"

"I am not Indian. I am of the Rom."

"Gypsy?"

"Yes. I am *cha*."

"Whatever that means. How come you're by yourself? I had the idea you folks travel in a bunch all the time, like the Indians do."

"Explaining would take too long. It will be light soon, and Reeder and the women will be up."

"You still ain't explained anything, Zara. Like what you're doing pussyfooting up on me. For all I know, you're the one that took them two shots at me a while ago."

"I could be, yes. But I did not shoot at you."

"You'd tell me that whether you had or not."

"There is no way I can prove what I say. If you think I have come to harm you, you can search me. You will find that I carry no weapon."

Longarm's instinct told him to believe her. But, after having been made a target once during the night, his common sense warned him to keep his guard up.

"You still ain't told me why you came sneaking over here."

"Only to talk with you."

"As far as I know, we ain't got anything to talk about."

"You are wrong," Zara replied.

"Go ahead and prove it, then. Start talking."

"You have come here to find—" Zara broke off suddenly as the sound of clanking metal came from the direction of the main building.

Longarm turned to look, and when his movement took the pressure of the gun muzzle from her back, Zara stepped around to look also. She took half a step ahead, as though to leave, but stopped when she saw what was holding Longarm's attention. During the time since she'd arrived the air outside had become faintly luminous with the arrival of the false dawn. The shabby buildings of the whiskey ranch loomed through it, not really visible yet, but no longer hidden in deep darkness. A light showed inside the main building now; neither Longarm nor Zara had seen it from inside the cabin where they stood talking. The door of the saloon was open and Reeder's bulky figure, unmistakable in silhouette, showed against the light. Zara turned to Longarm. He could see her face now as a pale blur in the darkness, vague shadowed areas marking her eyes and mouth.

Zara said quickly, "We cannot talk now. He is a very suspicious man, Reeder. And he is no friend of ours."

"If you got something to tell me, Zara, you better spill it right fast. I aim to be moving on at sunup."

"That will be soon. I must go now. I wish no trouble with Reeder."

"Wait a minute!" Longarm protested. "You say you got something to talk about. Go on, tell me what it is."

"No. Not now, and not here. You are going to leave soon, and so am I. Go west when you leave. In—"

"Hold up, Zara! I ain't about to—"

"Hush!" she interrupted. "Listen to me! Ride west. In two or three miles there is a little river. Follow it until you reach the first creek that flows into it from the north. Wait for me there. I will leave soon after you do, but my wagon moves less fast than your horse."

"Now, if you think I'm going to go off on some kind of wild goose chase—"

"You chase something wilder than the goose now, do you not?" she broke in. "Do as I ask. I try only to help you, United States Marshal Custis Long."

Longarm was totally unprepared to hear the gypsy woman call him by name. He stood staring at her. Ignoring the gun in his hand, Zara turned and left the cabin. Longarm could do nothing but stand gazing after her, his mouth agape with surprise, as she ran quickly across the short distance that separated the cabin from her wagon and disappeared inside the vehicle.

Chapter 9

Longarm recovered quickly from the shock, and started from the cabin to the wagon. Reeder's harsh hail stopped him before he'd taken a second step.

"Smith! You remember what I told you! You got till noon to clear outa here!"

"Don't worry, Reeder," Longarm called back. "I aim to be on my way as soon as I saddle up."

"I won't make any man ride off with his belly empty," Reeder said. "Stay for breakfast if you want to. The girls will have it ready in a few minutes."

"I'll find my own breakfast, thanks. All I want to do now is shake the dust of your damn whiskey ranch off my boot heels."

Reeder did not reply. He nodded curtly and walked on to the saloon, disappearing inside.

Longarm decided that his impulse to follow Zara's suggestion would be a mistake, with Reeder keeping an eye on him. He went back into the cabin and assembled his gear. When he lifted his canteen, he found it was almost empty. It was a prairie truism that only a fool rides out on the arid plains without water. He took the canteen and started to the well.

It was full daylight now, and Longarm had his first real chance to inspect the whiskey ranch. It was about like all the others of its kind he'd seen in the Indian Nation. Though it was built of raw lumber that had never seen paint, the main building looked to be reasonably solid. The cabins were less so, with holes sawed in them for doors and windows, their walls already begining to twist and lean. Two tin-roofed sheds stood a bit away from the cabins, to shelter some bales of hay and the horses. A spiderweb of trails fanned out from the cluster of buildings.

As he passed Zara's wagon, he examined it without seeming to do so. Having seen it only in the dark, he hadn't pictured it as being the gaily painted gypsy caravan it was. A small room had been built on the wagon bed. It had low wooden walls, a narrow door in the back, and tiny curtained windows in the sides. The outside was painted a soft green, the door and windowframes were outlined in maroon. The door was closed and the curtains drawn, but as Longarm passed a hand slid through the curtain and flicked a quick wave.

Longarm did not return the greeting. He carried the canteen on to the well, dropped in the bucket, let it fill, and drew it up, the unoiled pulley creaking as the spindle rotated. He was pouring water from the bucket into the canteen when Netta came out of the saloon and walked over to join him.

"I heard what you and Reeder said," she told him. "But if you'd just put off leaving long enough to come inside and sit down to breakfast with us, I think he'd change his mind."

Longarm shook his head. "Reeder might change his mind, Netta, but I won't."

"I was sort of counting on tonight," she said.

"You won't miss me. You still got Reeder, ain't you?"

Netta spat expressively. "I don't want Reeder."

"There'll likely be somebody else along, today or tomorrow."

"Where are you heading for, Smitty?"

"Oh, I'm just drifting along. Not much telling where I'll wind up."

"You wouldn't like to take me with you, I guess?"

"It ain't in the cards, Netta. The way I travel, I can't take a woman along."

"Well, maybe you'll drift back this way sometime. Or we might run into each other again, someplace else."

"Maybe. The country ain't all that big, you know."

Reeder appeared in the door of the saloon. He called, "You got work to do in here, Netta. Leave Smith alone; he's trying to get ready to leave."

Netta's face wrinkled with distaste. She said, "Goodbye, then, Smitty. Remember what I said."

"Sure," Longarm replied.

He watched Netta disappear into the saloon, finished filling his canteen, and rode off as quickly as possible. He did as the gypsy had told him, heading west along the faint trail that ran from the whiskey ranch. He stopped at one point to examine the trail, and found that the freshest hoofprints on it had been left a week or more before.

It was obviously a trail over which few travelers passed, and, as soon as he'd satisfied himself on that point, Longarm relaxed. He let the cavalry mount set its own pace and ate his breakfast in the saddle, munching on slivers of jerky and an occasional crunchy bite of parched corn. When he reached the river Zara had told him about, Longarm followed it until he came to the creek that flowed into the larger stream from the north.

Both watercourses were low. A few holes that looked knee-deep or less lay between shallow trickles over gravelly bottoms. There were small tufts of grass at the high-water mark in both streambeds, so Longarm took the bridle off the horse and hobbled it to let it graze and drink while he waited. As the sun rose higher and felt warm on his back, the water began to look more and more inviting.

You know, old son, this'd be a right nice place to take a bath, Longarm told himself as he stood gazing at the shrunken river's rippling surface. *No way of knowing how long that Zara woman's going to take getting here, if she shows up at all. But her knowing your name likely means she knows a lot more, so just be patient and bide your time. And that nice cool crick's as good a place to bide in as any.*

Levering off his boots, Longarm shed his clothes. As he did sometimes when he had to undress in uncertain territory, he opened the clasp that attached the chain of his derringer to his watch and returned the watch to the pocket of the vest. He fastened the clasp in the loop attached to the derringer and drew the chain over his head, so that the little snub-nosed pistol dangled just below his chin, like an oversized medallion on a necklace. Only then did he step into the stream.

There was a deep hole just a few yards from where he stood; at the point where the creek joined the main stream the crosscurrents had scoured out a sizable depression in the bed. He waded out, the stones on the bottom digging into his feet, and found that the hole was mid-thigh-deep in its center.

Moving a little up the side of the hole, he selected a place where the creek's current kept the bottom covered with soft sand. He studied the bank along which he'd just ridden and found that, even with his eyes a bit below the bank, he could see back along the trail for at least a mile.

Satisfied, Longarm sat down. The water was armpit-deep and he began splashing it over his head, letting it trickle down his face and shoulders. He kept an eye on the trail, intending to leave the stream when he saw the gypsy woman's wagon so he could be dressed and waiting when she arrived. But the water was pleasant and the sun was warm. The song of the rippling brook filled his ears, and he was taken by surprise when Zara's voice broke the silence.

"Marshal Long, you are either a very brave man or a very foolish one, to enjoy a bath at such a time."

Longarm did not change position. At Zara's first words he'd brought his hand up to free the derringer. Before she'd finished speaking he had turned quickly, swiveling his torso without standing up. Zara was standing on the bank beside his clothes and gunbelt. Her eyes grew wide when she saw the stubby derringer in his hand, its twin muzzles covering her.

She laughed. "I give you not enough credit, Marshal Long. You are ready for someone who tries to surprise you."

"You done pretty good at it. I was looking for you to come the same way I did."

"I did not take from Reeder's place the trail I saw you leave by," Zara explained. "I think he might be suspicious to see me if I follow you, so I go north when I leave. Then I circle to come back to here, but it was not to steal up behind you."

"A man in my job gets used to people coming at him from behind. If he wants to keep on living, he watches both ways."

"I understand now why Gilbert—" She pronounced the name with a soft "G" and dropped the last letter, making it sound like "Jil*bair*"—"feared because you have been sent to follow him."

"That's Gil Bright you're talking about?" Longarm frowned. "From what you said last night, I gather you know him."

"Yes. How else would I know who you are, when you come to the whiskey ranch?"

"That's what's been puzzling me ever since I rode away from the place. Where'd you know Gil? How long since you seen him?"

"You were very close to catching him. If you were to come to the ranch one day before, he would not then have left."

"Where'd he take off for?"

Zara shrugged. "He did not tell me—only that he would travel west."

"How far west?"

Again Zara shrugged, but this time she said nothing.

Longarm had been studying Zara while they talked. It was the first time he'd really gotten a look at her. She wore a full ankle-length skirt and a white blouse with a rounded, low-cut neckline. The blouse was very loose, and concealed her figure, but at the depth of the cleft at the lowest point of the deep-cut neck Longarm could see the generous swelling of her breasts.

Her chin was firm, her brightly scarlet lips full and pouting. They formed a wide oval, almost a circle, under a nose that was a bit too aquiline for her wide cheekbones. Her eyes were dark hazel with greenish flecks in their depths, and her brows were thick. Her forehead was narrow, her coal-black hair grew in a semicircle that ended at the tops of her ears.

"We got to have a talk, you and me," Longarm told her. His thoughts busy with what Zara had just said, he forgot that he was naked, and stood up. He saw her eyes leave the derringer and move up and down his body, and squatted down in the water again at once. He said, "If you'll just give me a chance to get out of here and put my clothes on—"

"I do not mean to make you embarrassed. My *gonyadota* is a small distance behind, along the creek. I will drive it closer while you dress."

"Go ahead, then. I'll be dressed when you get back."

Zara began walking upstream beside the creek. His mind busy with the puzzling relationship between the gypsy woman and Gil Bright, Longarm dried himself hurriedly on the suit of underwear he'd taken off and put on the fresh suit that had been wrapped around his telegraph key. He donned the rest of his clothes as quickly as possible, put his watch back on the chain, and put the watch and derringer in their accustomed pockets of his vest.

He'd rebuckled his gunbelt and was holding a cheroot, ready to light it, when Zara returned, driving the gypsy wagon. She pulled up the mule, took a turn with the reins around the whip-socket, and jumped from the seat.

"Now we can talk without fear of Reeder," she said. "Come sit by me in the wagon, where there is shade."

Longarm followed her into the caravan. The ceiling was low; he had to take off his hat and bend down. The interior

78

was dim and cool after the bright, hot sunshine. A bunklike bed spanned the front of the caravan, stretching across it from side to side. A bench ran along one side from the bed to the door. There were cabinet doors beneath the bench and below the narrow table or shelf that occupied half of the opposite wall. A cast-iron brazier stood in the corner near the door.

Zara sat down on the bed and Longarm settled on the bench. She said nothing, and was obviously waiting for him to speak first. Not wanting to show his eagerness, Longarm lighted the cheroot he was holding. When she still did not speak he said, "Suppose you do the talking for a while, Zara. Tell me how you got hooked up with Gil Bright and why he come to talk so free to you."

"Gilbert was kind to me when my husband is killed. This is two years, almost three, ago. Our *krif*—" Seeing Longarm's frown, she explained, *"Krif* is like a family, but has not family blood. I do not know the word you use for it."

"Something sorta like an Indian tribe? A clan, maybe?" Longarm asked.

Zara nodded. "Yes. Clan is the word I forget. So. We are then camped in the Indian Nation, my *krif*. They do not like us, the Indians. Gilbert has come to bring law after the fight, and he was kind to me. We go back to Fort Smith."

She fell silent again. Longarm waited. Finally he asked her, "You begun living with him then?"

"I am *phralia* to Gilbert, even if I am *cha* and he is *gajo*—" Zara paused. "Excuse me, Marshal. I think back and get angry with the sad memory. Then I forget and speak in Rom."

"It's all right," Longarm said. "I caught on to what you was saying. Go ahead."

"Gilbert becomes sick," Zara went on. "He changes; he is like a stranger to me." She stopped, frowned. "I do not know how to explain. He is angry with me. He is angry with everyone. He talks of revenge, and speaks names I have never heard. And I do not see until too late that this is because of a sickness he has. He leaves his work and goes away, but he does not say where he will go. And for a long time I know nothing, except that he is gone."

Zara paused, her face twisted into a worried frown. Longarm waited again, but as her silence grew prolonged he said, "But Gil come back right lately. You said he was at the whiskey ranch with you."

"Yes. But it was not like it had been with us before. He

79

was not Gilbert to me. You do not know our language, Marshal Long. In Romany is a word for one dead but still alive. *Mulo*. Gilbert is *mulo* when he comes back."

"A ghost?" Longarm suggested.

Zara nodded. "For what he had done for me, I am grateful to him. But between us, nothing."

"You must've talked about something."

"We talked, yes. But he does not tell me of where he has gone, what he had done, except he says you are following him, to arrest him." Zara looked at Longarm, frowning. "It is not easy to think you must do this. You understand, he has told me much of you, Marshal Long." She smiled. "It is hard for me to say your true name. Always Gilbert called you Longarm."

"If you feel that way, why don't you do the same?"

"You would not mind?"

"Not a bit."

"Then I will." Zara was silent for a moment, then went on. "Always Gilbert spoke of you as his friend, but when he came back to Fort Smith he said you are now enemies. He must run from you, he tells me, and I say I will go where he goes. He did not want me to, but I did. He said he must go west, but we got only this far. He knew Reeder. I do not know how or where before."

"Did they act friendly?"

Zara shook her head. "Not as friends, no. Gilbert said he must not stay long, but he was sick. He could not travel."

"He didn't tell you he was leaving? Or where he was going?"

"He told me nothing. We did not—" Zara hesitated. "We did not have love between us."

"You're trying to say you wasn't sleeping together," Longarm said bluntly.

Zara replied, "For a long time, even before he left me, Gilbert had no manhood. His sickness took away what a woman needs from a man. I came with him because of what he once did for me. I owed Gilbert a debt, and we of the Rom pay our debts."

"You don't feel like you're obliged to Gil for anything else, then?"

"No." Zara's eyes met Longarm's. "I know why you ask me that, Longarm. You want to know if I have told you everything he has told me of his plans. But he has told me nothing."

After a thoughtful pause, she added, "I think he trusted me not at all after he came back."

"I believe you, Zara," Longarm said.

"Then is it time we forget Gilbert?" she asked. "I have done for him all I can. I have paid him my debt. I will go now to some other place. I will not see him again."

"Where are you thinking about heading?"

Zara shrugged. "I do not know. I will just go. When I find the place where I should be, I will recognize it and stay."

"I got to be riding out, too," Longarm told her. "Maybe I can pick up Gil's trail before it gets cold."

"Would you not stay a while with me, Longarm? I told you how it has been with me. I need a man, and when I saw you naked in the stream, I knew that the man I want is you."

"You don't mind speaking right out, do you, Zara?"

"It is the way of Romany women." Zara leaned forward and ran her hand along Longarm's thigh. She stopped at his crotch and began caressing him. "When we wish to make love we do not wait for the man we want to ask us. We ask him."

While she talked, Zara had unbuttoned Longarm's pants and slid her hand inside his trousers. The feel of her warm fingers opening and closing around him was bringing him erect. Zara dropped to her knees on the floor in front of him. She shrugged the low-cut blouse off her shoulders and drew her arms from the sleeves.

Leaning forward, she began rubbing the globes of her bulging breasts over Longarm's swelling shaft. Her dark ruby rosettes were already budded, their tips protruding. She began swaying slowly from side to side, guiding Longarm's sensitive tip over the soft, warm spheres.

Zara traced a subtle pattern, one moment rasping the tip of his quickly hardening erection over the roughened circles of her rosettes, then guiding him to the soft warmth of the satiny skin of the quivering globes. She leaned down to rub his tip on her cheeks, and stroked it with her long eyelashes before she took him into her mouth. Holding him with her lips, her hands freed, she began working at the buckle of his gunbelt.

Longarm pushed her hands away and took the gunbelt off himself. Zara undid the remaining buttons of his fly, freeing his shaft completely, while her mobile tongue was busy bringing him to a full, throbbing erection.

She stood up. At some time she'd loosened the waistband

81

of her skirt, for the skirt slid to the floor, followed by her blouse. Straddling Longarm's thighs, kneeling on the bench, Zara mounted him. He felt her hot wetness engulfing him as she lowered her hips, moaning with pleasure as she felt him going deeper into her wet hot pulsing depths.

"*Ujesti m'ro!*" Zara sighed.

Longarm did not understand her words, but took them as a request. He lifted her, standing up, and took the short step to the bed. Zara screamed softly as he fell on top of her, driving his shaft still deeper. Her screams became a softly modulating medley, sighs and high-pitched cries of pleasure, as Longarm drove into her again and again.

Zara gyrated her hips beneath him, raising them to meet his lunges. The tempo of her lusty upward thrusts increased as her pleasure mounted, until Longarm felt that he was driving into a fleshly whirlwind. Then Zara's cries modulated into one throaty, continuing scream. She trembled under Longarm's plunging strokes, and locked her legs around his hips to pull him still deeper into her while her body writhed and jerked until he felt her muscles let go in total relaxation. Then he quit plunging and lay quiet, still pressing deeply into her with his firm erection.

After a few moments Zara opened her eyes and looked at Longarm's face, so close above her. "*Meery, meery, meery,*" she sighed. "*Tatchipen,* Longarm."

"I guess that means you're all right." He smiled.

"More than all right." Zara's eyes grew wide and then a small frown puckered her face. "But I still feel you big and hard inside me. You cannot be ready so soon again!"

"Whenever you are, Zara."

"Then now!" she exclaimed. "And do not stop until you must rest, even if I should beg you to!"

Chapter 10

"No, Billy," Longarm said firmly. "You can't just close this case and pull me off it. Damn it, you know that!"

A sudden flush of anger swept up the chief marshal's cheeks to his forehead and the little bulges of flesh that were creeping over the rim of his collar as he glared at Longarm across his paper-strewn desk.

"Don't tell me I can't do something!" Vail snapped. "Not until you're sitting on this side of my desk and I'm sitting where you are now!"

Longarm saw that he'd gone too far. He'd seldom seen his chief so angry. "I didn't mean to sound like I was telling you what to do, Billy. Sure, you can close the case any time you feel like it. But you can't tell Gil Bright to stop killing lawmen. He ain't done all the killing he's got in mind."

"How can you be sure?" Vail demanded. "Did Bright write you a letter?"

"You know better than that, Billy. But unless the gypsy woman—that Zara I told you about—was lying to me, Gil set out from No Man's Land to find somebody else to gun down."

"That was three weeks ago," Vail pointed out. "Bright's had all the time he'd need to murder anybody he had on his list."

"Maybe, maybe not. If he was after me, now, he'd've had to wait until I got back here. And I spent nearly two weeks after I left No Man's Land trying to pick up his trail."

"If his tracks were so cold you couldn't uncover them two weeks ago, they're even colder now," Vail said.

"Likely he's just moving around. I been trying to figure out what I'd do, was I in Gil's shoes. You know, Hays and Dodge and No Man's Land ain't all that far apart. If I'd stirred things

83

up as much as he did in such a little bitty area, I'd put a lot of miles between me and those places."

"I won't argue against that. He's almost certain to know we've found out who he is. Sure he's going to make a long move about now. The question is, in what direction?"

"My bet's west. It's the only way he ain't zigzagged so far, unless you count the little jog he made into No Man's Land. And that might've just been his first stop to someplace else."

"Even if you're right, we can only carry a case so far. You know, there's other offices besides this one, and the chances are good Bright's next move will carry him into another jurisdiction. Let them chase him for a while."

"Nobody in any of the other districts knows Gil inside and out, the way I do, Billy. Except maybe somebody in the Fort Smith office."

"You know how the Attorney General feels when we step into another district's territory. No. We'll call it quits."

Longarm said nothing. He simply fixed his gunmetal-blue eyes on the chief marshal and stared unblinkingly. Vail locked eyes with him for a long minute or so, then dropped his gaze to his desk. He shuffled the stacks of papers for a moment, then looked up at Longarm again.

"Oh, hell!" he exclaimed. "I know you're right about the damned case, Long. We've got a bad apple on our hands here, and he's not going to stop by himself."

"Not much use in me saying I look at it the same way, Billy. Gil's got to be caught, and that's all there is to it."

"It's still your case," Vail said. "Go ahead. I'll square things if one of the chief marshals in another district bellyaches. Damn it, if I took you off the case now and left Bright free to kill more lawmen, I'd feel as guilty as if I'd pulled the trigger on them myself."

"That's the way I'd feel, too." Longarm nodded. "Thanks, Billy."

Vail said, "Don't thank me too soon. Keeping the case open doesn't mean you're going to loaf around here in Denver until Bright comes out into the open again."

"I imagine you'll find something for me to do."

"You know I can't afford to have one of my deputies sitting around idle. While you're waiting, I'm putting you on the civil cases here in Denver and close by."

"You won't hear me complain about that one bit," Longarm

replied. He knew that Vail knew how little he liked the boring routine of serving civil complaints and summonses and shepherding jurors day after day. "But I'd take it real kindly if you'll do one more thing on Gil's case."

"What's that?"

"I been thinking about the places Gil's likely to head for. You know, he covered a lot of cases when he worked outa Denver, here. Wyoming Territory, Texas—New Mexico and Arizona Territories, too. When you sent out them wires right after Gil begun his killing rampage, did you send 'em to them places?"

"Some. I didn't cover the whole damned West like a blanket, if that's what you're driving at."

"Then send out a bunch more wires, Billy. Get the word to places you didn't warn when you sent that first batch. And if his trail opens up, and I'm out serving a summons or something, send that little pink-cheeked clerk of yours to find me, so I don't lose a minute getting on Gil's trail."

"That's reasonable enough," Vail nodded. "You've got my word on it."

Longarm was still out of sorts when he started up the steps to his rooming house that evening. The soft grey hush of the mile-high twilight was just giving way to the blue of a Rocky Mountain night, but Longarm's mind was far away from his familiar surroundings.

He spent the day trudging over the toe-catching bricks of Denver's uneven sidewalks, serving jury summonses in the downtown district. Some of the businessmen to whom the summonses were addressed had made him wait anywhere from ten minutes to half an hour before they'd see him, and almost all of them had put up an argument before accepting the documents.

A few of the prospective jurors had offered to pay him to report that he'd been unable to find them, and he'd had to explain that if they didn't answer the summons this time, they'd simply get another at the next court term. He was still chafing over Billy Vail's order to suspend his pursuit of Gil Bright when he opened the rooming-house door and started up the steep stairway to his second-floor room. The landlady hadn't yet lighted the hall lamp, and the narrow passageway at the head of the stairs was in semi-darkness.

Longarm took his key out of his pocket as he reached the head of the stairs and started down the hall to the door of his room. He stabbed at the lock, but the key hit an obstruction and dropped from his hand. Longarm bent down to pick it up just as a sharp, high-pitched pop sounded from the end of the hall and he heard the unmistakable thud of a bullet tearing into the doorframe at the level where his head had been a second earlier.

Instead of standing up, Longarm dropped flat. His move saved him from the second shot. Another pop broke the stillness in the second it took him to get to the floor, and another slug thunked into the doorframe above his head.

As he went down he whipped his Colt out of its holster while his eyes were searching the dark hallway for the source of the shots. There wasn't enough light in the direction of the stairwell for him to see anything. Even the newel post at the top of the banister was hidden in the gloom.

Still on his belly, Longarm wormed his way along the worn runner that covered the hall's floor. His ears caught the faint sound of retreating footsteps going down the stairs, and he jumped up. Covering the distance between the door of his room and the head of the stairs in a series of giant steps, he took the stairs two at a time going down. The outer door stood open. Crouching low, Longarm ran through the open door and looked along the street.

On the unfashionable side of Cherry Creek, the streetlights were few and spaced far apart. Streaks of brightness lay across the street at wide intervals from the windows and doors of the houses facing the street, but though Longarm stood on the dark porch of the rooming house and scanned the street in both directions for a good quarter of an hour, nothing moved except a dog chasing a stray cat. Finally he holstered his Colt and went back up the narrow stairs.

When he reached the door to his room, he struck a match with a flick of his thumbnail, located his key where he'd dropped it on the floor, and picked it up. When he tried to slide the key into the keyhole it met resistance, but Longarm forced it in. After the door had swung open, he looked on the floor inside his room and saw lying on the threshold the small wad of cardboard that the sniper had used to block the keyhole. He lighted the lamp on his bureau and took a quick swallow from the bottle of Tom Moore that stood next to the lamp before opening his clasp knife and going back to the door.

86

Though he knew he'd get a jawing from the landlady for damaging the woodwork, Longarm dug the two slugs out of the doorframe. He weighed the little leaden pellets in his callused palm as he closed and locked the door, picked up the bottle from the bureau, and put it on the floor beside the bed. Then he sat down on the bed and lighted a cheroot while he studied the bullets.

"Same gun," he muttered, turning the small cones on his flattened palm with the tip of the knife blade. The slugs had come from a .25 garter pistol, the same as the one used by the sniper in No Man's Land. It was a woman's gun, and Longarm couldn't recall making any woman mad enough at him to want to shoot him. But whoever this one was, she liked to hide in the dark and potshoot. Except she didn't aim very well, if she aimed at all.

He swallowed some of the smoothly biting rye and took a long puff on the cigar. He thought, *There ain't no way to figure out who she could be, old son. Likely somebody that's carrying a grudge over an outlaw you shot or put away in the pen. And about all you can do about it, is to keep looking over your shoulder and hope she keeps on missing.*

He finished his cigar, had a nightcap, and turned in. He went to sleep at once, and when he reported to the office the next day he said nothing about the attempt that had been made to kill him. As far as he knew, the effort stemmed from some case he'd closed long ago, and until he caught up with his would-be assassin there was no point in discussing the matter.

Longarm spent another boring day serving summonses, and the following day he almost welcomed being assigned to federal court as guardian of a jury hearing a land claims case that consisted mostly of lawyers arguing with one another in their own private language over the validity of some early survey boundaries. The court adjourned early and, for lack of anything better to do, Longarm decided to check in at the office before quitting for the day.

Instead of walking the length of the federal building to the wide marble stairs in the foyer that were used by the public, he took the service stairs at the rear, came out of the unmarked door on the second floor, and walked down the hall. A scrub-woman was on her knees a short distance from the door of the office, bending over with her brush, her bucket by her side. Her head was bound up in a cloth that formed an improvised cap and her shapeless grey skirt spread out on the floor behind her. Longarm stepped around the bucket and went into the office.

Vail was standing in the outer room when he went in, talking to the pink-cheeked young clerk. When he saw Longarm he said, "It's a little bit early for Judge Laney to adjourn court, isn't it?"

"I guess he just came to a good stopping place and decided he'd heard enough lawyer talk for one day," Longarm replied. He took a cheroot out of his pocket and dug out a match. "Any news from them wires you sent out, Billy?"

"Not a thing. Looks like Bright's holed up somewhere."

Longarm rasped his horn-hard thumbnail across the head of the match as Vail was speaking. Over the hissing of the match springing into flame he heard the soft click of the doorknob behind him being turned stealthily. Suddenly remembering that it was much too early in the day for the scrubwomen to be starting to clean the building, Longarm flipped the match from his hand in a flaming arc and dropped to the floor.

"Get down, Billy!" he called as he swiveled and reached for his holstered Colt.

He got a glimpse of a woman's face—a dark-skinned face, contorted in hatred—half hidden by her extended arm and the miniature revolver she held in her hand. The gun spat a bright needle of muzzle blast and he heard the now-familiar short, light pop as she pulled the trigger. She'd been expecting to find a standing target, though, and had not lowered the pistol's muzzle enough to hit Longarm.

Behind him Longarm heard the pink-cheeked young clerk give a high-pitched cry of pain as the revolver popped again. Longarm had his Colt out now, but seeing a woman in his sights was a strange experience to him. He hesitated for a split second before triggering off a shot and, in that brief eyewink of time, made his decision. He shifted the Colt's muzzle for a shot that would wound but not kill.

Longarm aimed at the woman's upper arm and the slug went true. It plowed into her flesh, her arm jerked back with the impact, and her elbow shattered the frosted glass pane that filled the upper half of the door. Uttering a sharp cry of pain, the woman dropped the little revolver and turned to run.

Longarm leaped to his feet and started after her. She had taken only a few steps down the hall when he caught up with her. The arm his bullet had hit was useless, dangling at her side, blood dripping from her fingertips. She was in too much pain to resist when his big hands reached her and clamped down on her shoulders.

Spinning the woman around to face him, Longarm stared at her dark face for a moment. Her features were strange, but at the same time strangely familiar. He reached up and pulled off the cloth that covered her head. Above the line where the cloth had been bound, her skin was white, and a cascade of streaked blonde hair dropped to her shoulders as he pulled the headcloth away. She turned her face up to glare at him defiantly.

"Netta?" Longarm exclaimed.

"Who in hell did you think I was?" she snarled.

"I didn't rightly know." Longarm suddenly became aware of the blood dripping from the bullet wound in Netta's arm. He took his bandanna from his pocket and wrapped it tightly around the arm to stop the flow. "Come on. We'll go back to the office and get a bandage on that arm so you won't bleed too bad before I can get you to a doctor."

"Aren't you going to arrest me?" she asked defiantly.

"Oh, you're already under arrest. Don't worry about that. But you'll have a doctor's care, just the same."

"Just my damned luck!" Netta said bitterly. "I missed the best chance I had to get you that night at the whiskey ranch."

Along the wide corridor, doors were opening as workers from the other offices on the floor were drawn out by the shooting. Longarm waved them back.

"The excitement's over," he called. "There won't be any more shooting, so you might as well get back to your jobs."

His words had little effect. A few of the federal workers did go back to their own offices, but most of them crowded up to the door of the marshal's office, peering through the jagged opening left in the frosted glass panel. Inside, Longarm found the pink-cheeked clerk sitting in a chair, his coat on the floor beside him, his sleeve pulled up above the elbow, while Vail wrapped a handkerchief around the young man's arm.

"Godamighty, Billy!" Longarm exclaimed as he guided Netta to one of the chairs that stood along the wall. "Maybe we better get a doctor up here instead of trying to take them outside, especially since there ain't no way to lock up the office right now."

Vail finished knotting the handkerchief and straightened up. He looked at the curious faces framed by the jagged edges of the broken door. Picking out a familiar face, Vail called, "Bob

Sanders! Go across the street and get one of the doctors out of the building there. Tell him to bring whatever he needs to tend to a couple of gunshot wounds. The rest of you people do what Marshal Long told you to. Get back to where you belong."

With the chief marshal's command reinforcing Longarm's earlier order, the crowd outside the door shrank rapidly, and in a few moments the last of the curious had gone. Vail turned to Longarm and jerked a thumb at Netta, who was sitting cradling her wounded arm in her lap, moaning softly.

"Who in hell is she? Some lady friend you jilted?" he asked.

"Nothing like that, Billy. This here's one of them girls from that whiskey ranch in No Man's Land that I told you about."

"She must've had a reason for wanting to shoot you," Vail suggested, his voice hard.

Longarm began, "Billy, I give you my word—"

Netta cut him short. She said bitterly, "You're damned right I had a reason! You're the son of a bitch who shot the best man I ever had. I swore I'd get even, and I did my best to. Only I just wasn't a good enough shot."

"Who're you talking about, Netta?" Longarm asked.

"Jack Carver, that's who!" she snapped. "Or maybe you've already forgot about him?"

Longarm shook his head. "No, I remember him. He had a bad eye. Everybody called him One-Eye Carver. Is he the one?"

"You know damned well he is!"

Longarm told Vail, "Carver was riding with Whiskers Cleburn and tried to hold up a train I was on. You oughta remember my report, Billy."

Vail nodded. "Yes. And I remember that Carver had a long record. Two murders while robbing a bank, another one in a train holdup, and I've got a hunch there were some more that never did get onto his record."

"Jack might've been on the wrong side of the law," Netta said, "but he was good to me. And I had to get even with this bastard for killing him."

"You knew who I was when I showed up at Reeder's whiskey ranch, didn't you?" Longarm asked her. "You tried to shoot me there, and you tried at my rooming house the other day, too."

"Wait a minute!" Vail broke in. "I didn't hear anything about that, Long. Why didn't you report it?"

"Well, there wasn't much you could do about it," Longarm replied. "Or me, either, till I found out who was after me."

He turned back to Netta. "You sure fooled me out in the hall with your face made up the way it is."

"I'd have gotten you sooner or later," Netta said bitterly. "I guess I missed the best chance I had there at Reeder's."

"Not that it's such a much of a matter now, but what was you doing there?" Longarm frowned. "You couldn't've known I was going to show up there."

"I didn't," she answered. "That was just luck. I was on my way to Denver to find you when I ran out of money. I had to stop there to make enough to travel on the rest of the way. But I guess I won't have another chance at you for a while, will I?" She turned to Vail. "You're going to put me in jail, aren't you?"

"You ought to know the answer to that," he replied. "You came up here to kill one of my deputies, and managed to miss him, but you wounded my clerk." He turned to indicate the wounded man and his jaw dropped. The clerk lay on the floor beside the chair in which he'd been sitting when the chief marshal bandaged his arm. While Vail and Longarm had been questioning Netta, the pink-cheeked youth had quietly fainted.

91

Chapter 11

Seated in the red morocco upholstered chair in Billy Vail's private office, Longarm puffed thoughtfully on one of his long slim cheroots while he looked at Vail across the chief marshal's paper-strewn desk. Vail was leaning back in his own chair, his hands folded over the small paunch he kept fighting to remove.

"I'll tell you what, Billy," Longarm said. "Soon as that fellow finishes putting in the new glass, I'll walk down to the corner with you and buy us both a drink. You look like you could use one after all the excitement."

"I won't turn down your offer," Vail replied. "But we don't have to wait." He opened the desk's bottom drawer and took out a half-filled bottle. He shoved some papers aside to make a clear space for it on the desk. "Except that bourbon's not your favorite liquor."

"Right now I ain't looking no gift horses in the mouth," Longarm said. "After you, Billy."

Vail tilted the bottle and swallowed twice, then passed it to Longarm. He said, "I know all that commotion wasn't your idea, but it's more than we've had in this office for a longer time than I can remember."

Longarm didn't reply until he'd gulped his own drink and put the bottle back on the desk. Then he grinned. "I ain't seen a to-do like that since grandma got her left tit caught in the wash wringer. But I guess it's all over and forgot now."

Vail slapped the desk with the flat of his hand and rose to his feet. He started for the outer office, saying over his shoulder, "Damned if I didn't forget! Just before you walked in and the shooting started the messenger brought up a batch of late wires from the telegraph room."

Denver's federal office building, like all such district headquarters across the nation, had its own telegraph terminal. The room in the basement not only had wires coming in from the fledgling Western Union Company that was beginning to expand its operations into the western states, but boasted a direct line to the Attorney General's office in Washington and terminals from the railroads that ran into Denver.

Carrying a small sheaf of flimsies, the chief marshal came back into the room.

Longarm asked, "You think there might be something I'd be interested in, Billy?"

"I'll know in a minute." Vail was thumbing through the tissue-thin sheets in his hand. He stopped, pulled one out, and passed it to Longarm. "Here. Read this."

Longarm read the flimsy:

DEPUTY CITY MARSHAL BRAINERD SHOT AND KILLED BY MAN ANSWERING DESCRIPTION YOUR TELEGRAM STOP REPORTING MURDER AS REQUESTED STOP CITY MARSHAL JOHNSON EL PASO

"Looks like I was right about Gil heading west," Longarm told Vail. "I didn't figure on him winding up in El Paso, though."

"You remember Brainerd, don't you?" Vail asked.

"Can't say I do." Longarm frowned.

"No, I guess he was before your time," Vail said. "Damned near before mine, come to think about it. He was one of the tough old boys, quick on the trigger and mean as sin. He was a little too tough for the Attorney General to stomach as a deputy U. S. marshal, I guess. He was dismissed about a year after the new administration came in, and I'd heard a while back that he wound up in El Paso."

Longarm nodded absently. He was already thinking about train schedules and distances. He said, "If I get moving right away, I can get a connection on the D&RG to the Santa Fe at Trinidad that'll put me in Albuquerque tomorrow. The stage out of Albuquerque only takes two days to get to El Paso."

"It seems to me you'd do better staying with the trains," Vail suggested.

Longarm shook his head. "Last time I was down that way, Billy, it took a week to get down to the Rio Grande. What's bothering me is that Gil might be figuring on dodging across into Mexico. You know what that means."

"I don't want you in Mexico again, Long!" Vail said firmly. "Every time you've stepped across the border you've stirred up enough trouble with the *rurales* to keep Washington on my neck for a month of Sundays. If Bright does go to Mexico, you're not to follow him—and that's an order!"

"Whatever you say, Billy," Longarm answered mildly.

"This time I mean it!" Vail said. "All right. If you need anything before you leave—"

"I still got vouchers and requisitions left in my wallet. Enough to see me through this trip, anyhow."

"Get on your way, then," Vail nodded. "If any later word about Bright comes in, I'll wire you in care of Johnson."

Longarm swung off the stagecoach at the El Paso station, his bones still rattling from the long trip south. He waited while the driver took his saddle from the boot and started down Piedras Street toward the river. The town was just beginning to wake up for the evening, and as he got closer to the Rio Grande the number of men on the sidewalk grew steadily larger and the sound of one tinny piano after another drifted from the swinging doors of the saloons and caught his ears as he walked along.

Though a considerable amount of time had passed since Longarm's last visit, El Paso's city hall and the police station that occupied part of its ground floor had changed little. He saw a grizzle-faced man with bulldog jaws sitting beside the station door, his chair tilted against the wall, his ankles crossed, feet dangling off the ground.

"I'm looking for Marshal Johnson," Longarm said, coming to a halt in front of the door. "Think he might be inside?"

"Nope." The man spoke around the stub of an unlighted cigar clenched between his teeth. "Outside. I'm Johnson."

"My name's Long. Deputy U. S. Marshal from Denver."

"Hell you say!" Johnson spat out the cigar stub. "How's my old friend Billy Vail? Ain't seen him for a spell, not since he was with the Rangers."

"Billy's fine. Said to tell you hello."

"You say your name's Long? You wouldn't be the one they call Longarm, would you?"

"Some folks call me that."

"Well, now. You federals must want the fellow Billy wired about pretty bad, to send you all the way down here, even if you're not sure he's the one that killed Jess Brainerd."

"We're certain enough it's the man we're looking for, if he fitted the description in the wire you got from Billy. And we want him bad enough, or I wouldn't be here." Longarm took out the sketch of Gil Bright and passed it to Johnson. "Can you tell from this whether I'm on a water haul, or have I got a hot trail?"

Johnson squinted at the sketch. "I'd say you got a hot trail. Put a set of black whiskers on this fellow, and he'd be the man that gunned Jess down, all right. Real thin fellow, is he? Tall, long legs?"

"Sure sounds like him. What kind of gun did he use?"

"Damned little nickel-plated .32 belly-gun. Jess was having hisself a drink at the Acme Saloon, and this fellow was standing at the bar next to him. Jess turned away from him and the son of a bitch taken out that little peashooter from the bellyband of his pants and shot old Jess in the back of the head."

Longarm nodded. "That's him, all right. He murdered a town marshal up in Dodge the same way."

"Who is he, anyhow?" Johnson asked.

"His name's Gil Bright. He used to be one of Billy Vail's deputies before he got transferred to the Fort Smith district. For the last six months he's been out shooting lawmen."

Johnson whistled through his teeth. "Don't wonder you're after him hot and heavy. Wish my boys had caught up with him so I could hand him over to you, but it looks like he's got clean away. Not that we didn't try to find him."

"I imagine you did all you could."

"You're damn right we did! I'll tell you something, Long." Johnson dropped his voice, so that Longarm had to lean closer to hear him. "There's a mean bastard named Dallas Stoudenmire who's out after my job. Every one of the selectmen's keeping an eye on me, and I've got to convince 'em I'm the best man. I can't afford to miss a bet when it comes to finding out who killed Jess Brainerd."

"You're sure it was Gil Bright?"

"I'm sure enough, now you've told me Bright's running around the country killing lawmen. Allowing for the beard, that picture you showed me fits the man that was in the saloon."

"But he got away," Longarm said flatly.

"No fault of me or my boys! We went over this damn town like a pack of hounds after a coon. Shit! The bastard had got away before we ever begun looking for him."

"You must've found out something about him if you turned

El Paso upside down, like you say," Longarm suggested.

"We found out a few things. Not anything that'd help us after he'd got away—like where he'd come from and where he might be headed."

"You feel like telling me what you picked up? It'd help me out a lot. Things like how long he'd been in El Paso, where he hung out, how he got away."

"Well." Johnson took a new cigar from his shirt pocket and jabbed it in his mouth, bit down on it, but did not light it. He went on, "He was after Jess Brainerd, all right. He'd asked the barkeep at the Acme and two or three other saloons about him. And he come into the stationhouse once to ask about Jess."

"Did he talk to you the time he was in the station?"

"No. It was a mite early for me to be here. About six in the morning, as I recall."

"After he shot your deputy, when you were shaking the town down trying to find him, did you come up with anything?"

"Oh, we found the hotel where he'd stayed. Got to it the morning after he killed Jess. But he'd gone by then. Bed hadn't been slept in. All there was in the room was a bunch of dirty, snotty handkerchiefs. He must've had a nosebleed sometime or other. There was blood on one or two of 'em."

"If you traced him back to a room he'd rented, your men must do a pretty good job of work."

"Well, he'd killed Jess on an army payday, so the military police helped us a little bit."

"Wait a minute," Longarm broke in. "How'd they come into the case?"

"You know Fort Bliss is back in business, I guess?"

"I didn't know it'd ever been *out* of business."

"Oh, hell, yes. The army shut it down and moved out till we had that little dustup with Mexico over them salt beds up the river a couple years ago. That brought the sojers back, and it looks like they'll stay this time." Johnson bit off an inch of the cigar stub and spat it out, then returned the rest of the stogie to his mouth.

"I was asking about the MP's," Longarm reminded him.

"Sure. Well, on paydays, all the sojers flock into town to blow their money and raise a little hell. Some of 'em get into trouble. We don't want our jail all cluttered up, so the MP's patrol with my boys and any of the Fort Bliss boys they arrest go right on out to the guardhouse at the fort."

"What's that got to do with Gil Bright?"

"I'm getting to it," Johnson said. "One of the MP's was with Jess Brainerd and got a good look at your man Bright. He said he'd seen him out at the fort just the day before, asking where the dispensary was at."

Longarm remembered his conversation with the doctor in Hays City, where Bright had also discarded a number of dirty handkerchiefs. "What'd he want at the dispensary?" he asked Johnson.

"Damned if I know. The MP didn't say anything about it till after we knew we'd let the fellow get away, so I didn't ask."

"I don't guess you'd have any objection if I'd go out to the fort and nose around a little?"

"Not a bit. It ain't far from here. You can walk it in ten minutes. I'd go along, but it's getting on toward the part of the evening when I make a round of the stores and show everybody I'm right on the job."

"I guess you won't mind if I leave my saddle here?"

"Just drop it inside the door, and tell the desk man I said to keep an eye on it."

After he'd wasted the better part of an hour going from one house to another in Fort Bliss's officers' row, Longarm finally found the doctor Bright had consulted.

"Yes, of course I remember the man," Major Cleary said after looking at the sketch Longarm showed him. "It's not often that one of us gets a visit from a discharged veteran who claims he's still entitled to consult us about an illness."

"That's what Bright did?"

"He didn't give me that name, Marshal Long. He called himself Parker. But it's the same man, I'm positive of that— even though he wore a beard when he was here."

"You mind telling me what he wanted?"

"Advice on his condition. He's tubercular, you know."

"I been told that, but this is the first time I've had a chance to make sure."

"You can be sure now. His symptoms were quite definite. Recurring coughing, sputum discharge, wasting of body tissue, spells of weakness. All symptomatic of the disease."

"You examined him, Major?"

"Of course. Quite thoroughly, even though his claim to army medical care wasn't justified by regulations. Tuberculosis isn't classed as a service-connected injury, but I feel sorry for veterans who can't afford to pay for the care they need. I bent the rules a little and gave him an examination."

"What's your judgment on his case, if you don't mind telling me?"

"Well . . ." The major thought for a moment. "I don't suppose there's anything wrong with telling you, under the circumstances. The man's illness is definitely approaching a terminal stage."

"If I translate that into the kind of talk I understand, don't it mean he ain't got much longer to live?"

"I'd go a bit further, Marshal. What I'm telling you is that, for all practical purposes, you're chasing a dead man."

"How close to being dead is he? A week, maybe? A month? I need some facts, Major."

"I'm afraid I'll have to disappoint you. Tuberculosis is a very deceitful disease, Marshal Long. The man I examined could have a major hemorrhage tomorrow and die within twenty-four hours. I asked him whether he'd started coughing up blood yet, and he said he had."

"Ain't that going to make him weak?" Longarm frowned. "I been shot a time or two, and I know what bleeding does to a man."

"I'm not trying to evade any of your questions," Major Cleary replied. "But that's another one I can't pin down with a direct answer."

"Meaning what?"

"As I just said, tuberculosis is deceptive. A tubercular person can be as weak as a kitten for a while—a day, a week, even a month or so—and then suddenly recover his strength almost miraculously overnight."

"And stay strong how long?"

"All I can do is repeat what I just said. A day or so, a week—perhaps, in some cases, as long as a month."

"He'd be able to travel and all that while he was feeling strong, then?"

"Of course. He might even think he was getting well. He'd be wrong, of course."

For another moment Longarm sat in thoughtful silence. Then he asked, "I don't suppose he said anything about what he was aiming to do when he left, did he?"

Cleary shook his head. "No. Nothing definite. He did say he had a few things to take care of and that he hoped he wouldn't get sick before he got to where he was going."

"But he didn't mention where that was?"

"I'm sorry, Marshal," Cleary replied. "I was interested in the man's illness, not his traveling plans. He didn't say where he might be going, and I didn't ask."

Longarm stood up. "I thank you for your time, Major. You've been a real big help."

Longarm had time to think while he was walking back to downtown El Paso. So far, his efforts at trying to put himself into Gil Bright's shoes had been a mixture of success and failure. He couldn't avoid feeling that the successes had for the most part been accidental.

You might as well face up to it, old son, he told himself as he reached the dead end of Copia Street and turned into Piedras, with the city hall only a short distance away. *You just ain't been figuring Gil out too good, or you'd've caught up with him before now. What you got to do is get a jump ahead of him. Now, there ain't no place he'd go from here but east, and after what that doctor told him, he's likely heading home to see his mother. Which means you better cut a shuck towards Missouri, or he'll get so far ahead of you again that you won't catch up with him until he's made his visit home and set out again to kill some other poor devil.*

As Longarm walked along Piedras Street, Bill Johnson came out of a saloon and fell into step with him. Johnson said, "I hope you found out something that'd help you at the fort, Long."

"I did and I didn't. But the doctor I talked to there told me enough so I'm betting Gil headed east for Missouri when he left here. Now I got to figure how I can catch up with him."

"Why don't you just get on the train and go?"

"Hell, you know the Southern Pacific ain't built more'n ten miles of track east of here. I found that out before I left Denver. That's why I took the Santa Fe to Albuquerque and rode that slow, miserable stage the rest of the way here."

"Way up there in Denver where you're headquartered, I guess you must not've heard about the Katy," Johnson said.

"That'd be the MK&T, I guess. Sure. I heard about 'em, but their trackage stops at Laredo, and that's twice as far from here as Albuquerque."

"You're behind the times, Long. The Katy and the SP was in such a hurry to beat each other to El Paso that both of 'em built track faster than you'd think possible. The Katy railhead's only about twenty miles east of here now, and it'll get you to

San Antonio. Once you're there, you can hop a train that'll connect to just about anyplace east you might name."

"That being the case, I better figure out a way to get to the Katy railhead," Longarm said thoughtfully.

"Now that ain't no problem. You got a saddle, I'll lend you a horse out of the city stable. Leave the horse at the Katy railhead stable and tell the boys there I said for one of 'em to bring it into town when they get around to it. Why, damn it, you can be halfway to Missouri by this time tomorrow."

Chapter 12

Stretched out in the chair, his face swathed with a steaming towel, Longarm could feel the travel grime melting away. The barber lifted the towel off and began lathering the three-day growth of stubble that coated Longarm's cheeks and chin.

"Stranger in town, ain't you?" the barber asked as he rubbed the lather in. Without waiting for a reply, he went on, "Planning to stay awhile, or just passing through?"

"Visiting," Longarm said. As always when he was in a strange town, he welcomed a garrulous barber. He'd found them almost as good as barkeeps as a source of local information. "I guess you'd know the family. The Brights?"

"Oh, sure, I know 'em. Her boy used to come in for a shave and a trim when he was in town, but I ain't seen him for a while. You're acquainted with Gil, I suppose?"

"I know him," Longarm said, raising his voice to be heard above the noise made by the razor the barber had begun stropping.

"Widow Bright's poorly right now," the barber went on, drawing the blade down Longarm's cheek. "Been ailing quite a while. Has her ups and downs, I'd imagine." He lifted Longarm's chin to shave his lower jaw. "You just making a friendly visit, or have you got business?"

"Just a visit. Matter of fact, I was hoping her boy would be home, so I could see him while I'm in town."

"I guess Gil's been too busy to come back for a visit of late." Deftly, the barber switched the angle of Longarm's face to attend to the cheek that was still unshaven. "He's a government man, you know. Works down at Fort Smith."

"So I heard. You ain't seen him for a spell, then?"

"Better part of a year, I'd say. Heard he was in town a few

101

months ago, but I guess he didn't stay long enough to come in and say hello."

"I reckon you can tell me how to get to the Brights' house?"

"Why, you can't miss it. Town ain't all that big. Just go east on Main Street past the store and turn left at the next street. It'll be the— Let's see, the fifth house on the west side. Little cottage painted white. But that ain't much help, I guess, seeing most all the houses in town's painted white."

"I'll find it all right."

"You ought not to have any trouble." The barber's shears were snipping away at Longarm's moustache, trimming it smooth. He put a dab of pomatum on his fingertips and rubbed them over the steerhorn curves that swept up to a tip on each cheek. "Now, then. I think that'll fix you up, mister."

Longarm fished a quarter out of his pocket, handed it to the barber, and stepped over to the coat tree where his gunbelt hung on the hook over his coat. The man dropped the coin in the till behind the barber chair and took out a dime. Longarm had buckled on his gunbelt by now and was sliding his arms into his coatsleeves. He waved the coin away.

"Keep the change. You was good enough to steer me to the Bright house. I appreciate it."

"Well, thank you, mister. Easy to see you ain't from around here. Folks in Lamar don't go in much for tipping."

As the barber had predicted, Longarm had no trouble finding the Bright house. He started up the brick walk that led to the porch of the neat one-story dwelling without any enthusiasm for the visit he was about to make. A young woman wearing a gingham apron over a housedress answered his knock.

"My name's Long, miss," Longarm said. "Custis Long. I'd like to visit a minute with Mrs. Bright, if she ain't busy."

"Are you the Long we've heard Gil speak of so often? The one he calls Longarm?"

"I suppose I am. Him and me was together for quite a spell. I guess he's mentioned me a time or two."

"I'm Gil's sister, Marshal Long. Maybe he's said something to you about me. Sue?"

"Oh, I heard quite a bit about you when me and Gil was working together. But that was a while back, you know."

"I guess you haven't forgotten, have you? Sue Gardner's my married name."

"I'm right glad to meet you, Mrs. Gardner."

"Please call me Sue. And, if you don't mind, I'm going to

call you what Gil always does. Goodness, I wish I had a penny for every time I've heard him mention your name. You don't mind if I call you Longarm, do you?"

"Of course not."

"Well, step inside, Longarm," she said. Then, as she held the door open for him to enter, she went on with a frown, "You are still a U.S. marshal, aren't you? Like Gil?"

"Oh, sure." Sue Gardner had stopped in the hallway after closing the door. Longarm took off his hat and stood waiting.

"It's too bad you didn't get here a few days ago," Sue went on. "Gil stopped in, but he was going somewhere on an important case, and he could only stay between trains."

Longarm hid his surprise and curiosity. He said, "I didn't pass through Fort Smith on my way here, but I'll be dropping in there right after I leave. Maybe I'll see him then."

"I don't think so. Gil doesn't tell us anything about his work, you know. I guess you don't talk about your cases, either, do you? When you're with your family?"

"Well, I ain't got a family, Sue. But if I did have, I'd be the same way. A U.S. marshal ain't allowed to talk about his work, you know."

"Yes, Gil explained all that to us." She hesitated for a moment, then dropped her voice. "You—you're not bringing us bad news, are you? I mean, nothing's happened to Gil? I know the job is dangerous."

"Why, me and Gil don't work out of the same headquarters, haven't for a long time. And I ain't seen him for two or three years. I . . ." Now it was Longarm who hesitated. "I was in the neighborhood, and it struck me that I'd oughta visit his folks since I was so close by."

"I'm sure Mother will be glad to see you. She's old, and not very well, you know. Rheumatism. It settled in her joints and she can barely walk. But she can sit and talk, and I know she'll be right glad to see somebody Gil's told her about so often."

When he settled down on the horsehair-upholstered sofa in the parlor, Longarm was thankful he'd gotten some cues from his brief conversation with Gil's sister. Mrs. Bright sat in a rocking chair at the end of the sofa. Sue had left them after an introduction and a brief explanation to her mother of the reason Longarm had given for his visit.

Even in the dim light that trickled through the slats of the room's shuttered windows, Longarm could tell that Gil's mother was not in good health. Her age-seamed face was waxen, her lips colorless, and her deep-set eyes were filmed. She kept a knitted woolen shawl pulled closely around her face; the shawl was draped over her shoulders and tucked around her body.

"My laws, my laws!" she exclaimed after Sue had left them. "Marshal Longarm! After all this time you've finally come to pay us a visit. You know, I've told Gil he'd ought to bring you with him sometimes, when he's come home to see us, but he never did seem to get around to doing it."

Longarm decided not to try to explain the difference between his actual name and his nickname. She'd probably heard her son refer to him by the nickname so often that it was small wonder she'd gotten confused. He wasn't looking forward to the next few minutes, and he didn't want to prolong their conversation any longer than was actually necessary.

Even before entering his former partner's childhood home, Longarm had been wondering if he was going to be able to do his duty and deceive Gil Bright's trusting family. He hadn't been able to deceive himself, though. He'd known while he was wondering that no matter what his own feelings might be, he'd put his duty first.

He told her truthfully, "When me and Gil was working together all the time, he told me a lot about you, Mrs. Bright. I wished a lot of times I could've come here with him, but it ain't always easy for two men to get leave at the same time."

"I do hope you've brought me some news about my boy," Mrs. Bright said, leaning forward in the rocking chair.

Longarm understood at once that Mrs. Bright still had the idea he and Gil had continued to be close colleagues even after they'd been assigned to different headquarters, almost a thousand miles apart.

"I'm afraid I ain't seen Gil for a long time, Mrs. Bright," Longarm said. "Matter of fact, I was hoping I'd run into him here or in Fort Smith."

"Dear knows, he hasn't had time to stay for a real visit for almost a year, now," she went on, as though Longarm had not spoken. "I don't know what I'd do if it wasn't for Sue. She didn't have to leave to take a job, like Gil did. Sue lives here in town and spends the daytimes with me while her husband is at his work."

"You're lucky she can do that," Longarm said. "Sue told me Gil was here for a visit not too long ago, though."

"A visit!" She snorted. "Some dinky little visit it was, Marshal Longarm. He got in on the day train from Fort Smith at noon and had to take the night train out at seven that same evening. Why, goodness me, I thought I'd brought Gil up better than that! My daddy and mama always told me that children didn't call it a visit if they didn't stay with their mother for a week or more. I'd've been spanked if I'd made my mother a visit like that one Gil made me, even if he is a grown man with a lot of responsibility."

Longarm tried to get back to the subject that interested him most. "Gil didn't say where he was going from here, did he?"

"Oh, no!" Mrs. Bright seemed shocked at the question. "All he did was leave the names."

Longarm was surprised by her reply, but did not let it show in his face or voice. "What names did he leave you, Mrs. Bright?"

"Why, the same ones he left the last three or four times he's had to go away on a case." Mrs. Bright shook her head and added, "I didn't mean to say it the way it come out, Marshal Longarm. They wasn't the same names all the time, but the same *kind* of names."

Longarm felt himself sinking deeper into a mystery he didn't understand. He said carefully, "You mean that Gil's been leaving you some names when he's made a trip lately?"

"Of course that's what I mean! Just exactly like he did before, when he knew he'd have to be gone a long time, so I can answer his letters. And I will say this much for Gil. He's right good about sending me letters when he can't come home to visit. But it's not the same as seeing him."

"Did he leave the same names every trip?"

"Now, I just said he didn't. Or did I forget and only think I said they wasn't?" She stopped for a moment, frowning, and shook her head, then looked questioningly at Longarm. "But you oughta know all about the names, Marshal Longarm. Your work's just like Gil's, ain't it?"

"More or less," Longarm replied carefully. "But there's a few things different in all our jobs. Maybe if you'd explain a little more about them names Gil left, I'd understand."

"They're the ones the government makes marshals use when you can't use your own because you're out on a case."

"Oh, sure. Them names."

Longarm had never heard of a list of names such as Mrs. Bright described. It wasn't an official policy of the Justice Department to allow deputy marshals to travel under aliases, though the deputies did so occasionally. He had a pretty shrewd idea that he knew what Gil had been doing, however.

Nodding, he said, "What you're talking about is the false names Gil uses when he's out chasing some crook, so they won't recognize him like they would if he used his real one."

"Of course. I knew you'd understand about it, even if I don't see why he has to do it."

"A man can't be too careful when he's after a mean crook. I know Gil's sure he can trust you with a list like that."

"Well, I should hope he can! My son not trust his own mother! And I take real good care of the list, like my boy told me to." Mrs. Bright said. She slipped a hand inside her shawl and fumbled between her hips and the arm of the rocking chair for a moment, then brought out a bulging envelope. "I keep it by me all the time, where it's handy, in the same envelope with Gil's insurance policy. I don't even let Sue look at it. You know how children are. They talk before they think."

Sue Gardner, Longarm thought, was a long way from being a child. Then, not relishing what he felt he was duty-bound to do, he said, "I'd sorta like to see Gil's list, Mrs. Bright, see how it compares with mine. You know you don't have to worry that I'll tell anybody about it."

"Well—I don't know," Mrs. Bright said tentatively. "Gil always told me I had to be real careful not to show it to anybody else."

"Oh, that wouldn't apply to another marshal," Longarm said quickly. "Seeing as I know about the names already."

"Well, I guess you're right. Here." Mrs. Bright opened the envelope and took out a folded slip of paper. She handed it to Longarm. "This is the list he left the other day."

Taking the paper, Longarm unfolded it and scanned the names, written in Gil Bright's neat script: *Frank Martin. Martin Frank. William Edwards. Edward Williams. Robert Blake. Blake Roberts.* As he read them, he memorized each of the combinations. All of them were ordinary names, names easily forgotten by one who'd encountered them casually, easily remembered by a man who was accustomed to carrying such detail in his mind. All of them were names that could be reversed, which made each set easier to recall and doubly useful. He returned the list to Mrs. Blake.

"It looks fine to me, Mrs. Bright."

"I'm glad to hear you say that, Marshal Longarm. You know

how I am—like any mother, worrying about her boy."

"I'd say Gil's been a real thoughtful son. Didn't you say something a minute ago about him taking out insurance on you?"

"Not on me, on him. Like he explained it, if anything was to happen to him, I'll be taken care of without being a burden on Sue and her man." She leaned closer to Longarm and dropped her voice. "It's a big policy, too, Marshal Longarm. Ten thousand dollars! What do you think about that!"

"I sure hope Gil didn't get hold of a bad agent," Longarm frowned. "There's some insurance companies these days that ain't as good as others."

"Oh, Gil wouldn't make no mistakes." Mrs. Bright pulled the flap of the envelope back and brought it up to her face. She said, "The company's called the Quaker Life Insurance Association. Quakers are religious folks, you know, so it's bound to be honest. Gil bought the policy in Fort Smith, but the main office is back East, in Boston, where there's lots of money."

"I'm sure it's a fine company," Longarm assured her. He took out his watch and looked at it. "Well, I hate to make such a short visit, Mrs. Bright, but I've got to be at the depot in time to catch the train."

"Laws, is it that late? I guess sitting talking a body loses track of how fast time passes." Longarm stood up, and she said, "Well, it was real thoughtful of you to stop and say hello to an old lady, Marshal Longarm. I guess you'll be seeing Gil when you go to Fort Smith?"

"I sure hope so," Longarm replied truthfully.

"You give him my love, then, and tell him to come visit me again whenever he's got time."

"I'll do that," he promised. "Now, don't disturb your daughter. I'll just let myself out and be on my way."

Retracing his steps to the main street, Longarm lighted a cheroot and trailed a cloud of smoke behind him as he scanned the signs above the fronts of the buildings while walking toward the railroad station. He'd almost given up when he saw the one he was looking for: POST OFFICE. LAMAR, MISSOURI.

He went inside. It was a typical one-man office, with a partition built across the center of the narrow building into which a window had been cut. Through the window he could see the pigeonholes for mail and a man with his back turned sorting letters and placing them in the cubicles.

Longarm raised his voice a bit. "You'd be the postmaster, I guess?"

"Sure am. Do something for you?" When Longarm produced his wallet and flipped it open to show his badge, he went on, "Well, now, a U. S. Marshal! I guess you know one of our Lamar boys that's on the same force you are. Name of Gil Bright."

"Of course I do. Matter of fact, I stopped in to see you because of a case that's got something to do with Gil."

"That so? Nothing happened to him, I hope?"

Longarm evaded the question by saying, "I'm more concerned about Gil's mother right this minute, Mr.—"

"Green. Horatio Green." The postmaster frowned. "I'd hate to hear the Widow Bright was having some kind of trouble."

"So would I. Now, Mr. Green, I can't tell you all the ins and outs of this case, but it concerns both Gil and his mother. And the department needs your help."

"Well, I'll sure do what I can."

"I'm glad to hear you say that." Dropping his voice, Longarm went on, "We're trying to run down some names that are connected with a case that concerns Gil. There might be some letters coming to Mrs. Bright that'd upset her."

"You mean the crooks Gil's after might threaten that nice old lady?"

"Well, like I said, I can't tell you too much. But I'm going to give you some names, and if you handle any letters with them names on 'em for return addresses, I want you to wire me at the marshal's office in Fort Smith, and tell me where the letters was postmarked."

Green scratched his chin. "I ain't so sure I can do that, Marshal. You know the Post Office has got rules about us postmasters not talking about anybody's mail unless it's on orders of one of the postal inspectors."

"I know all about that." Longarm nodded. "You'll get an order from a postal inspector as soon as I get back to Fort Smith."

"Well, in that case, I guess it's all right," Green said.

"I sorta figured you'd see it that way. Now, let me have one of your pens and a piece of paper, and I'll write down the names I want you to be on the lookout for."

Longarm wrote the names twice, tearing the sheet of paper in halves and tucking the second set away in his wallet in case he forgot them. He gave Green the other half-sheet.

"Now, you know enough so you won't be talking to anybody about this, I guess," he told the postmaster. "If anything that might concern Gil got back to his mother, it might worry her."

"Don't worry, Marshal. I'll be silent as the grave."

"Good. And thank you for your help."

Longarm walked on to the station. He still had half an hour to wait before the southbound train was due, but the deserted depot was as good a place as any to sit and think, and he had a lot of heavy thinking ahead of him.

Chapter 13

Longarm reached Fort Smith too late in the day to visit the federal courthouse and talk to the district's chief marshal. He checked into the Fenolio Hotel, had dinner in the hotel dining room and a drink in the adjoining bar, then bought a bottle of Tom Moore to carry up to his room.

His visit with Gil Bright's mother had depressed him. Though he knew he'd done no more than was required of him by his oath of office, he felt sorry for Mrs. Bright, and wondered if she could survive the shock that awaited her when her son was finally captured.

Damn that Gil, anyhow, for turning renegade! his thoughts ran as he made his preparations to go to bed. *He's bound to be clear out of his head to hare off and go around killing lawmen the way he's been doing. And it looks like he's setting out to do some more killing, unless you can stop him in time, old son.*

Ordinarily, after he'd put several days of hard travel behind him, Longarm had no trouble sleeping when he came to a stop. But tonight sleep didn't come easily. After smoking a cheroot down to the butt he lay awake, reviewing in his mind the seemingly aimless pattern that Gil Bright had woven on the map as he moved from one murder to the next.

Gil's covered one hell of a lot of miles since he started this murdering spree, his thoughts ran. *And he ain't been just running wild. Everyplace he's gone he's had a reason, even if it wasn't more'n laying down a false trail to throw off pursuit.*

Because he knows damn well you're trying to catch him, according to what Zara said. And he's a sick man. Running the way Gil's been doing, he's bound to be dog-tired by now. He's likely ready to hole up and rest awhile.

Indian Nation? It's right handy, but it ain't likely he'd go there. Too many of Judge Parker's men prowling through it. Gil could've headed north from Lamar, but it ain't likely. The Missouri brakes ain't what they was when the Jameses and the Youngers was using 'em.

Now, the Arkansas brakes ain't been bothered much since old Judge Parker cleaned 'em up, and that was before he started in on the Nation. Gil would know his way around in 'em; he worked outa this office long enough. And they're close to where his family lives. If I was wearing his boots, that's just about where I'd make tracks for.

After going over Bright's cross-country moves three or four times without finding any reason to them other than the random running of a fugitive trying to lay false trails, Longarm was still as wide awake as he'd been at high noon. He got out of bed and lighted a cheroot, drew the cork from the whiskey bottle, and went to stand at the window. The fresh, cool night breeze was billowing the curtains inward. He pulled up a chair, took a swallow of Tom Moore, and looked down on the street.

Fort Smith was in the quiet of the after-midnight doldrums. The portion of the street Longarm could see was virtually deserted. From one or another of the three saloons visible from the window only an occasional straggler reeled out and wove along the sidewalk. A hackney cab was disappearing in the distance when Longarm first glanced out, and as he watched a second hack stopped in front of the hotel. The driver wrapped the reins around the whip-socket and went across the street into a saloon.

When he'd finished his cheroot, Longarm still was not sleepy. He went to the bureau, tossed the butt of the cigar into the spittoon that stood handy, and lit another. Going back to his chair, he picked up the bottle of Tom Moore from the floor beside it. A thin stream of the pungent rye was just starting to trickle into his mouth when he saw a man push through the batwings of one of the saloons down the street.

As the man turned and began walking away from the saloon Longarm paid little attention. Then he almost dropped the bottle when the man turned to look back over his shoulder. In spite of the beard that covered his cheeks and chin, the profile Longarm glimpsed so fleetingly was one he knew well. It was Gil Bright.

Longarm leaped to his feet, overturning the chair and almost dropping the bottle. A single giant stride took him to the side of the bed where he could grab his trousers. He pulled the breeches up and jammed his feet into the boots that stood by the bed. His gunbelt hung, as usual, from the bedpost, and while he buckled it on Longarm went back to the window. He leaned out until he was almost overbalanced, but Bright had disappeared in the darkness.

Pausing only long enough to slide his arms into his coatsleeves, Longarm took two steps at a time as he ran down the stairs and through the deserted lobby into the street. Bright was nowhere in sight. The few gaslights on the street were spaced far apart, with long pools of darkness between them. The cabbie who'd left his hackney standing in front of the hotel was nowhere to be seen, and Longarm was not in the mood to waste time looking for him. He stepped up into the driver's seat, freed the reins, and slapped them across the horse's back.

Feeling strange hands on the reins, the horse refused to move at first. Longarm shook the reins again and the animal plodded ahead. The carriage rolled down the street. Behind him Longarm heard a shout as the cabbie, hearing his hack moving away, burst out of the saloon with an angry shout and began running after the vehicle.

Longarm paid no attention to the pursuit. He slapped the horse over the back with the reins again and again, trying to get the tired animal to move faster, but the horse had its own ideas about proper speed.

At the third cross street from the hotel, the streetlights ended. Ahead was total darkness. Longarm went on to the next street, then turned the horse into it. There were no gaslights on the cross streets; the only illumination came from an occasional dim light trickling from the back of a store through the front windows. There was no one around.

Longarm searched in a pattern, covering two blocks on each side of the main street before moving to the next intersecting street. Twice he pulled up to inspect a late walker, but neither of the two men was Bright. When he gave up and returned to the Fenolio Hotel, the irate cabbie was pacing back and forth in front of its doors.

"I'll have the law on you, you dirty horse thief!" the cabbie shouted, leaping up to the seat, his fists flailing.

Longarm let the reins drop and managed to grab the angry hackman's wrists before he'd landed a blow.

"Just hold your temper," he snapped. "I'll pay you for the use of your hack."

"Keep your money and be damned!" the cabman gritted, struggling to free his wrists. "Jail's the place for horse thieves!"

"You'd have trouble trying to get me put in jail. If you'll cool your damned temper, I'll get out my badge and prove it."

"You're saying *you're* the law?" The cabbie's voice held doubt, but he stopped struggling.

Longarm released the man's wrists and took out his wallet. He flipped it open to show the badge pinned inside its folds. The cabbie grunted and shook his head.

"One of the old hangman's posse riders, are you? Maybe I'm lucky all you did was take my horse and hack."

"Judge Parker's not my boss," Longarm told the man. "I work outa the Denver office. I was trying to catch up with a man who's wanted for murder, so I borrowed your rig." He dug a silver cartwheel from his pocket and held it out for the cabman. "Here. I'll be glad to pay you for the use of it. This oughta cover the ten minutes I had it."

"It's fair pay," the cabbie nodded, taking the coin. "If you was one of Parker's bully boys, I'd get nothing."

Back in his room, Longarm undressed for the second time and stretched out on the bed. This time he had no trouble going to sleep at once.

Morning found him walking down Third Street to the old army barracks that was now occupied by federal offices. The marshal's office on the ground floor was deserted except for one man, who sat leaning back in a chair. One leg, swathed in bandages, rested on another. A deputy marshal's badge was pinned on his blue flannel shirt.

"You looking for somebody?" he asked.

Longarm did not answer at once. He was examining the office layout, which had been changed since his last visit. He took out his wallet and showed his own badge. "Name's Long, outa the Denver office."

"I'm Frank Dalton," the man said, extending his hand.

Longarm shook the extended hand. "If you'll just tell me where to find your chief, I need to have a word with him."

"Sorry, Long, I'm afraid you'll have to settle for telling me what's on your mind. All hell's busted loose down on the Choctaw lands over in the Nation, and everybody else is on their way over there to give the Indian police a hand." He indicated his bandaged leg. "I'd be with 'em, if it wasn't for this."

"Well, what I have to say ain't no secret," Longarm told

113

Dalton. "Likely you know I been after Gil Bright since he—"

"Wait a minute!" Dalton broke in. "You'd be the fellow they call Longarm!"

"I answer to that when somebody calls me," Longarm admitted.

"I'll be damned! Sure—I've heard a lot about you, even if I am the newest deputy here. Have you found Bright yet?"

"I ain't nabbed him, if that's what you mean, but I got a hunch I'm coming close. That's what I need to talk to the chief marshal about." Longarm settled down into a vacant chair that stood nearby. "Hell's bells, you can pass on what little I got to say to your chief when he gets back. I guess you know about Gil Bright?"

"What there is to know, which isn't much. It's been your outfit's case, but we've been keeping an eye out for him. Damn shame when one of our own men goes bad."

Longarm nodded. "I seen Gil in town last night, from my window at the Fenolio."

"And he got away?"

"I didn't do more'n see him. I never did rightly have him. I was looking outa the window up in my room at the Fenolio, and he came out of a saloon down the street. Time I got my pants and boots on, he was gone, and I never managed to turn him up."

"You're going to stick around and look some more, I guess?" Dalton asked.

"You can bet on that." Longarm nodded. "I figure he might be holed up in the Arkansas brakes, if there's any hidey-holes you boys left out there. I recall Judge Parker cleaned 'em up before he started in to tame the Indian Nation."

"I can't tell you a lot about the brakes." Dalton frowned. "There's whiskey stills out there, and I guess some hideouts, too. When I first come to work here I heard something about the judge cleaning 'em out again soon as they get things in hand over in the Nation, but that talk's kinda died down now."

"From what I gather, the Nation's turned into a pretty big bite for you boys here to chew."

"Oh, we keep on biting." Dalton shrugged. "I guess it'll all be whupped into shape, sooner or later."

"You've got no regular man prowling around out there?"

"Longarm, between the raids and the hangings, not a deputy on this force has any time to spare for the damn brakes."

"Then please tell your chief I'd consider it a favor if he'll keep it that way. If I can get out and prowl by myself, I might have a better chance of turning Gil up."

"I'll pass the word to him, soon as he gets back," Dalton promised. "Anything else?"

"One thing." Longarm quickly outlined the arrangement he'd made with the postmaster at Lamar. "If your chief will get word to the postal inspector to tell that Lamar postmaster it's all right, there might be a wire come for me. I'd like for one of your men to come tell me, if one does."

"How's he going to find you?"

"Oh, I won't be invisible."

"Maybe not, but from what I've heard, them brakes is right wild," Dalton frowned. "I got a passel of kid brothers—Bobby and Grat and Emmet—that go deer hunting in the brakes. They know 'em about as good as anybody can, and if they get too deep in them thickets they get lost sometimes."

"I ain't going out there to hide. Matter of fact, I want to make myself real easy to find."

"Couldn't that be dangerous?"

"You're new to the force, Dalton. You'll find out soon enough that we don't have no Sunday School picnics." Longarm thought for a moment, then said, "Tell you what. I'll make camp at the first creek that runs into the river on this side. That'll make it easy for anybody that knows the brakes to find me."

Dalton nodded. "All right, Longarm. I'll remember what you've said, and I'll tell the chief when he gets back."

"You do that. And I don't guess I need to tell you that if any word about Gil Bright being someplace else comes in, I'll want to know about it."

"I'll remember that, too," Dalton promised.

"Seems to me I recall hearing you got a string of horses here for deputies who don't have their own," Longarm said. "Reckon I'd have any trouble getting one?"

"Show the stableman your badge and sign one out. That's what I do."

"I'll be on my way, then." Longarm stood up. "Take care of that game leg, now."

Longarm's planning the night before had saved him from wasting time in preparations. He'd brought his saddle and saddlebags with him, and one stop at a grocery store on the way out of Fort Smith provided him with the necessities he'd need to

115

camp in the brakes for a week. There was a well-used road leading east from town. It ran straight across an old alluvial plain and met the river where the stream looped into a horseshoe bend. Then the road paralleled the watercourse over the low hump that had deflected the current into its horseshoe, and Longarm followed it as long as it ran roughly parallel to the river.

When the river bent to the north, Longarm left the road and took the narrow trail that stayed close to the stream. The horseshoe bend in the river ended; its course was eastward again. Longarm kept the stream in sight until he reached the low-lying land, subject to periodic flooding, where the brakes began.

A wide belt of tall sycamores and spreading white oaks, blackgum and hickory and spindly straggling persimmon trees, rose from the ground that was largely covered with low-growing grassy brush broken by almost-bare stretches covered with creeping, ground-hugging berry and chokecherry bushes. Clumps of sumac and wild grasses, tall and still green, swayed in the wind that came off the river.

Between the belt of trees and the river the land was a tangle of higher-growing brush, May-apple bushes, sumac and red-bud, with stretches of wetland where the tall canes grew. They were thick as well as high, and just beginning to dry now and to rattle in the breeze that blew across the surface of the Arkansas River, rolling green and half a mile wide as it flowed in its course to join the Mississippi three hundred miles away.

Longarm let the horse set its own pace, and noon had come and gone before he reached the first brook. A fainter trail than the one he'd been following broke off to meander beside the small stream. It led through the tree belt, where the brook coursed up almost to the canes before deepening and widening. Ahead, Longarm could see that the stream wove through the brush-grown strip for a half or three-quarters of a mile. There the brush vanished in the roots of a clump of oaks where the trees and the brakes came together. The brook wound through the grove and disappeared in the thick growth beyond.

Pulling up at the oak grove, Longarm looked around. The place had been used as a camp before. In the center of the grove where the brush petered out and disappeared, a dozen or so flat stones had been shaped into a crude V. Long-dead black nubbins of coals and a grey area of rain-washed ashes told of a cooking fire. On the trunks of the oaks there were

116

axe and hatchet cuts, and a few short branches with chopped ends still lay at one side of the fireplace. A bigger heap of uncut dried branches lay at the edge of the clearing.

A man couldn't ask for more'n a ready-made place to camp, old son, Longarm told himself, surveying his surroundings. *If the ones that used it before got along here, you can, too.*

Looking at the sun, which was just beginning to slide down, Longarm decided to make camp later. He dismounted, unsaddled the horse, and tethered it where there was grass. Then he made a neat pile of his gear and, taking his rifle, walked through the glade and set out to follow the brook on foot.

A scant half-mile away he came on the burned-out boards of what had once been a shanty. The ruins were old and looked as though they had not been disturbed for years. Moving on, the trail only faintly visible now, he found the wrecked coil and pot of a still in a second glade a quarter of a mile past the charred shanty.

There was still the vestige of a seldom-used trail beyond the battered ruins of the still. Longarm pushed ahead, following it. Once or twice he encountered signs that a horse had passed in recent weeks, drying piles of dung in the brush. There was deer sign, too, and always ahead of him as he walked deliberately along, the rustle of the undergrowth signaled to his keen ears the retreat of small forest animals—rabbits, raccoons, possums.

He'd covered almost two miles and was about to turn back when he smelled wood smoke in the air. He stopped at once and stood silently, gauging the wind currents. Leaves rustled overhead. Their movement gave Longarm the direction of the wind. He moved on, changing direction, taking only a few slow steps at a time. Even so, he lost the scent of the smoke in the fitful, faint breeze more than once, and was forced to zigzag through the thin brush that grew between the trees until he caught the acrid odor again.

He did not see the cabin until he was almost at the edge of the clearing in which it sat—or rather, squatted; the structure was barely head-high. A stovepipe protruded from one wall, a thin thread of smoke issuing from it. Standing sheltered by the rough grey-barked bole of a white oak, Longarm examined the tiny glade. The cabin had a window, but it was covered with board shutters, and the door was on the side away from him.

As he peered around the tree, Longarm saw brush across

117

the glade swaying, though there was no wind. There was no sign of human movement, but though no voice hailed him and no footsteps reached his ears, Longarm's finely honed sixth sense told him that he was being watched. He made no effort to go up to the cabin, but stood quietly behind the tree for several minutes. Then he used its thick trunk to shield his retreat, his ears straining for a sound he did not hear as he dodged from tree to tree until he was well away from the vicinity of the cabin.

A quarter of a mile from the glade he stopped and hunkered down to watch his back path. He waited for almost an hour before giving up and going back to camp.

Well, you've made a start, old son, he mused silently as he prepared his supper. *Somebody knows you're here now, and they mightn't know who you are or what you're after. But in a hideout like these brakes, word gets spread fast. Chances are you'll get a visitor or so right soon. You might not see 'em, and maybe it'd be best if they don't see you. Just give it time to work. It might not take more'n two or three days, or it might take a week or so. But it ain't going to be long before you'll know if your hunch that Gil's hiding out here's good or sour.*

Chapter 14

In the darkness, a noise that didn't belong to the quiet night roused Longarm. He woke, instantly alert, but he did not stir. He lay with his eyes open, letting them adjust to the starshine that shed a faint radiance under the canopy of branches that arched above his camp. With no night breeze to fan them and keep them alive, the last coals of his cooking fire had long ago faded and died. There was not even the hint of a glow from the stone V of the firepit.

Just hang on to your patience, old son, Longarm cautioned himself. *You been working hard enough trying to toll somebody up here. Don't get itchy now and spook 'em off.*

For the three days Longarm had been in his camp in the brakes of the Arkansas he'd worked diligently at making himself visible without seeming to do so. He knew he was taking the risk of being recognized by some wanted criminal he'd encountered in the past, but he counted on the outlaws hiding in the brakes knowing that all the federal marshals in Fort Smith were occupied in the Indian Nation.

Longarm was gambling that only the man he was after would recognize him from the description that he was sure must be working its way along the outlaw grapevine. He'd prowled the brakes downstream from his camp on foot and on horseback, going several miles beyond the occupied cabin he'd discovered on the day he arrived. There'd been no signs of the loosely knit gangs that in past years had used the brakes as their headquarters. All the evidence he'd seen convinced him that the thickets were now being used by loners.

Twice he'd found shanties that were either occupied or had been in the recent past, and once he'd nearly walked into a clearing where a still was in operation. On half a dozen occasions his instinct more than anything he'd heard or seen had told him he was being observed, and on two such occasions he'd gotten quick glimpses of the men watching him. Now, lying motionless in his blankets, Longarm waited for what he hoped would be proof that his careful maneuverings of the past few days had not been wasted.

The proof was not long in coming. A voice behind him spoke quietly, only a shade above a whisper.

"Longarm. Don't move. I'd hate to have to shoot you, but you oughta know damned well I will if you try any stunts."

"I ain't any more anxious to get shot than you are to shoot me, Gil," Longarm said. "I been wondering when you'd show up."

"I wasn't positive it was you until yesterday. Then I saw you myself, when you stopped to light a cigar a couple of miles downriver, by that big blasted sycamore."

"That was you skulking out there, was it? I didn't get a good enough look to recognize you."

"We might as well get to the point, Longarm, and save a lot of time. I'm not surrendering. But I don't suppose you really expected me to."

"No, not after what you been doing."

"How'd you pick up my trail? I knew you'd been after me, pretty close behind me once or twice, I guess. But I thought I could outguess you by stopping so close to Fort Smith instead of taking off for the next place on my list."

"I got acquainted with your gypsy lady friend in the Nation, Gil. She give me the first hint of what you was setting out to do. It wasn't hard to figure out what she couldn't tell me."

"Zara never did have anything to do with this!"

"I think she knew more'n you figured she did. But she ain't the only one I talked to."

"Who else?"

"I had a talk with that army doctor in Fort Bliss. I knew you wouldn't be able to go too far after that long haul from El Paso. And I figured you'd think like you did—that I wouldn't believe you'd stop too close to where a lot of folks know you by sight. It wasn't such a much to pick out the brakes, here."

"I ought've known. You always were good at outguessing a man on the prod."

"Ain't you getting tired of running, Gil? It's a game you can't win at, you know." Longarm moved involuntarily, but

120

froze instantly when he heard the metallic click of Bright's pistol hammer being drawn back to full cock. He said quickly, "I wasn't going for a gun. You know I got more sense than that. Besides, I feel the same way you do. I wouldn't want to cut you down any more'n you said you'd want to shoot me."

"Not wanting to do a thing and having to do it are two different things, Longarm."

"Sure." For a moment there was silence. Then Longarm asked, "Is my word still good with you, Gil?"

"It always has been. I don't see that us being on different sides of the fence now changes that."

"It changes everything else, though, don't it?"

"Yes, I suppose so."

Gil stopped talking and Longarm heard the rasping of his breath as he inhaled deeply several times. Longarm waited until the fugitive's breathing was back to normal. Then he said, "What I started out to say was, I want a cigar. If I give you my word I won't go for my gun, can I light one?"

After a moment's hesitation, Bright said, "Sure. Go ahead."

Releasing the butt of his Colt, which he'd been holding beside his thigh under the blanket from the moment he'd first been aware he was watched, Longarm sat up. He leaned over to his vest, neatly folded beside his bedroll, and took out a long, slim cheroot from one pocket and a match from the other. He clenched his teeth on the cigar, but kept holding it between the forked forefingers of his left hand.

Closing his eyes, he flicked the horn-hard thumbnail of his right hand across the match head and brought the hand holding the match up to the hand touching the cheroot. He puffed until it was drawing well and flicked out the match. Only then did Longarm open his eyes.

In the inky darkness of the clearing, the glowing tip of the cheroot lighted the area around the bedroll with the effect of a lantern. Longarm's pupils were dilated in night vision, and he could see for a yard or two in any direction he turned his head. He made no effort to swivel around and look at Bright, though.

"I guess you know why I'm here," the fugitive said.

"No, I can't say I do, Gil. Not unless being so sick's made you a little bit lightheaded."

"Stop talking like that!" Bright snapped angrily. "There's not a damned thing wrong with my head. I've proved that to

121

you these last few months, Longarm. I've been a move or two
ahead of you all the time, and we wouldn't be talking face to
face right now if I hadn't wanted to."

"Settle down, Gil, and don't go getting riled up," Longarm
said soothingly. "I ain't bad-mouthing you when I say you're
sick. Remember, I talked to that doctor back at Bliss."

"Being sick's got nothing to do with my brain. I set out to
do a job that needed doing. So far I've done just what I meant
to, and I aim to finish it without being stopped."

Longarm decided he could risk taking advantage of Gil's
outburst. He took his cigar out of his mouth and used the
movement to mask a shift of his position, until Gil was no
longer squarely behind him. But he found he'd underestimated
the other man's alertness.

"Damn it, I told you not to move, Longarm!" the renegade
deputy snarled.

"I ain't used to talking to you over my shoulder," Longarm
replied calmly. "If you wasn't all on edge, you'd know that I
just moved without thinking."

"Oh, no!" Gil chuckled, but it was an ugly chuckle, not a
friendly one. "I know you too well! When you're in a tight
spot, like you are now, you don't do *anything* without thinking
about it."

"We'd both talk a lot easier if we was sitting face to face,"
Longarm suggested.

"That's a chance I'm not fool enough to take. I might,
though, if you'll hand over that Colt you've got under your
blanket."

Longarm hesitated for only a split second. Within a few
seconds after he and Gil had begun their conversation he'd
become convinced that the ex-lawman had come to talk, not
to kill. If murder had been his aim, he'd have come in shooting.

"I might as well," he told Bright. "The way things stand
now, you'd be able to put a slug in me before I could use it."

"I'm glad you see it that way, Longarm. Push the blanket
down until I can see your gun, and then pick it up by the
muzzle. If you try to get your hand on the butt, you're a dead
man."

Longarm followed instructions. He picked his Colt up with
his fingers just grasping the muzzle and held it up where Bright
could see it.

"Just lift it up over your head," Bright commanded.

When Longarm raised the weapon, he heard a scraping of

boot soles on the ground, and at once Bright pulled the revolver out of his grasp. The fugitive deputy walked around Longarm's bedroll and squatted on the ground facing him. Longarm drew deeply on the cigar that was still clamped in his teeth. The tip glowed brighter as he inhaled and he got his first look at the former companion whom he'd been pursuing over so many miles.

"That's better, ain't it, now?" Longarm asked. He drew on the cigar again while he studied his old companion's face.

Bright's beard had grown full now. It masked his features from cheekbones to chin, but it did not hide his sunken cheeks or the unnatural thinness of his face. He'd trimmed his moustache, and his lips showed pale, almost as light in hue as the area of skin that was revealed between the upper edge of his beard and the strip of his forehead below the brim of his hat.

His eyes were unnaturally large, much bigger than Longarm remembered them, and the vertical wrinkle of what seemed to be a perpetual scowl cut between his brows. In moving, he'd turned his head for a moment, and Longarm got another glimpse of his profile, still the same straight nose that extended without the usual bump between nose and brow; the profile that had enabled him to identify Bright from his window in the Fenolio Hotel.

"Well?" Bright asked. "Have I changed all that much?"

"Oh, you've changed some. It'd be unnatural if you hadn't, being sick the way you are, and on the run for such a long time," Longarm replied. "But I'd still know you."

They sat silently for a moment, each man studying the face of the other through the gloom. Gil broke the silence.

"Damn it, aren't you interested in why I've been—" He did not seem able to pronounce either of the words which most accurately described his recent activities, and he finished, somewhat lamely, "—been rampaging around?"

"I think I know without you telling me, Gil."

"Like hell you do. Go on and prove it, then."

"You've been around lawmen long enough to see that all of 'em ain't good. Matter of fact, some that we both know about are nasty, mean sons of bitches." Longarm paused a moment while he puffed his cheroot, then went on, "Now, what I figure is that you decided to clean out the worst ones— at least the worst ones you'd run across."

"How the hell did you figure that out, Longarm?"

"It wasn't all that hard. I'd only met two out of the five

you've cut down, but I'd heard about the other three."

"Well?" Gil asked, a challenge in his tone. When Longarm did not reply, he said, "You've shot your share of men. I've been with you when you did it. What makes you think you're fit to judge me?"

"Oh, I've shot men down, like you say, Gil. But they was all crooks. And I never shot a man that wasn't a killer himself, and every last one of 'em I shot was holding a gun, most of the time aimed at me."

"Those men I put out of the way deserved to be shot just as much as the ones you killed."

"Well, granted they wasn't much good, I still ain't going to say you done the right thing by killing 'em."

By the glow of his cheroot, Longarm saw Bright's eyes grow wide and wild, glaring fixedly. His beard waggled and he started snapping his jaws, opening and closing his mouth like a beached fish gasping. His body trembled and his arms began swinging wildly, as though he had no control over them. For a moment Longarm thought he was watching the beginning of an epileptic seizure. Then Bright's trembling stopped as quickly as it had begun, the movements of his head and mouth ended, and his eyes returned to normal. He stared at Longarm for a moment, then shook his head as though to relieve it of a headache.

His voice pitched high, Gil said, "I did the world a favor by killing them trash."

"That's as might be," Longarm said, keeping his voice low and soothing, hoping to keep the unpredictable Bright calm. "You sure didn't do yourself no favor, though, Gil."

"You don't deny they deserved killing, do you?"

"I don't deny they was miserable bastards, going by what I know and what I've heard."

"Clark was behind two gangs of Indian looters," Gil burst out. "Barnes was taking bribes from the outlaws us deputies brought in and going so easy on 'em when he testified that they'd get off scot free. That Jimmy Bob let three killers go free because they paid him to. Brainerd shot three innocent men I know of. I was with him twice when he shot and didn't have to."

"That still don't give you the right to set up as a court all by yourself and judge 'em guilty without trials."

"Damn it, they were bad apples, Longarm! They deserved what they got!"

Longarm waited for a long moment, debating with himself. To gain time, he carefully took the stub of his cigar from his mouth and tossed it in the direction of the stone firepit. He said at last, "You've made yourself into a bad apple, Gil. Didn't that ever occur to you?"

Bright leaped to his feet. While they'd talked he'd let the muzzle of his revolver sag. Now he brought it up, and Longarm found himself staring into a threatening black hole. Bright's face was twisted with anger, but this time he was in full control of himself. Longarm gazed at the gun muzzle and said nothing. He'd seen enough wild killers to know that his life was hanging by the thinnest possible thread.

For perhaps a full minute the two men remained as motionless as statues. Then Bright's gun hand began trembling. The muzzle of his pistol wavered, and Longarm wondered if he was about to have a second attack. The trembling was only momentary this time, however. Recognizing that the moment of danger had passed, Longarm began to breathe normally again.

"I still haven't finished my job, you know," Bright said matter-of-factly.

"Give it over, Gil, whether you think you've finished or not. Hadn't you rather I take you in than somebody you don't know? Maybe somebody who'd backshoot you and say you tried to run away?"

"Nobody's going to take me in, Longarm." Bright's eyes were slitted now, his face contorted. "Not you, and not anybody else."

"You know better. You was on the right side of the law long enough to know what's going to happen to you."

"Then it'll just have to happen." Bringing his revolver up again to cover Longarm, Bright stood up. "But not until I've done all I can to finish what I've started."

"Give it over, Gil!" Longarm repeated, his voice sharper and more urgent this time. Instinct told him there was more behind Gil's recent actions than had come to the surface yet, and he wanted to keep their conversation alive.

Gil did not seem to hear him. Turning his head, the fugitive called, "All right, Charley. You can come out now!"

There was a rustle in the brush a few yards from the clearing. Longarm strained his eyes through the darkness. A man's figure took shape, and as he got closer Longarm saw that he carried a rifle.

125

Bright spoke sharply when the newcomer was still a dozen feet from them. "Stop right there, Charley. Don't get any closer to this fellow, regardless of what he says. He's as full of tricks as a circus monkey and as dangerous as a rattlesnake."

Obediently, Charley stopped. "Is this the one you been looking for to get here?" he asked.

"Yes. He's the one, all right."

Longarm could see Charley only dimly, but from the man's way of walking and speaking he took him to be a halfbreed. He asked Gil, "You got any objection to telling me what you got in mind?"

"No. I was getting ready to, anyhow. I've got business over past the Nation, so I need to get a move on. Charley's going to stand guard so you can't stop me getting away."

"Why don't you just shoot me yourself and be done with it, Gil?" Longarm asked. "You know damned well that's what you've told him to do, soon as you're gone."

"Why would I have any reason to kill you, Longarm?" Bright asked. "After all the time we worked together, I know you're not like the ones that don't deserve to live."

Longarm recognized Bright's careful evasion for what it was. He said, "I'll be coming on after you as soon as I get free. You know that."

"Sure I do." Bright walked over to Charley and handed him Longarm's Colt. "Give me the rifle, Charley. Use this to guard him with. Don't let him get away, now. Remember what I told you to do."

"I remember, Gil," Charley said placidly. The two men exchanged weapons. Charley covered Longarm with the Colt. "I'll keep a good watch over him, just like you said."

"Goodbye, Longarm," Bright said. "I'm sorry things had to work out this way, but you can see it's the only thing I can do."

"Oh, we'll run into each other again, Gil." Longarm put all the confidence he could muster into his voice. "We ain't done with each other yet. But I aim to finish my job up as quick as I can, now that I know what a real bad apple you've turned into."

Bright started to speak, but thought better of it. He turned and walked away and, in a moment, had disappeared in the darkness. A short while later, Longarm heard the hoofbeats of a horse galloping away through the brush. The noise diminished and silence returned to the glade.

While several minutes ticked slowly away, Longarm lay still, propped up on his elbow, studying his new guard, standing motionless as only an Indian can. He held the Colt steady, with its muzzle trained on Longarm. When he judged that Gil had gotten safely out of hearing, Longarm spoke.

"You might as well sit down and take it easy, Charley," he said. "You're going to get awful tired if you don't. I ain't got no idea how long Gil told you to stand watch over me, but I'd imagine he give you some kind of time."

"Until noon."

"That's when you're supposed to kill me?"

"Gil said not to tell you anything."

"You don't have to tell me something I already figured out. Noon's a long time away." Longarm was grasping at straws. He knew that he must somehow get Charley off guard. He went on, "Go ahead, sit down. I won't jump you."

Charley hesitated, peering around the clearing through the dimness. He saw the V of stones and looked at them for what seemed to Longarm a very long time. Finally he said, "All right. I will sit down there, where you can't reach me." He started for the stones, and halfway there he saw the cigar butt Longarm had tossed away. Its tip still glowed in the dark. Without taking his eyes off Longarm he bent down and picked up the butt, brushed the dust off its end, and put it in his mouth.

"Hell, Charley, there ain't enough left of that butt to give you any kind of smoke," Longarm told him. "If you want a whole new cigar, I got plenty. Be glad to give you one."

"No. Gil said not to get close to you."

"Well, now, you don't have to get close. My cigars are right here in my vest pocket. I can get one out and throw it over to you." Longarm watched Charley's face as it wrinkled into a frown of indecision. He pressed the thin wedge deeper. "Gil didn't say I couldn't smoke a cigar, did he?"

"No."

"And he didn't say you wasn't to take one if I offered it?"

"No."

"Then that makes it all right, don't it?" Longarm risked making a small movement. He sat up straight and nodded toward his folded vest. "Look there, you can see my vest. I don't have to get close to you to toss you a brand-new cigar."

At last Charley reached a decision. "All right. A whole new cigar will be good."

Longarm picked up his vest. Without unfolding it, he took

two cigars from one of the top pockets. He put one in his mouth and tossed the other to Charley while he slid his derringer out of the bottom vest pocket. Charley was smart enough not to try to catch the thrown cigar. He let it fall to the ground at his feet and kept his eyes and the Colt fixed on Longarm while he picked up the cheroot.

"You got a match, I guess?" Longarm asked casually.

"Sure. Plenty of matches."

Longarm waited, holding the vest over the derringer, until Charley struck the match to light his cigar. While the big halfbreed's eyes were dazzled by the match flaring in the darkness, he aimed quickly and triggered the derringer. Charley slumped to the ground, the Colt and the flaring match dropping from his lifeless hands.

Chapter 15

With Charley's body lashed across the horse's back behind the saddle, Longarm ignored the pedestrians who stared curiously as he rode into the center of Fort Smith. There were fewer of the curious to stare after he'd turned onto Third Street, and by the time he reached the high, dressed-stone wall surrounding the Federal Building the street was deserted. He guided the horse through the open gate and rode into the stable yard behind the main building. The stableman who came out was not the same man who'd been on duty when Longarm got the horse not quite a week earlier. He looked at the corpse, then at Longarm, leaned on his pitchfork, and shook his head.

"Seeing as you're a new man, I guess nobody's told you, but whenever you bring a body in, this ain't where you deliver it," he said.

"What am I supposed to do with it, then?" Longarm asked.

"Ride on through that gate." The stableman pointed across the yard to a wide gate in a ten-foot-high board fence that ran between the dressed-stone walls of the old building and the high stone wall enclosing the yard. "There's a shed on the far side. That's where all the bodies go."

Nodding, Longarm walked the horse through the gate. The first thing that drew his eyes was the stark bulk of a high, narrow platform that filled the far end of the enclosure. For a moment Longarm stared at the skeletonized structure, which at first glance looked like the framework of a house in the first stage of its construction. Then suddenly he realized that he was looking at Judge Isaac Parker's notorious twelve-trap gallows.

As he guided the horse to the low, unpainted shed at the side of the enclosure, separated by a few feet from the gallows,

Longarm studied the execution device. He'd seen gallows before, but never one like this.

At both ends of the platform, which rose eight feet above the ground, steps wide enough for three persons to mount abreast rose from the flagstone-paved courtyard. Stretching from end to end of the platform was a sturdily braced two-foot-thick oak beam with heavy bolts spaced along its length. Below each bolt was a trapdoor; these trapdoors hung open now, and hid the trigger mechanism that was tripped by a lever at one end.

A rat-a-tat of hammers pounding nails assailed Longarm's ears as he reined up the horse in front of the shed and swung out of the saddle. He peered in the open door. In the center of the shed stood a coffin supported on sawhorses; two men worked over it, putting on the finishing touches. At one end of the shed half a dozen more coffins were stacked, their freshly milled pine boards filling the air with the scent of rosin.

Longarm raised his voice to override the noise of the hammering. "You the men that take care of the bodies?"

"How many you got?" asked one of the workmen straightening up and putting his hammer aside.

"Just one."

"How ripe is it?"

"It ain't ripe at all," Longarm replied, taking out a cigar and lighting it. "It's an outlaw I had to shoot last night out in the Arkansas brakes."

"Why in hell didn't you just leave him out there where you shot him?" the man grumbled. "We got our hands full getting these coffins finished. The damned trial starts tomorrow."

Longarm eyed the coffins stacked in the end of the shed. "It looks like you got enough already."

"You're new here," the workman said with a mirthless grin. "They brought ten renegades back from the Nation yesterday, and eight or nine of 'em are likely to hang."

"One more body won't make all that much difference, will it?" Longarm asked. "I'd appreciate it if you'd take care of the one I brought in. I got business to tend to."

"Go ahead and tend to it, then. By the time you're through, we'll have him outa your way. You can pick up your nag on your way out."

Longarm went inside the building and found the office of the chief marshal. Mart Wimberly looked up from his desk, which was piled almost as high with paperwork as Billy Vail's. He said, "Frank Dalton told me you were in the neighborhood, Longarm. I don't guess you had any luck out in the brakes?"

"You might say I did and I didn't," Longarm replied, taking out a cheroot and lighting it. "Gil caught up with me out there. He sorta took me by surprise, so both of us walked away."

Wimberly grunted. "I don't know what it is gets into these bad apples we have every now and then. Seems like whatever turns 'em bad gives 'em extra smarts. What happened?"

Longarm gave the chief marshal a condensed account of his meeting with Bright and how he'd managed to outsmart his guard. "I brought Charley's body in," he concluded. "Figured you might know something about how him and Gil got together."

"That'd be Charley Broadbear," Wimberly nodded. "He was one of Gil's stool pigeons. Outside of that, I don't know a hell of a lot about him that'd help you. We haven't been doing much lately in the brakes on this side of the Arkansas line. There's been too much going on over in the Nation."

"Gil let something drop while we was talking out in the brakes." Longarm frowned. "He said he had some business over past the Nation. I figured that meant he's picked himself out another target out to the west. You got any idea who he might've been talking about?"

Wimberly was silent while he rolled and lighted a Bull Durham cigarette, his forehead creased thoughtfully. Finally he shook his head.

"Hell, he could've meant a lot of men. You know how this office is, Longarm. It's a lot different from what you're used to, working for Billy up in Denver. We get men who blow in and work a while and move on. A lot of 'em just got itchy feet, but there's some that can't stand working for the old judge."

"I ain't so sure I'd wanta work for him myself."

"Well, somebody's got to." Wimberly shrugged. "But I'll grant you, a lot of men do get a bellyful pretty fast. There's plenty of them who'll move on after two or three months. Gil didn't give you a hint except saying he was going past the Nation when he left the brakes?"

"That's about the size of it. I been thinking, though, ever since he let drop what he had in mind. If he'd been going very far, he'd've been more likely to say he had business out West.

I figure when he said 'past the Nation' he must've meant Texas, or maybe New Mexico Territory."

Wimberly considered this for a moment, then nodded. "When you put it that way, I guess that's what I'd have thought, too."

"Well, then, Mart, can you come up with the name of any men that used to be in your office here and might be in Texas or New Mexico Territory now?"

"Damn it, deputies come and go so fast here that I can't recall offhand. Give me a minute to think about it."

"There can't be such a lot. Instead of just thinking about it, why don't you write me out a list?" Longarm suggested.

"Now, you know how it is," the chief marshal said. "Once a man leaves a job and goes looking, he's liable to keep moving till he finally lands one that suits him. I guess I could send out some telegrams and check, if you think it'd help."

"That might be a good idea. Maybe it'd save me some time."

"You're not in a big hurry to move on, are you?"

Longarm shook his head. "I got something else I need to find out before I go. You might know something about it. Gil took out a big life insurance policy a year or so ago. He ever talk to you about why?"

"That's an easy one. Some big insurance outfit back East opened up an office here about that time. The head man must've figured us for pretty good prospects, because he was after us from the start to insure our lives. Three or four of us did, me included. So did Gil, I recall."

"They're still in business, I suppose?"

"Sure. The office is on Garrison Street. You won't have any trouble finding it, if that's what you got in mind."

"You know what they say about any old port being a good one in a storm, Mart. I ain't finding the sailing none too good, so I'm sorta looking under any rock I see in hopes I'll turn up something. No use me chasing after Gil unless I got some idea of where he might be heading."

"I'll send the wires, then. Come on back later on. I ought to have some answers for you."

Longarm rode back to the business section, found the insurance company office, and went in. A counter stretched across the narrow room the company occupied; a young man sat at a desk behind the counter, making entries in a ledger. At the rear, a partition broken by a door closed off the back area.

When the youth looked up from the ledger, Longarm said,

"I don't guess you'd be the boss here, would you?"

"Your guess would be right, sir." The youth's voice was high-pitched and almost girlish. "I'm just the clerk. Mr. Adams is in charge of the office."

"Then I guess he's the one I need to talk to."

Adams emerged from the office in response to the clerk's knock. He was an incongruity in Fort Smith, wearing an unusually high starched collar, a puffed-out cravat with a pearl stickpin, a dark morning coat, striped trousers, and patent-leather shoes. He looked at Longarm, who wore his long black city coat but still had on his camp-stained covert-cloth jeans and travel-scarred boots, with a pained frown which he tried unsuccessfully to hide. When he spoke, his voice had the twang of New England.

"You wanted to see me, Mr.—"

"Long. Deputy U.S. marshal." Longarm showed his badge.

"To be sure. We've written a number of policies for your colleagues, Marshal Long. Have you come to inquire about one for yourself?"

"Not exactly. I'm interested in finding out about a policy taken out by a man named Gil Bright. Gilbert's his full first name. He's another deputy, or was at the time."

"Yes. I remember Mr. Bright." Adams frowned. "I'm afraid I can't help you, though. It's company policy not to discuss the terms of a policy with anyone but the insured or a beneficiary."

"Now, hold on, Mr. Adams," Longarm said sternly. "I ain't just noseying around because I'm curious. This is official business."

"That doesn't alter company policy, Marshal Long. Our rules are very strict. If you want to look at our files, I'm afraid you'll have to get a court order."

"You and me both know I can do that, Mr. Adams. It'll take a day or two, though, and I ain't got time to waste. Now, why don't you just let me take a sorta unofficial look at Bright's policy? Nobody's going to know about it but the two of us."

Adams shook his head. "That's impossible. Get your order and come back later, Marshal, if you want me to open our files."

Without awaiting a reply, Adams turned his back on Longarm and returned to his office, closing the door with a firmness that just fell short of being a slam. Longarm stood looking at

Adams's office door for a moment, then turned to go. Before he reached the front door, a whisper from the clerk stopped him.

"Marshal Long? Wait just a minute."

Longarm stopped and turned back to the office. The clerk was tiptoeing up to the counter. Still whispering, the fair-cheeked youth said, "Anything you'd like to know about Gil Bright's insurance file, I'll be glad to tell you."

"Well, that'd be a big help. Now, what I was wondering—"

"Not here! Mr. Adams might come out. I'll come to see you in a day or so. Mr. Adams will be going out of town on Thursday. The office closes at six o'clock. Where can I find you then?"

"I'm staying at the Fenolio Hotel."

"I'll be there right after six, then."

"I'll be waiting for you," Longarm promised.

With the prospect of settling the question of Bright's insurance policy, Longarm went back to the main stream of his investigation. Between the time he'd spent delivering Charley's body and his visit to the insurance office, he'd used up the whole morning. He found a restaurant and had the first good meal he'd enjoyed since starting for the brakes, then returned to the federal building and found Mart Wimberly.

"You're looking for that list, I guess," Wimberly said.

"If you got it ready."

"You got here just in time. Judge Parker decided not to wait until tomorrow to convene court. I'm due to start getting the defendants upstairs in about fifteen minutes."

"I guess you'll be using all the coffins I saw out in the shed this morning, then."

"More than likely. The judge only seems to know how to say one thing when an outlaw's found guilty. But I'll give him one thing," Wimberly went on. "He's sure cut down on the killing and outlawry hereabouts."

"Being strung up is a pretty sure way to stop the bad ones from doing any more killing," Longarm nodded. "Well, if you'll give me them names, Mart, I'll get out from underfoot and let you go about your business."

Wimberly took a folded sheet of paper from his pocket and opened it out. "I got five names here," he told Longarm. "All of 'em're the kind of men you said Gil called bad apples. He knew three of 'em, and the other one hadn't been gone long

134

when Gil came on duty here, so I guess he had plenty of chance to hear about what kind of man he was."

The list read:

Sam Franklin	range detective	XIT Ranch, Texas
Cal Givens	Arizona Ranger	Prescott
Jim McInerny	town constable	Albuquerque
Otho Keller	Texas Ranger	Fort Worth
Mike Provo		Winnemucca

Longarm looked up at Wimberly. "Damned if they don't scatter pretty good when they leave here, Mart."

"They do," Wimberly agreed. "But there's not too many men who've worked this district that have trouble landing a job—even the ones who leave here with a bad name."

"I guess these fellows are still in the places you wrote by their names?" Longarm asked.

"As far as I know, they are. But I won't guarantee it. You know how men in our trade move around."

"Is there something strikes you about this list, Mart?" Long-arm frowned.

"Not especially. I copied the names and places from the files. You know we try to keep track of a man after he leaves here."

"Them files is like the ones we keep up in Denver, I guess? The letters just the way they come in the alphabet?"

"Sure. That's how every file I ever saw was kept. Why?"

"It just struck me as sorta funny, Mart. If you was to shuffle 'em around and put the towns in line, the way you'd get to 'em was you moving west, what'd you have?"

Wimberly looked at the paper over Longarm's shoulder. "Why, I guess you'd have Fort Worth, then the XIT—it's up in the Texas Panhandle—then Albuquerque, Prescott, and Winnemucca."

"Pretty much of a straight line west, wouldn't you say?"

"About as straight as you could draw it, given the lay of the land," Wimberly agreed. "Why?"

"Put yourself in Gil's place for a minute. We got no way to know, of course, but let's say for a minute he's got all of these names on his list. He'd be cutting a shuck right now for Fort Worth, wouldn't he?"

Wimberly looked for a moment at Longarm, then nodded slowly. "Yes. I suppose he would."

"Then I'm going to take a gamble and do the same."

"What if you're wrong?"

"Then I ain't no worse off than I am now. And if I'm right, I'm way ahead."

"You'll be leaving right away, then?"

"Soon as I can get a train to Fort Worth. Maybe with this list I can get ahead of Gil instead of following him."

"That won't be until Friday morning, I'm afraid. The St. Louis–Southwestern doesn't go to Fort Worth, and the first train east on the Katy is at eight in the morning."

"That won't put me too far behind him. Gil didn't leave the brakes until late last night. Besides, I got one more thing I still got to find out about, and I can't do that till six o'clock Thursday evening."

"Anything I can do to help?"

"Not a damn thing. And I'm obliged to you, Mart," Longarm said, tucking the list in his pocket. "If you're anyplace close to Denver on a case, I'll do all I can to give you a hand."

"Sure. Well, good luck to you, Longarm. I hope you catch up with Gil before he does any more killing. When one of us goes bad, it gives all of us a bad name."

"That's what I keep reminding myself, Mart. It ain't easy to hunt down a man you've partnered with."

Longarm was sitting at the window puffing a cheroot and enjoying a sip of Tom Moore when a knock sounded at the door.

He opened the door and saw the young clerk from the insurance office standing there. "You're right on time, I must say. Come on in and we'll have our little talk." As he closed the door, he added, "You know, I didn't get your name this morning when I was in your office."

"It's George. George Baker."

"You already know mine, so now we're acquainted," Longarm said. The clerk was looking around the room, holding his derby hat in his hands. Longarm took the hat and put it on the bureau, then motioned to the table and chairs in front of the window. "I was just having a little sip of Maryland rye before supper. Maybe you'd like to join me?"

"Why, I . . ." The clerk hesitated.

"If you're temperance, I won't think nothing of it," Longarm

136

said quickly. "But if you ain't, I've found a little tot sure helps break the ice when a couple of strangers sit down to have a talk."

"Why, yes," the youth said. "I guess that's right."

Longarm picked up two glasses from the bureau and put them on the table. He poured a generous quantity of the rye into each glass and held his own up in salute.

"To your good health, George Baker," Longarm said.

Duplicating Longarm's gesture, the clerk lifted his glass, and in the soft, high-pitched voice Longarm had noted earlier replied, "And to yours, Marshal Long."

Longarm drained his glass in a single big swallow. The clerk hesitated, then tried to duplicate the feat, but as the pungent, sharp-edged rye trickled down his throat he exploded into a convulsive cough. The glass fell from his hand, spilling liquor down the front of his coat and vest and soaking his shirt.

"Now, I'm real sorry," Longarm apologized. "I guess you ain't used to the way rye whiskey bites into a man's guzzle. Here, let me give you a hand."

Longarm stepped up to the youth and stripped off his coat and vest. He tossed the wet garments on the bed and turned back, saying, "I'll sponge off your coat and vest and they'll be good as new. But we better get off that soaked shirt—"

He stopped short and stared, his eyes fixed on the clerk's shirt front. The liquor had spread into a wide wet stain that covered the youth's chest. Longarm blinked. Where the white fabric of the shirt was clinging to his visitor's chest he saw the bulges of small but perfectly formed breasts.

Chapter 16

"Well, I'll be damned and double damned!" Longarm gasped. "You ain't a boy at all—you're a woman."

"Of course I am!" she snapped angrily. "And if I hadn't been silly enough to try to drink with you because I was afraid you might not think I was a man, you never would've found out. Now I've gone and ruined everything."

"It ain't that bad," Longarm said. "Your coat and vest are going to smell like rye whiskey for a day or two, but if you sponge 'em off and air 'em out, the smell won't last long. And your shirt won't smell after it's washed."

"That's not what I mean!" Tears started flowing from her eyes and a sob crept into her voice. "When you arrest me, it'll all come out in the open, and—"

"Hold on!" Longarm broke in. "What gave you the idea I was going to arrest you?"

"Well, isn't it against the law for a woman to make people think she's a man?"

"It ain't against any law I ever heard of."

As suddenly as the tears had started to flow, they stopped. She wiped her eyes with the sleeve of her shirt and asked, "Do you mean I've been worrying about nothing for more than a year, since I've been pretending I'm a man?"

"You sure have, if that's all you've been doing. You didn't dress that way so you could steal from that insurance company, or anything like that, did you?"

"No. All I did it for was to get back at that outfit, Marshal. They're a bunch of crooks!"

"You mean they stole from you?"

She nodded vigorously.

Longarm said, "Maybe we better sit down and talk about all this. You want another drink of whiskey to make up for the one you spilled?"

"I don't know. This is stronger than any whiskey I've tasted before. Not that I've drunk all that much."

"It ain't really stronger, it just tastes like it." He suddenly remembered the coat and vest and said, "Before we start talking, we better sponge the whiskey off your clothes, though. There's water in that pitcher and towels hanging on the end of the stand. What we need to do is—"

"I know what we need to do," she interrupted. "You don't have to help me. I can take care of it."

"Go ahead, then. Likely you'll do better by yourself than if I was to try helping you, so I'll just sit while you do it."

Longarm lighted a cheroot and leaned back in his chair, sipping his Tom Moore, while she went very efficiently about the task of sponging off her coat and vest with a moistened towel.

While she worked, he studied her absorbed features, trying to visualize her as a woman. Her close-cropped hair made it just a bit difficult, as did her male clothing. Except for the small globes of her breasts, she had disguised her sex almost perfectly.

She was small in stature, with a thin nose that flared at the nostrils. Her brows were thick under a high forehead. Her lips, pursed now as she gave frowning attention to what she was doing, were full, the lower lip perhaps a trifle too full. Her cheeks were thin and high-colored, her chin full and rounded. She finished the job quickly and hung the garments on the bedposts to dry, then came back to the window.

"I guess we're ready to talk now," she told him. "And I've been watching how you enjoy that—what did you call it? Maryland rye? I need something to get me over my nervousness, so I think I will try a little bit."

Longarm got a clean glass from the bureau and poured an inch of Tom Moore into it. "Now, don't try to take all this in one swallow," he suggested. "Just sip a little at a time."

Sipping cautiously, she took a small swallow of the pungent whiskey, then another. Holding her glass up to the light, she studied the amber-hued liquor and said thoughtfully, "It tastes pretty good when you drink it this way."

"Drinking whiskey's like a lot of other things," Longarm

said. "It's something you got to get used to." He refilled his own glass. "Now, then. Maybe the best way for us to start talking would be for you to tell me your name. I don't imagine it's really George, is it?"

She shook her head. "Georgette. I shortened it when I went to work for the insurance company."

"How'd that come about, anyhow? You must've had a real good reason." Longarm flicked a finger at her masculine haircut. "I imagine you did a lot of thinking before you cut off your hair."

"Not a great deal." Georgette's lips turned down at the corners in a sour half-smile. "I was so mad at the company that I'd've done anything to get even with them."

"What'd they do to you?"

"They cheated my mother." She shook her head. "No. That's not exactly true. Since I've been working for them, I've found out a lot of things I didn't know before. I guess, by their rules, they really didn't cheat."

"How'd you figure that out?"

"Well, you see, Father worked for the railroad, and when he took out the policy he was just on a track gang. Then he shifted to the blasting crew, and it was dangerous. But he didn't notify the insurance company when his job changed, so when he got killed they refused to pay."

"And you set out to get even?"

"Yes. When Father got killed we were living up in Alma. I guess you know where that is—about twenty miles north of here, on the other side of the river." She waited for Longarm's nod, then went on. "The company's closest office was in Little Rock, but I heard they were going to open one here in Fort Smith."

"So you decided to go to work for them and steal the money you figured they'd cheated you out of?"

"Yes. It wasn't a very smart thing for me to do, I guess."

"No, it wasn't. People get put in jail for stealing when they get caught."

"Oh, I thought about that. As it turned out, I didn't have a chance to steal anything. But I got even in other ways."

"I ain't going to ask you how," Longarm said. "You look like too nice a girl for me to have to put in jail, Georgette."

"I guess that's a compliment, Marshal. I'll take it as one, anyhow."

"What I can't figure is how you passed yourself off as a

140

man all this time. Or even why you bothered to try."

"Companies don't hire women to work in offices. Hadn't you noticed? And they really don't like to hire very young men. But around here there aren't many men who can write at all, let alone write the kind of hand you need to keep ledgers. So, I cut down some of Father's clothes to fit me, and fixed it up for Mama to go stay with her sister, and—well, I got the job, and that's about all there is to tell."

"Except what you came up here to tell me. About that policy Gil Bright took out."

"Oh, that."

Georgette sat silently for a moment. She drank the small amount of whiskey that remained of her drink. Longarm picked up the bottle and held it out, questioning her with his eyes. She hesitated for a moment, then nodded. He poured an inch of rye into her glass and replenished his own. He took out a fresh cheroot and lighted it and, as he flicked the match to extinguish it, looked at Georgette. She was studying him with a frown.

"What's wrong?" he asked her. "Something you'd rather not tell me about?"

"Talking about that policy isn't very easy, Marshal Long. It's all mixed up with Gil and me, and telling you makes me feel a little bit embarrassed."

"Look here, Georgette, I ain't out to pry, but if it's something I need to know in my job, I'd oughta hear it." He took a puff from the cheroot and, thinking he might make it easier for her to talk to him, went on, "There's something else. I got a sorta nickname my friends call me. Maybe if you'd stop calling me Marshal Long and just call me Longarm, it'd make things a little friendlier between us."

"It might. All right, I'll try, Longarm."

"Good. Now, don't feel like you got to bust right out with what you got on your mind, either. We can talk about the weather or something else for a while, if it'll help."

"I don't think it would. The quicker I start, the quicker I'll get it off my mind," she replied.

"Go on, then."

"You see, Longarm, Gil and I were going to be married at one time. We—well, we didn't quite wait for the preacher."

"That ain't so uncommon," Longarm smiled. "Some folks I know that call themselves married never have got around to standing up in front of one."

Georgette sighed. "I'm glad you understand. Well, Gil was still a deputy U. S. marshal at that time, and I thought he ought to have insurance. I guess that's natural, since I worked for a company that sold it. So he signed up for a policy—"

"Ten thousand dollars, I heard," Longarm put in.

"Yes. But I don't know how you know that."

"Never mind. Go on, Georgette."

"Well, the trouble was, Gil didn't pass the doctor's examination. Dr. Fellers found out that he had tuberculosis."

Longarm could see what she was getting around to confessing. He said, "So you changed some papers so that Gil could get the policy."

Georgette's jaw dropped. "How on earth did you know that?"

"It wasn't all that hard to figure out. What'd you do, fix up the doctor's report so the TB wouldn't show?" When Georgette nodded, Longarm asked, "And that bothers you, does it?"

"Oh, I don't guess it does, really. After working for the company for over a year, I've gotten to the point where I can see that Gil's more likely to be shot or something like that than he is to die of an uncertain disease like TB."

"I'd say you're right about that," Longarm agreed.

"Besides," Georgette added, "even if Gil did throw me over, I still feel sorry for him and for his mother."

"There ain't nothing between the two of you now?"

Georgette shook her head. "Not a thing, if you mean do I still love him. I'm not even sure now that I ever did love him."

"I don't guess there was anything special about the policy Gil bought, was there?"

"No. I'd learned enough by then to make him fill out all the blanks right, saying that he had a dangerous job. But it was just a standard policy, with the regular disclaimers that say the company won't pay if he's lied about having a dangerous job or if he's killed in a war or if he commits suicide or—"

"Wait a minute," Longarm broke in. "You mean if Gil was to kill himself, the company wouldn't pay off?"

"Of course not. Unless that clause was in there, somebody—well, somebody like Gil, who knows he has TB, might make his mind up to go ahead and kill himself if he knew his family wouldn't have him to depend on any longer."

"That makes sense," Longarm agreed.

Georgette lifted her glass to her lips to take another sip of whiskey, but found it empty.

"It's hard to drink out of a glass that's empty." Longarm smiled, picking up the bottle. "I better pour you a drop more."

"I'm not sure that I . . ." Georgette hesitated, then held out her glass. "I might as well have another swallow, now that you've taught me how to enjoy it."

"Mind, now, I ain't encouraging you. I wouldn't want you to blame me for getting you drunk."

"Oh, I wouldn't blame you, Longarm. Besides, I'm a long way from that," she assured him, sipping from her replenished glass. "Not that I don't feel like getting drunk, now and then. Why, there are times—"

"Times when what?" he asked, when Georgette stopped short.

"I'd better not say it," she answered. She sat for a moment, looking at him over the rim of her glass. Then she asked, "Tell me something, Longarm. Don't you feel sometimes like you've just got to go out and kick up your heels?"

"Why, sure. I imagine everybody does."

"And do you? Go out and kick them up, I mean."

"If I ain't on a case that I can't turn my back on, I do. If I feel like having a fling, I generally go on and have it. It's my own business, nobody else's."

"And you don't feel bad later?"

"Of course not. As long as what I do doesn't get somebody else in trouble, or hurt anyone, why should I? There's nobody but me I got to answer to."

"Even when you feel like doing something you know you ought not do?"

"Who's to say what I ought not do except me?"

"I guess that's one way to look at it," Georgette said thoughtfully. "And you don't seem to be a man who's easy to surprise or shock."

"If you're getting at what I think you are, I've been thinking the same thing the past few minutes," Longarm told her.

"You're not going to be the first to say it, though, are you?"

When Longarm did not reply, Georgette got up and put her empty glass on the table. She took a step that brought her to his side and stood beside him for a moment before leaning over him. Longarm raised his head. Georgette bent down a bit further and sought his lips with hers. Her tongue parted his lips and darted inside his mouth, twisting and groping. Longarm

143

met it with his. Georgette slid down into his lap.

"Is this one of the times you didn't feel like telling me about a while ago?" he asked when they broke the kiss.

"You know it is. Now, please don't ask any more questions, Longarm. You're not any stranger to women. Anybody can look at you and tell that. You know what I want you to do. So go ahead and do it."

"As long as you're certain that's what you want."

"I'm certain. I have been for quite a while."

Longarm freed the knot of her cravat and unbuttoned her shirt. Georgette's breasts were bound with a corselet that flattened them, but not very effectively. When he undid the snaps, the globes that had seemed so small under the concealing fullness of her shirt sprung free. Their soft, bulging firmness invited his lips and he bent to kiss their rosy tips. He felt them budding at his touch, began caressing their rosettes with his tongue, and their tips popped erect in his mouth.

Georgette was lying back in his arms, her eyes closed, her lips curled in a smile of sensual anticipation. She did not protest when Longarm stood up, lifting her with him, and carried her to the bed. He stood holding her for a moment while he levered off his boots and pushed them aside. When he lowered her to the bed and lay beside her, Georgette's hands sought his crotch and began caressing him. She felt him beginning to swell and her fingers moved to his fly, unbuttoning it. She reached in and freed the shaft she'd felt growing firm under her hands.

"Oh, my!" she breathed.

Longarm's lips were closed on one of her breasts, his tongue busy circling its jutting tip.

With one hand clasping Longarm's upthrust shaft, Georgette quickly unbuttoned the fly of her own trousers and slid them off. She wore knee-length knit knickers under the trousers, and she pushed them quickly down below her knees. Turning on one side, she parted her smooth, full thighs and slid his erection between them, then clamped her legs together, holding him cradled in the warm softness of her flesh.

Longarm was caressing one breast and then the other with the agile tip of his tongue. Georgette pulled herself closer to him and began to rotate her hips.

"Don't you want to put it in me?" she whispered urgently.

Longarm stopped caressing her breasts. He propped himself up on an elbow and looked at her for a moment before asking, "You're real sure you want me to?"

"Yes, damn it! I wouldn't've gone this far if I wasn't."

"All right, Georgette, just as long as you're sure."

Rolling away from her, Longarm kicked out of his trousers and balbriggans. When he turned back, Georgette was lying naked, her legs sprawled, waiting. She grasped his jutting erection and thrust it down into her crotch as he lowered himself. Guiding him into her, she moaned softly as Longarm sank down. Then she cried out and, before he had entered her fully, her hips began rising and falling spasmodically.

Surprised at this reaction from a woman who'd seemed almost timid and hesitant only moments earlier, Longarm did not stop. He buried himself with one sudden lunge, and Georgette gasped as she felt him fully in her for the first time. While Longarm held himself motionless at the end of his first full plunge, her small body quivered, and even before he could start stroking Georgette writhed and shook convulsively, breathing out small, gasping whimpers of delight.

She had not stopped shaking when Longarm started driving, sinking full length at each hard stroke, while her small body continued to quiver. The quivering grew more violent, then once more she began crying out, small gasps from deep in her throat, while her hips bounced furiously as she tried to meet Longarm's plunges. Even when the quivering of her orgasm had ended she did not stop, but kept jerking her hips upward as he continued to drive into her with slow, even lunges.

After several minutes Georgette cried out again, a smothered sob that became a small scream, and her hips writhed as another orgasm seized her. She raised herself frantically to meet his lunges, holding a hand over her mouth to stifle her throaty cries, but long after her fierce, jerking spasms had passed and her cries trailed off, her body continued twitching.

"What are you doing to me, Longarm?" she gasped. "I've never felt like this before! I just can't stop!"

"Don't, then, unless you don't like it."

"I like it too much!" Georgette panted. "Oh, please keep on going! I'm just about there again!"

Longarm did not stop, then or later. He lost track of the number of times Georgette went from one orgasm to another, but her excitement communicated itself to him and he kept on pounding into her steadily until her urgency brought him up to the point where his own control vanished. He did not even try to hold back, but let go as he peaked and joined her in another of her frenzied, frantic spasms.

145

As he lay inert, still erect inside her, Georgette whispered, "I don't know what you've done to me, Longarm, but I love it! If you want to start again, I'd love that, too."

"Oh, I'll start again, after you've rested. Right now, we better stop long enough to eat. I'll pull the call-cord and get the bellboy to bring us up some supper from the restaurant downstairs. I don't guess you got someplace else to go?"

"Even if I did, I wouldn't leave. I don't intend to get out of this bed until I've got to. I didn't know there was a man like you anywhere on earth. This is the most wonderful thing that's ever happened to me!"

Chapter 17

Longarm and Georgette were sleeping soundly when a sharp knocking at the door broke the pre-dawn hush. Longarm rolled out of the bed at once, instantly alert, and Georgette sat up with a start, blinking sleepily, still only half awake.

Before the echo of the knock had faded, a habit that by now was almost instinct had sent Longarm's hand to the Colt that hung in its holster from the headboard. His feet hit the floor and he stood with the gun ready in his hand by the time the second sharp rapping followed the first.

"Who is it?" he asked.

There was no need for him to raise his voice in the stillness that hung over the sleeping hotel.

"Mart Wimberly, Longarm. Got a wire for you."

"All right. Just a minute."

"What about me?" Georgette whispered as Longarm began pulling on his trousers. "I can't afford to let anybody see me in here, Longarm! I'd lose my job!"

"Don't worry. I got enough sense not to bring Mart in here. I'll talk to him in the hall."

Barefoot and wearing only his trousers, with his Colt still in his hand, Longarm opened the door. The Fort Smith federal district's chief marshal stood there alone, but Longarm glanced quickly in each direction along the hall to make sure it was deserted, and that no doors were cracked open along the corridor.

"Damned if you're not about the carefullest cuss I ever run into," Wimberly said as Longarm stuck his Colt into the waistband of his trousers. "Hell, you act like your face is on every 'WANTED' flyer that's circulating west of the Mississippi."

"Being careful's one way to stay alive, Mart," Longarm replied. "I found out a long time ago that outlaws carry grudges, even if they don't put out no flyers."

Wimberly grunted, but he said, "I guess you're right."

"You're out early, ain't you, Mart?"

"Got to be. It's hanging day. Judge Parker sentenced seven of that bunch we brought in day before yesterday. Not that I've got anything to do with it, except sign the papers after it's over." He jerked a thumb toward the door, which Longarm had left ajar only a tiny crack. "Any reason we're standing talking out here in the hall?"

"It's as good a place as any, ain't it?"

"Oh." Wimberly winked and nodded wisely. "I ought've tumbled before that you been entertaining company. Well, what I came up for won't take long. Here." He handed Longarm a telegraph flimsy. "This was the first message on the wire this morning. I wanted to get it to you before you checked out of the hotel."

Longarm had unfolded the message at once and was reading it while Wimberly talked.

LETTER ADDRESSED MRS ELLEN BRIGHT PASSED THROUGH OFFICE TODAY STOP POSTMARK TUSKAHOMA IT STOP RETURN ADDRESSEE ROBERT BLAKE TUSKAHOMA STOP LETTER UNDELIVERABLE AS MRS BRIGHT DIED YESTERDAY STOP POSTMASTER LAMAR MISSOURI

Looking up at Wimberly, Longarm said, "I reckon you read the wire, Mart."

Wimberly nodded. "I can't see it's much of a surprise, though. His mother was way up in years."

"That ain't what I was driving at. He mailed that letter outa Indian Territory."

"It shows you're probably right when you said he'd be moving west. After I heard you lay out the reasons, I was pretty sure you were right. All this wire does is to prove it."

Longarm glanced at the wire again. "You don't imagine he'd stop there any length of time, do you?"

"I can't see any reason he would. There ain't a hell of a lot for anybody to stop at Tuskahoma for."

Longarm scratched his head. "Just exactly where is the damn place? If I ever knew, I've forgot by now."

148

"Oh, Tuskahoma's to the southwest. More south than west, I guess you'd say."

"It can't be much of a town, or I'd remember it."

Wimberly's face twitched into a half-smile. "Tuskahoma's just a town by name. Ten, fifteen houses. It's a whistle stop on the St. Louis & San Francisco."

"How far away is it?"

"From here, about a hundred miles as the crow flies, and the railroad makes a pretty straight shoot there. Call it a short day's ride."

"Then how far to Fort Worth?" Longarm frowned. "I don't recall that I ever rode the train that way."

"Well, the railroad meanders a right smart before it hits Texas. It has to kink back on itself three or four times, going through the bad spots along the Muddy Boggy."

"Gil would've passed through there about a day after he left from the brakes, then," Longarm said thoughtfully. "And get to Fort Worth sometime the following day. He's a couple of days ahead of me."

"At least you figured him right." Wimberly nodded. "Now it comes down to one thing: you getting to him before he can get to Otho Keller."

"Which might be easier to say than do. Well, thanks, Mart. I got almost two hours before my train pulls out, but there ain't much way I can see to move faster."

There were only half a dozen passengers on the mixed train Longarm boarded later in the morning. Fifteen or twenty box-cars, a baggage car and day coach made up the string. Most of the stops were little more than sidings, with a one-room depot partitioned off from the freight shed and a few widely scattered houses on both sides of the rails, wide apart.

More passengers alighted from the train than boarded it, and after the fourth or fifth stop, Longarm had the coach to himself. He made up some of the sleep he'd lost the night before, dozing in his seat. A quarter of an hour before they were due to pull into Tuskahoma, Longarm walked to the back of the coach where the conductor was playing Canfield solitaire.

"How long we stopping in Tuskahoma?" Longarm asked.

"Unless there's a passenger flag out, we won't stop there at all, this trip," the conductor replied, stripping three cards off the deck he held in his left hand and looking at the top card.

"How come?"

"Oh, Tuskahoma's just a flag stop," the trainman said. He took the top card off the three he'd just laid down and put it on one of the suit layouts. The play made it possible for him to lift a card off the foundation and turn up a fresh one.

"I got to stop there about ten minutes," Longarm explained.

"Your ticket says you're traveling through to Fort Worth." The conductor did not take his eyes off the cards as he slid three more from the deck and laid them on the stack.

"Look here, I'm a deputy U. S. marshal," Longarm said. "I'm trailing a man that's wanted for half a dozen murders, and I need to talk to the postmaster at Tuskahoma, to find out for sure that my man stopped there."

"Well, I'm sorry about that, Marshal." The conductor slid three fresh cards off the deck. "I've got standing orders to follow, and train orders, too. But I guess you know that." He lifted the top card of the three he'd just removed from the deck and placed it on a suit layout. "My standing orders are, no stops at flag stations except to discharge or board ticketed passengers or manifested freight. And we don't have any of either one for Tuskahoma."

Longarm eyed the brake cord that ran through its stanchions on the ceiling of the coach. He asked the conductor, "Suppose there's a passenger getting on? How long do you stop then?"

"Just long enough to get him in the coach." The conductor had dealt the last three cards from the deck in his hand without finding a new play. He picked up the deck and straightened the edges in his hand preparatory to running through it again.

Longarm glanced out the window, and saw ahead the yellow and brown end of the Tuskahoma station coming closer by the minute. Without saying anything more, he reached up and yanked the brake cord. The train jarred as the engineer began to apply the brakes. The conductor looked up angrily, his anger turning to shock when he found himself staring into the muzzle of Longarm's Colt.

"Now, what in hell do you think you're pulling?" he demanded hotly. He started to stand up, thought better of it, and stayed in his seat.

"Looks to me like I already pulled it," Longarm replied. "You made it pretty clear that the only way I was going to get you to change your mule head about stopping was to stop this damn train myself."

"Why, you can't do that, even if you are a U.S. marshal!"

"Looks like I just did," Longarm said coldly. He waggled the muzzle of the Colt. "Now, you stand up. And get your hands out to your sides while I relieve you of your gun." Longarm pulled the conductor's weapon from its holster and tossed it on the seat, then commanded, "Now, march!"

"Where to?"

"Right up the aisle to the front of the car."

With an angry glare, the conductor started walking. The train was grinding to a halt now, and Longarm saw that it would stop with its center cars even with the little depot. They went into the vestibule and Longarm motioned for the conductor to alight on the side opposite the station. On the ground, he started the man walking toward the locomotive along the oil-stained gravel that covered the ground between the main right of way and a short siding.

The conductor asked, "What've you got in mind to do?"

"You'll find out soon enough," Longarm snapped curtly. He said nothing more until they reached the locomotive cab. Both the engineer and fireman were at the opposite side of the cab, their heads out, looking back along the train on the side where the conductor usually alighted. Longarm poked the conductor's ribs with his Colt and said, "Tell the engineer to come here."

Not inclined to argue with the pressure of the muzzle digging into him, the conductor obeyed. The engineer appeared in the cab and looked down on Longarm and the conductor.

"What the hell's going on, Sam?" he frowned.

Longarm showed his Colt. "Come on down here and you'll find out," he told the engineer.

"This damned yahoo claims he's a federal marshal," the conductor began as the engineer's feet hit the gravel. "He wants—"

"Shut up!" Longarm snapped. "I'll do whatever talking's needed." Facing the engineer, he went on, "Like your friend here says, I'm a deputy U.S. marshal on a case. He wouldn't stop here at Tuskahoma when I asked him as nice as I knew how, so I had to commandeer your train."

"Listen, mister, this'll put us late by the board—" the engineer began.

Longarm cut him short. "What I got to do won't take ten minutes, and you can make that up easy enough. Now, just so you two don't get no ideas about pulling away while I'm gone, both of you step over against that back driver."

151

Apprehension written on their faces, the railroaders did as Longarm ordered. When they were both standing with their faces to the five-foot-high driving wheel, Longarm took out his handcuffs and shackled the engineer's right wrist, passed the open cuff on its chain around one of the wheel's massive spokes, and snapped the other shackle on the conductor's left wrist. The two men were prisoners of the wheel. It could not turn without the spoke to which their wrists were looped lifting them from the ground.

"I don't guess I need to tell you what'll happen if this wheel turns," Longarm told his captives. "Now, you just hold your water till I take care of my business here. Then I'll take off the cuffs and we'll be on our way again."

Walking around the cowcatcher of the locomotive, Longarm ignored the fireman, who was on the ground by now, engaged in a hand-waving conversation with the stationmaster. He looked at the eight or ten houses that made up the town of Tuskahoma. The post office stood less than a hundred yards from the depot.

Longarm covered the distance with giant strides. The front room had a table along one wall. Some sheets of stamps, a rubber cancellaton stamp, and a pad lay on the table, and above it on the wall hung a set of pigeonholes made from a grocery crate. There was no mail in any of them. A man came in from the rear of the house.

"You'd be the postmaster, I guess?" Longarm asked.

"Sure am. You need stamps or something?"

"Not today. What I need is for you to look at this picture and tell me if you ever seen the fellow before."

Longarm took out his wallet and extracted the sketch of Gil Bright. Unfolding it, he handed it to the postmaster, saying, "He might've grown a beard since that picture was drawn."

Giving the portrait a quick glance, the man nodded. "I'll swear it's the same fellow that was in here the other day, and he didn't have no beard then. He mailed a letter." The postmaster stopped. "What right you got to be asking me questions, mister? You a postal inspector?"

"No." Longarm held out his wallet so the postmaster could see his badge. "Deputy U.S. marshal. This man's a fugitive I'm after. You say he mailed a letter here the other day?"

"He sure did," the postmaster confirmed. "Letter to Lamar, Missouri. Had to borrow my pen to write the address on it."

"You're positive it was the same man?"

"Certain sure. Listen, Marshal, when you don't see more'n

152

a dozen new faces a year, you remember them you do see, and where they send a letter to. Besides, I recall this fellow was in a hurry. He'd just stepped over here to mail his letter while the train picked up a freight car that was on the siding."

"If you're sure, that's good enough for me," Longarm said. "He got back on the train, did you say?"

"I don't recall saying, but that's what he did, all right."

Longarm restored Bright's picture to his wallet and returned it to his pocket. "I'm much obliged to you. Now, I got a couple of men waiting at the station for me to get back, so I'd best be moving along."

Wasting no time, ignoring their angry looks and angrier words, Longarm freed the engineer and conductor. "Now, then," he told them, "if you men ain't got coal dust in your heads instead of brains, you'll act like this never happened. You didn't lose more'n ten minutes stopping here because of me, and you can make that up easy between here and Fort Worth. But if you go complaining to your bosses about it, they'll have to go complain to my boss, and we'll all waste a lot of time getting things squared away. I leave it up to you which way it'll be."

Apparently the two railroaders had talked things over during their brief period of imprisonment and decided they'd been in the wrong. "We'll forget it if you will," the engineer said. "Now, if you'll get aboard, Marshal, we'll see how fast we can make up the time we lost and get you into Fort Worth on time."

For the first hour or more after leaving Tuskahoma the engineer was as good as his word, and the train chugged along at a speed matching that of a limited express. In midafternoon, though, the rails left red-dirt country and began weaving in wide, swinging arcs, where the track layers had been forced to keep to the narrow streaks of solid earth that lay between the treacherously shifting sandy soil stretching on both sides of the Muddy Boggy River. Progress was slow, and Longarm grew more and more impatient as the train crawled along the meandering tracks.

Darkness had fallen before the roadbed straightened out again, and knowing that he was almost certainly facing a period of strenuous activity, Longarm lowered the back of his seat and went to sleep with the all-pervading odor of stale coal dust from the green plush seat in his nostrils.

Dawn had broken over the Trinity bottoms but the sun was just rising when the train chuffed along the rails that cut a

153

straight line north of the looping curves of the Trinity River. Longarm had napped much of the night. He lighted a cheroot and looked out the windows where lights had not yet been turned out in the untidy straggle of houses along the riverbank that marked the little village of Dallas. Stepping into the aisle, Longarm stretched the stiffness out of his joints.

At the back of the coach the conductor looked up from his seemingly unending game of solitaire when he saw Longarm. He called above the thunking clickety-click of the train, "We'll be pulling into Fort Worth in another twenty minutes or so, Marshal. And I hope you won't carry no grudge over the mistake I made yesterday."

"No grudge," Longarm agreed. "Far as I'm concerned, there wasn't a thing happened."

Sitting down again, Longarm looked out the window. Below the tracks to the south the Trinity Bottoms stretched, a three- to five-mile border on both sides of the lazy green stream. As the morning brightened, Longarm could see that the sloping bottoms were covered with a dense growth of tangled mesquite and low-crowned scrub oak, and dense patches of head-high Johnson grass.

Except for a few cattle trails that wound from the edges of the flatland, vanished and reappeared at intervals in their course to the water's edge, only a few dilapidated squatter's shacks broke the broad expanse, and most of these were closer to the edges of the bottoms than to the stream. He eyed the thickly vegetated area and shook his head.

Old son, he told himself, *the Arkansas brakes is about like a desert compared to that. If Gil Bright takes cover in that mess of stuff down there, it's going to take the whole damned U. S. Army to flush him out.*

Beyond the stockyards that stretched for three miles around a bend in the river, the train pulled up at the depot and Longarm swung off. His stomach was growling, but he did not stop at any of the cafés that had sprung up to handle the cowhand trade. Loaded with his gear, Longarm thunked across the Twelfth Street bridge and turned down Commerce Street, heading for the spot that he'd learned on earlier visits was the place where the latest news and gossip were on tap, the White Elephant Saloon.

As he drew closer to the saloon, the streets grew crowded with men hurrying in the same direction, gathering in knots on corners, and talking excitedly. When he was passing one such group, a man running by him to join the others called out, "We better find Jim Courtright and tell him to hold up organizing a posse! McNelly's on the way from Austin in a special train with a bunch of his men to get the son of a bitch that shot the Ranger!"

Longarm spurted ahead and caught up with the man. Grabbing him by the shoulder, he said, "I just got off the train. You mind telling me the name of that Ranger I heard you say got shot?"

Panting, the man gasped, "I guess you wouldn't've heard, but it's true enough. Somebody bushwhacked and killed Otho Keller, the Ranger that's in charge of the Fort Worth station."

Chapter 18

"Who was it shot the Ranger?" Longarm asked.

"Hell, mister, nobody knows that yet! All I know is he got bushwhacked. They say it happened in the Trinity bottoms. And I guess you heard what I just said, about Captain McNelly bringing up some Rangers on a special train."

"You're sure the dead Ranger's name was Keller?"

"That's what they called him."

"Who called him that?"

"Why, the fellows that told me about it, down at the White Elephant. That's all anybody's talking about."

"Well, many thanks, friend." Longarm nodded. "You been right helpful."

Leaving the man to go on and join the crowd, Longarm continued to his destination. As he walked on along Commerce Street he thought of the Trinity bottoms. Seeing them from the train window, they'd reminded him of the Arkansas brakes.

Old son, he mused as he dodged around groups of men gathered in knots on the board sidewalk, *them bottoms is just the kind of place Gil Bright's been used to. They'd pull him to 'em like a honey pot pulls a swarm of flies.*

Outside the White Elephant, Longarm stopped for a moment. The street was packed. Men bustled around, jostling one another as they tried to get inside the saloon.

Someone in the crowd saw him standing holding his rifle and saddle gear and called out, "Here's one of the Rangers now! Let him get through! He's prob'ly looking for Longhaired Jim!"

Longarm saw that any effort to correct the mistaken iden-

156

tification would be useless. He let the crowd part, shaking his head in response to shouted questions from all sides, and finally he was able to get inside.

The White Elephant was a large saloon, with a long bar that stretched along one side from front to back. Tables occupied the front section, and the rear was taken up by the gambling layouts.

Close to the wall opposite the bar there was a small cleared space around a table where two men sat. One was thin-faced, with an aquiline nose between high cheekbones; he had a pointed jaw and wore a sandy moustache that drooped at each end. As he lifted his glass to sip from it, Longarm got a glimpse of the crescent-enclosed star that had become identified with police chiefs in that region, though his sandy hair was trimmed shorter than Longarm's was. The second man was bulky, with a protruding, rounded chin and a full, untrimmed black moustache that curled down to hide his entire mouth. They watched Longarm's approach.

"Where's McNelly?" the thin man asked as Longarm reached the table and dropped his saddle at his feet.

"I wouldn't know," Longarm replied. "I thought maybe you might. Ain't you Jim Courtright?"

"I'm Courtright, but I'm damned if I know you. You're on the Ranger force, aren't you?"

Longarm shook his head. "No. My name's Long. Deputy U. S. marshal, outa Denver."

"Denver." Courtright frowned. "You'd be the one they call Longarm, then?"

"I answer to that sometimes."

"Well, I don't know how you got here so quick, but sit down and have one with us," the Fort Worth police chief said. He looked at the half-dozen glasses on the table, selected one that seemed clean, and filled it from one of the bottles clustered in the center. "Oh, this is Heck Thomas. He's ready to give us a hand, too."

"I haven't got any real business here," Thomas explained in a voice that was surprisingly thin for such a big man. "I'm a special investigator for the Texas Express Company, but when I heard Oth had got shot, I came on down to see if Jim might need an extra man or two."

"How'd you hear about Keller getting killed, Long?" Courtright frowned. "They didn't find him until just before dark yesterday evening. You ain't had time to get here from Denver."

"I didn't hear about the killing till I got off the train from Fort Smith," Longarm replied. Sipping the whiskey Courtright had poured for him, Longarm's taste buds rebelled at the sweet taste of the bourbon. He took out a cheroot and lighted it before asking the police chief, "You got any idea who might've done it?"

"That's what we were just talking about," Courtright said. "It could've been anybody. Out in the bottoms there's a hundred places where wanted men hide out. Keller could've gone out there on a tip somebody passed on to him, or he could've been tracking somebody."

"You men went out and looked at the place where he was shot, I guess?"

Heck Thomas answered, "I was there before Jim was. In my job, I've got to know the bottoms, but they're outside of his jurisdiction."

"You're a detective for the express company, I gather?"

"Texas Express. Company handles money shipped by banks, high-priced merchandise like jewelry, things of that sort. I've found that half the crooks that rob the express company know a place in the bottoms where they can turn their loot into cash."

"If you were there, I guess you saw Keller's body before it was brought to town?" Longarm asked.

"Both of us saw it," Courtright said. "Two shots at close range. One in the belly, the other one in the head. It was the one in the head that finished him, I'd say."

"But there wasn't anything that'd give you a lead to who pulled the trigger?" Longarm persisted. He was certain he knew the identity of the murderer, but it was too soon to muddy up the investigative waters by revealing what he suspected.

"Not a damn thing," the police chief replied.

"Like Jim said, both of us figure Keller was out there after some wanted man," Thomas put in. "And I'd bet whoever did it is long gone by now, making dust for somewhere else. My guess is the Nation—it's closer than any other hideouts."

"You never did say what your business was with Keller," the police chief said to Longarm. "Some federal case, was it?"

Longarm hesitated for a moment, decided that no good purpose would be served by revealing details. He was more positive than ever now that Gil Bright had added another killing

158

to his string and he wanted to get on the trail now. He finally said, "I was going to ask Keller if he had any ideas about the case I'm on."

"That's right," Courtright said. "I'd forgotten Keller was with the U.S. marshal's outfit in Fort Smith before he came here." His light blue eyes narrowed as he looked at Longarm across the table and his mouth opened as he started to say something more, but he thought better of it and said nothing.

Longarm broke the silence. "If you don't mind me asking, Courtright, what in hell are you doing sitting here in a saloon when you oughta be out looking for whoever it was gunned down Otho Keller?"

"Well, like Heck said a minute ago, the Trinity bottoms are out of my jurisdiction." Under his sandy moustache, the police chief's thin lips twisted into a sour grin. He slid a telegraph flimsy from his coat pocket and handed it to Longarm. "But a better reason is I made the mistake of bucking McNelly and Armstrong before, and I'm not about to get crossways of them again."

Longarm read the message scrawled in a hard-pointed pencil on the thin paper.

TAKING FULL CHARGE OF KELLER MURDER CASE STOP LEAVING AT ONCE SPECIAL TRAIN STOP MCNELLY CAPTAIN RANGER CO B

Looking up from the telegram, he said, "All I know about McNelly is that my boss, Billy Vail, has mentioned him a time or two. Billy used to be a Texas Ranger, you know."

"If I did know, I didn't remember," Courtright said. "He was here before my time, I guess."

Longarm went on, "Now, I don't see nothing in this wire about Armstrong. And I can't say I've heard his name before."

"You would have, if you were a lawman in Texas," Courtright replied. "He's McNelly's second in command. McNelly gives the orders and Armstrong does the work. That's how he's come to be called 'McNelly's Bulldog.' Once he gets his teeth into a case, he won't let go till it's closed."

Longarm returned the flimsy to Courtright and asked, "How many men do you figure McNelly's bringing with him?"

"Besides Armstrong?" The police chief said, "Two. Maybe three."

"And he's ordered up a special train for that?"

"It's easy to see you don't know McNelly, Long," Heck Thomas put in. "Or the Rangers, either."

"Maybe I better learn, then," Longarm suggested.

"I guess maybe you had, because that special train ought to be pulling into town inside of the next half hour. Now, the first thing to get straight is that when McNelly says the Rangers are taking over a case, that means nobody else butts in. Not even the federal marshal's office."

"I get what you're driving at," Longarm said.

"Don't get the idea McNelly's a fool, Long. He's tough and smart, even if he hasn't got much use for local lawmen. And where he falls short, Armstrong picks up."

"I'll keep that in mind," Longarm said. "But even if all I come down here for was to talk about my case with Otho Keller, now he's been bushwhacked, I aim to stick around and be what help I can. I don't guess anybody'd object if I sorta nosey around and ask a few questions while everybody's waiting."

"It's your neck, if you want to stick it out." Heck Thomas shrugged. "But if I was you, I'd stick right here in the White Elephant until McNelly gets here and lays down the law."

Longarm stood up. "My neck's been stuck out so many times it's got calluses on it, Heck. Now I think I'll walk around and ask a question or two. I'd like not to have to lug my saddle along, though. Would you know a place close by where it'd be safe for me to leave it?"

"You'll find Jake Johnson around the bar, I'd imagine," Jim Courtright replied. "He owns this place. Just tell him I said I'll take it as a favor if he'll put your gear in his storeroom or office for you. It'll be safe if he's taking care of it."

Freed from the burden of his saddle gear and rifle, which made him conspicuous in the crowd, Longarm walked out and along the street. He'd left Courtright and Thomas in order to avoid being distracted as he planned his next move. He wanted to put himself inside Gil Bright's mind and decide what a fugitive fleeing after murdering a lawman would be most likely to do.

As he strolled, he told himself, *What McNelly don't know, and won't know until you tell him, old son, is that whatever he does, Gil's going to have figured out the moves another lawman would make. And Gil's just smart enough to find a hole in them moves big enough to wiggle through. Now, if this*

McNelly's as good as they make him out to be, the first thing he's going to do is to send men along all the roads leading out from town, asking if anybody has noticed a man riding away from Fort Worth in a hurry.

He don't need a description of Gil to do that, but he's going to have to get one, so his next move's going to be digging up somebody that seen Keller with a stranger. He'd have to turn the Trinity bottoms upside down before he'd have any luck, but if he's as good at his job as they say, he'll have a description of Gil before the day's out. Then he'll go to all the railroad stations and get wires sent ahead to watch the trains.

Except, while McNelly's bustling around, Gil's going to be on his way. Likely he already is. And he'll be moving west, that's one sure thing. The next man on his list is bound to be that Sam Franklin. He's up on the XIT, in the Panhandle. It wouldn't be outa Gil's way a mite for him to swing by there and go on to Albuquerque, then Prescott and Winnemucca. And he sure won't be going horseback or riding a passenger train, because he'll know McNelly's got them being watched.

Now, was I Gil, I'd hop me a freight. There ain't much way for a train crew to search a freight. Too many places to hide. More'n likely he can get a freight outa here that'd take him right where he's heading. Just about every railroad that hauls cattle is going to figure a way to get their trains running into them big stockyards I seen coming into town.

Old son, you got it licked. All you got to do now is get McNelly to see it the same way you do.

Satisfied that his deductions were sound, Longarm reversed his course and went back to the White Elephant. If anything, the crowd around the front of the saloon had grown thicker. He shoved through with difficulty to the batwings, not swinging now, but held open by the curious trying to look inside. Shouldering his way through the onlookers, Longarm stopped just inside the doorway.

At the table by the wall, Jim Courtright and Heck Thomas were standing talking to two newcomers. Guessing their identities, Longarm pushed his way to the table and stopped behind the new arrivals.

"Well, here he is now," Longarm heard Courtright say as he came up to the table. The police chief went on, "I was just saying you'd stepped out for a breath of fresh air and oughta be back any minute. I don't guess you-all have met before."

Before Longarm could speak, the smaller of the two men had swivelled around to face him. "McNelly," he snapped. His eyes were as cold as a snowy winter sky at daybreak and were flicking over Longarm in a quick evaluation. "Captain, Texas Rangers. And my lieutenant, John Armstrong. You'd be Long, deputy U.S. marshal out of Denver."

"That's right, Captain McNelly. My chief used to ride with your outfit—Billy Vail."

Longarm extended his hand. Armstrong took it with a firm grip, but McNelly made no move to raise his own hand.

"Yes, I remember Vail," the Ranger captain said. His voice was surprisingly deep and had a harsh edge. "I've heard your name, too, Long. Called Longarm, I understand. And you've made fools of some of my men with your damned tricks a time or two."

Longarm suppressed a grin, recalling the differences he'd had with the Texas Rangers and how they'd come out second best. He chose his words carefully. "Well, there was a time when I held on to some prisoners I'd taken that your boys wanted, Captain. I disremember that we've had any other run-ins. And there's been times your men and me have rode and fought side by side, too."

"I've heard that as well." McNelly's tone was a bit more moderate. "What's your interest in this case, Long?"

"Well, I never did partner up with Keller when he was on the U.S. marshal's force, but this morning when I got to town and heard he'd been killed, I figured—"

"Just a minute," McNelly broke in. "Were you sent here to Texas on a federal case?"

Truthfully and literally enough, Longarm replied, "No. But I heard about Keller being killed, and I thought—"

McNelly interrupted again. "I know what you thought, Long! You're the big federal man, the famous Longarm, and you thought you might stop off and help us poor ignorant Texas Rangers to—"

This time it was Longarm who interrupted. "Now, you hold on, Captain McNelly! What I had in mind was—" His attempt to explain was again halted by McNelly's sharp voice.

"Long! I'm not used to having anybody interrupt me. Let me go on with what I was saying."

Longarm decided that, since he was on McNelly's home grounds, he'd better not point out that McNelly had been the first to interrupt a moment earlier. He pressed his lips into a tight, straight line and said nothing.

McNelly continued to scowl at Longarm for a moment before he said anything more. Then he asked, "Where are you from, Long?"

"Why, from Denver. You know that, Captain."

"That's not what I meant. Where were you born?"

Puzzled, but still nettled at the Ranger captain's rudeness, Longarm snapped, "I don't see what that's got to do with anything we been talking about, but I was born in West-by-God-Virginia."

McNelly snorted. "A Border state. I suspected as much. You fought in the War, I suppose?"

"I got in a skirmish or two."

"Under which flag?" McNelly pressed.

"Look here, Captain McNelly, I don't see that the War's got anything to do with what we're talking about."

"Possibly you don't. I do. Long, I'll tell you something I don't expect you know. Before the War there were five Ranger companies, a force of almost two hundred damned fine men. The Rangers got started fighting Comanches, and made Texas a safe place for white men to settle in. Rangers fought the Mexican Army to make Texas a state, and fought outlaws to make it a decent state. Then, during the Reconstruction, the damned carpetbaggers did away with the Rangers and set up the State Police, mostly a bunch of ignorant ex-slaves. Now, I've had a hand in building up the Rangers again, and we're the finest damned law enforcement outfit in the world, barring none."

Longarm took advantagge of McNelly's pause for breath to say, "I ain't running down your Ranger force, Captain McNelly. All I'm trying to tell you is—"

McNelly had gotten his second wind by this time. Ignoring Longarm again, he overrode his efforts to explain. "The Rangers don't need any help in running down a man who killed one of our own, Long! There's only forty of us to keep law and order in this whole damned state, but if thirty-nine of us get killed looking for the man who murdered Otho Keller, the fortieth Ranger will bring in the killer's dead body! And we'll do it without any help from U. S. marshals or Longhaired Jim Courtright's police force, or Heck Thomas and his private detective outfit. Do you understand me, Long?"

When McNelly ran out of breath again and paused, Longarm gave the Ranger's temper and his own time to cool down by lighting a cheroot. McNelly glared at him the whole time that he was lighting up, and Longarm returned the Ranger's angry stare unflinchingly. When the cigar he'd taken his time in lighting was drawing satisfactorily, he took it from his mouth.

"Now, I heard you out, Captain McNelly," he said levelly. "Maybe you'll let me finish what I been trying to say without busting in and stopping me. I didn't set out to meddle in your case. I never did aim to do anything but try and help."

Armstrong had stood in silence while McNelly was giving Longarm the dressing-down. Now he snapped, "You heard what the captain said, Long. We don't need your damned help. The Texas Rangers take care of their own."

McNelly added quickly, "All right, Long, you've admitted you're out of your jurisdiction. Courtright, since Keller didn't get killed inside the Fort Worth town limits, you're out of yours, too. Thomas, you never had any. From now on, this case is in the hands of my Rangers. Long, I think the best thing you can do, since you're not here on a federal case, is to get on the next train out of town. Courtright, I don't want you or Thomas getting underfoot, either." He turned to Armstrong. "Come on, Lieutenant. Now that we won't be bothered by these men any longer, we can get busy."

Silently, Longarm, Courtright, and Thomas watched the two Rangers leave the saloon.

Longarm was the first to speak. "I'm sorry I let you men in for all that, but I didn't have no idea he was such a feisty little cuss."

"It wasn't your fault, Long," Courtright said. "McNelly's trying to put the Ranger force together again the way it was before the Reconstruction, but I'm afraid he won't be able to. Times are different now. Texas is too settled."

"Well, Jim," Thomas said, "I guess all of us got put in our place. And mine's at the express office."

"Yep," Courtright agreed. "I've got work to be done, too. What about you, Long?"

"I'll tell you men what I'm going to do," Longarm replied thoughtfully. "I'm just going to take Captain McNelly's advice and get out of town on the next train. Because I know right now that, wherever my business is, it sure ain't here in Fort Worth!"

164

Chapter 19

Longarm stayed at the White Elephant only long enough to ease his hunger. The lavish free lunch table for which the big saloon was noted had been badly depleted by the unusually large crowd, but he found two hard-boiled eggs surviving under a heap of shells, and there were a few slices of meat and a bite or two of cheese that had been overlooked. He washed down his impromptu meal with a drink of Tom Moore, then left his gear at the saloon while he went to check on freight train schedules.

After his long session of putting himself in Gil Bright's shoes, Longarm felt certain that his deductions were correct. He had assumed first that Bright would seek the men remaining on his list in geographical order; working west from Fort Worth, his next target should be Sam Franklin, the XIT Ranch range detective. His second assumption was that Bright would be shrewd enough to have killed Keller at a time that would make a getaway easy. Third, he was sure the fugitive would use the most readily available and reasonably safe transportation, a freight train headed for the Panhandle.

As the center of Texas ranching shifted north from the thin strip of early settlements along the Gulf coast and spread over the vast grassy plains north and west of the Colorado River, Fort Worth had displaced San Antonio as the heart of the state's cattle trade. The stockyards north of the Trinity River loop which dated back to the beginning of the ranching expansion had in a few short years grown to be the biggest in the nation.

When the western railroad boom began pulsing at the end

of the Civil War, nearly every railroad that pushed west from the Mississippi made Fort Worth its target, lured by the prospects of lucrative cattle shipments. Those roads which could not swing their main-line franchises to include Fort Worth on their principal routes built spurs to the town. Passengers might have had trouble getting in or out of Fort Worth during the cattle boom, but a herd of steers could be despatched overnight from the sprawling stockyards to almost any point in the world.

Cattle cars made up the major haul of almost all the freight trains leaving Fort Worth, and most of the shipments were to the big Midwestern and Eastern packing-houses. In fact, Longarm found very quickly that four of the nine railroads shipped no cattle at all to the west.

Knowing the approximate time of the shooting, Longarm could scratch off any freight train that had left earlier. He spent two hours going from one freight station to another before discovering that a train consisting principally of empty cattle cars consigned to the XIT loading spur at Dalhart had left the yards of the Fort Worth & Denver City Railroad not quite three hours after the time established for Keller's murder.

He put in another hour making sure there'd been no other train Gil Bright could have taken to get to the destination for which he was sure the bad apple was heading. There was none. His calculations showed him that the fugitive now held a ten-hour lead over him. He tried to figure a way to get to Dalhart himself and at the same time shorten or even overcome Bright's lead, but Longarm found himself butting against what seemed to be a wall of solid stone.

"Damn it, there's got to be a train on your schedule that'll get me up to the Panhandle by noon tomorrow!" he repeated to each of the stationmasters he asked.

In the first eight railroad offices he visited the response had been the same. "Sorry, Marshal. We'd like to help, but there's not a thing we can do for you."

When he reached the last hope he had, the new and struggling little St. Louis & Southwestern Railway, Blunt, the trainmaster, first repeated the dreary phrase Longarm had heard at each of the other roads. But then he added, "It's too bad you need to get up to the Panhandle right now, Marshal. In just a few weeks we'll have trains running up there on a faster schedule than the Rock Island & Denver City."

"You mean you're building tracks that near to where I need

to go?" Longarm asked. "If you are, why can't I get a ride on one of your work trains?"

"Normally, I'd say you could, but we've had to pull our work gangs off and shut down construction on the new line."

"You mind telling me why?"

"It'll be easier to show you than to try to explain," Blunt replied. He started toward the big map hanging on his office wall. "Come over here."

Longarm had seen similar maps on the walls of the other offices he'd visited. He looked at the one now in front of him. It showed the St. Louis & Southwestern rails as a red line angling northwest from Fort Worth in a straight line almost to the corner of the Texas–New Mexico boundary. The line ended there, but a second line, this one of red dots, extended due north, paralleling the border. This line ran all the way to the top of the Panhandle.

Accustomed as he was to reading maps, Longarm grasped the situation at a glance. He told Blunt disgustedly, "Hell, if that red line's where your rails end and you still got to build up along them dots, it'll be more'n any few weeks before you'll have trains running to where I got to get."

"Those dots don't represent rails that have to be laid, Marshal. The rails are already there. But our trains can't run on them until there's been some repair work done."

"I've ridden railroads all over this part of the country," Longarm said. "And I sure don't recall that one ever went where the dots are."

"There's no reason why you should've known about it," the trainmaster replied. "It never was a public line."

"Now, any man smart enough to make as much money as it'd take to build that much of a railroad would be too smart to build it if he didn't intend to make more money out of it."

"Usually, I'd agree with you," Blunt smiled. "But that was a private railroad." When he saw Longarm's bewildered frown, he went on, "How much do you know about the XIT Ranch, Marshal?"

"I know it was put together in a swap. The men that own the XIT made a trade. They built the Texas capital and Texas gave them a whole hell of a lot of land. I've heard the XIT takes in most of ten counties."

"Well, you're very close to being right. What most people don't know, and never did know, is that the XIT's owners built

167

their own private railroad from the north of their spread to the south. That's what the dotted line is."

"And you folks bought that right-of-way from the XIT?"

"Exactly. We came into Texas late, you know, which put us in a spot. We had the Fort Worth & Denver City boxing us in to the east, but their right of way goes up north in a big curve." Blunt traced the FW&DC line on the map and went on, "Our route's not much shorter, but it's a hell of a lot faster, because we don't have the grades to pull that they do."

"How much faster?"

"Oh, we figure we'll cut almost a full day off the run of a freight train hauling a full string of loaded cattle cars from the top of the Panhandle down here to Forth Worth. That means the cattle won't lose as much weight on the trip, so it'll pay the shippers to leave the Fort Worth & Denver City and ship with us."

"You say it cuts a full day off coming here. How much does it cut off going up there?"

"Hauling empties it should cut eight to ten hours off the run from here to Dalhart."

"Mister, that's just about how much time I need. You sure there ain't no trains running up that line right now?"

Shaking his head, the trainmaster said, "I'm not even sure the old XIT line is in shape to be used yet. That's why we haven't scheduled anything up there for another two weeks."

"Damn it! Right about now I'd sure like to be in McNelly's boots and be able to order up a special." Longarm stopped short. In his mind's eye he saw Billy Vail hand him the fat envelope containing expense vouchers, and heard Vail saying: *"Use these any way you have to. This is one time you won't be asked questions about anything you do."*

"How much—" Longarm began, then stopped. He set his jaw and went on in a rush, "How much would it cost me to get a special train to carry me up that straight line to Dalhart?"

For a moment Blunt stared at him. "I'd have to do some figuring. What kind of train?"

"About the least you can put together in a hurry. Engine, tender, one caboose. There won't be anybody going but me."

"Usually our rates require at least twenty-five first-class fares for a special, plus the extra pay for the crew, and a few other things."

"That sounds like a lot of money—" Longarm began.

168

"But I'll cut the price to the bone for you, Marshal," the trainmaster interrupted. "It'll be worth something to the St. Louis & Southwestern to set a record on that run that will make the FW&DC look like a backwoods jerkwater line."

Going to his desk, Blunt scribbled on a pad for a moment. He looked up at Longarm and named a figure. Longarm gulped, then nodded.

"I guess a government travel voucher's as good as cash?" he asked.

"Of course. So far the U. S. government's always paid us on the dot."

"Go ahead, then," Longarm said. "We got a deal, provided you can get me rolling in an hour or less, and provided you tell your train crew that they're going to have to make a faster run than they ever did before."

With the engineer tooting the whistle every ten or fifteen miles out of sheer high spirits, the special train rocketed over the uneven countryside.

Riding in the cupola of the caboose, Longarm gazed at the scenery rushing past. By high noon they'd pulled out of the shallow troughs of the Trinity and Brazos watersheds and mounted to the long, narrow flat-topped plateau that divided the Colorado and its tributaries from the Double Mountain Fork of the Brazos.

Grasslands and towns had been left behind after the special rolled with whistle shrieking through the little cowtown of Abilene. The rails ran due west now, chuffing across a landscape barren of growth, the beginning of short-grass country. An occasional ranch house could be seen in the distance, and once or twice the tracks skirted small settlements. The ground rose gradually in a western uptilt so gentle that the engineer needed to give the swaying special only a bit more throttle to maintain full speed.

Once news of the run had spread through the yards at Fort Worth, the railroad employees had worked with infectious enthusiasm. By the time Longarm returned from the White Elephant Saloon carrying his gear, the yards were buzzing with activity.

"I've got the board cleared for your special all the way to railhead," the trainmaster had said when Longarm came into his office to check on the progress being made. "After you get on the old XIT tracks, the road's clear anyhow. There won't be a thing to slow you down between here and where you're going."

"We've thought of a few things that should make your run faster, Marshal Long," the yardmaster had told Longarm. "We're putting on a pair of extra tenders to save you having to stop for coal and water. When one of the tenders is emptied, the engineer will just shunt it off on the first siding you pass. That ought to cut almost an hour off your time."

Just before the special pulled out, the engineer had come up to Longarm and said, "Mister, I'm going to give you a ride you never will forget. There's nothing but a few long easy grades up to where we switch to the XIT iron, and damn few curves. But if you wear false teeth, you better take 'em out and put 'em in your pocket, or you're apt to swallow 'em."

Gazing at the barren landscape, Longarm lighted a fresh cheroot from the butt of the one he'd smoked to a stub. The bottle of Tom Moore he'd bought at the White Elephant rested on the leather seat beside him. He'd already taken a few heart-warming sips, and now he tilted the bottle for another.

Old son, he told himself, *if this damn train don't fall apart, and if that stretch of old XIT track ain't gone to pot or busted up, you're liable to get to Dalhart in time to give Gil Bright the biggest surprise he's ever had in his whole life.*

Shortly before mid-afternoon the special switched to the old XIT trackage and headed north. By Longarm's rough reckoning, about 250 miles still lay between him and his destination. As he recalled the country from a long-ago case that had brought him there, the land ahead was tabletop-flat and rose in an upslope that was too regular and gentle to be called a grade. Both the spare tenders had been discarded now, and only the single tender that remained swayed between Longarm and the locomotive cab. He looked down on the engineer, who leaned far out to watch the uncertain roadbed while the fireman kept adding fresh coal to the bright red bed that crammed the firebox.

In spite of the speed the special was making, time seemed to pass faster and faster as the sun dropped lower in the west. Longarm looked out at the train's lengthening shadow flitting along the bare brown ground on his right and shook his head. He glanced at the tracks in front of the engine. They still stretched across the flat, featureless land. There was no sign of a house or building anywhere he looked. Indeed, the only man-made structures he'd seen since the train switched to the XIT line had been several holding corrals and loading chutes at trackside.

Far ahead, visible as a square-edged hump against the northern horizon, Longarm saw the outline of another loading chute. He watched it take shape, still distant. Beyond the chute he could see the rooflines of houses beginning to rise above the ragged edge of the flat prairie.

Damned if it don't look like you got it made, old son, he congratulated himself silently as he swung down from the cupola. *That's bound to be Dalhart on past that loading chute, and we ain't more'n ten, twelve miles from it now. Seems as though things are working out your way for a change.*

Longarm started toward the front of the caboose, intending to swing across to the tender and join the engineer and fireman in the locomotive when the chugging of the engine faltered and became a broken, thumping hiss instead of the steady song of power it had been until now. The caboose swayed and the metallic rasp of brakes being applied reached his ears. Slowly, the train came to a halt.

Swinging out of the caboose to the roadbed, Longarm ran along the tender. He arrived at the back of the locomotive just as the engineer was dropping from its cab.

"What's wrong?" Longarm asked anxiously.

"Water," the engineer said disconsolately. "We figured there'd be enough to get us there without much to spare, but it looks like we figured wrong."

"You mean there ain't any way we can keep going?"

"It takes steam to run the old hog," the engineer replied. "And nobody's figured out yet how to get steam without water."

Longarm looked ahead along the track. From his vantage point in the caboose, a dozen feet above the ground, he'd been able to see the loading chute and town. Now they lay out of sight below the horizon. The sun had dropped since the chute and the town fist came into sight. Reddening to sunset hue, its bottom edge already touched the jagged rim of the distant hills that thrust up to the west.

"Ten miles or more," Longarm said under his breath, more to himself than to the engineer. "A man on a horse can see seven miles in this flat country, but not more'n about three or four miles when he's standing flat-footed on the ground."

From the locomotive cab, where he'd been vainly twisting

171

knobs trying to get life back into the engine, the fireman called, "Marshal, you better come up here and take a look. I'm afraid we're about to get beat."

Longarm mounted the steps to the cab. The fireman had gone up the rungs that led to the tender and stood atop the water tank, gazing to the northeast. He pointed as Longarm joined him.

"Right over there."

Longarm followed the man's extended finger with his eyes. From the height at which he now stood, a thin plume of smoke above a long black line was visible on the horizon. "That'd be the train we been trying to beat?" Longarm asked.

"That's it. Fort Worth & Denver City."

Longarm was measuring distances with his eyes. He asked the fireman, "How does that train run from where it's at now? Looks to me like it'll miss the XIT chute up ahead, and the town, too."

"It won't. The track curves to the west about a mile from where the drag is now," the engineer explained. "It'll pull off the mainline and back into a siding to cut off the cattle cars at the chute. Then it'll ease along on another siding that goes to Dalhart. After it drops its freight and passengers, it comes back on the siding and hits the mainline again."

"Sorta doing it the hard way, I'd say," Longarm commented, his eyes on the distant train.

"Oh, they're going to move the town to the mainline, I've heard. There ain't more'n a dozen houses in the place."

"I make it about eight or nine miles to the chute," Longarm said thoughtfully. "How long's it going to take that train to get there?"

"Oh, about an hour an' a half, maybe a little longer."

"A man oughta be able to walk to that chute and get there about the time the train does," Longarm said. He started for the ladder. "You men do what you can here. I got business with that train when it gets to the chute."

Stopping only long enough to grab his rifle from the caboose, Longarm started for the chute. In the fading light of sunset he hurried along the tracks, getting off the gravelled right-of-way after the first few steps and making his way along the unbroken ground beside it. Now and then he broke into a run for a short distance, but he did not want to arrive at the chute winded and tired.

He had covered half the distance to the chute when the Fort Worth & Denver City train came into sight. It had changed direction since he first sighted it. The engine was now heading due west, toward the loading chute, its headlight catching the sunset's rays and glowing redly.

Longarm speeded up, but he was still a hundred yards from the chute when the train reached it and ground to a squealing halt. As a precaution, he dropped to the ground and lay flat, peering across the bare earth. He could see the chute and its surroundings clearly now. The chute stood beside a siding, with a series of small board corrals behind it. While Longarm watched the train it began moving, backing to shunt its string of cattle cars onto the siding beside the chute. It was a long train, with at least twenty boxcars and two passenger coaches in addition to the string of empty cattle cars.

There were three men moving around the cars now, brakemen who had jumped off as the train slowed. They were signaling to the engineer as the cars inched carefully back. Longarm studied the men on the ground. Though the light was fading, he could tell that none of them was Gil Bright. But he had not expected Bright to show himself yet. If the fugitive was on the train—and Longarm was confident of it—he would be holed up in one of the cattle cars. Stretched out on the ground, Longarm waited.

Spotting the cars took less time than Longarm had expected. Ten minutes after the train had pulled to a stop, it edged out of the siding that served the loading chute. It was much shorter now, but still had twenty or more boxcars and the passenger coaches behind the locomotive. The brakemen threw more switches and the train began backing on the siding that led to Dalhart, almost two miles from the chute.

With the departure of the chuffing train, the evening hush settled over the scene. Longarm began inching forward on his belly, snaking across the bare earth, his rifle in one hand. He did not stop until he was within fifty yards of the chute and the first cattle cars that stood on the siding in front of it.

In the deep silence and the fading light sounds were magnified. Longarm heard the scraping of feet on wood and the rasping of a cattle-car door sliding open. He brought his rifle up even before he saw the dark outline of a man emerge from the space between the cars and the chute. The man was carrying a rifle and moved slowly, favoring his right leg.

173

Longarm could not see his face in the growing dusk, but he did not need to. The limp was identification enough. He rose to his knees and leveled his Winchester.

"I'll give you one chance to give up, Gil!" he called across the distance that separated him. "You're covered. Don't make me kill you!"

Bright did not answer. He snapped his rifle up. His shot and Longarm's shattered the dusky silence only a split-second apart.

Chapter 20

Longarm heard the report of Gil Bright's rifle and felt the wind of the bullet's passage. He registered both the sound and sensation only subconsciously, for his eyes were fixed on the bad apple. He saw Bright's rifle fly from his hands as though it had been yanked away suddenly, and sail through the air. He heard the weapon clatter to the hard ground, but his eyes were watching Bright spin in his tracks and begin to crumple. The fugitive dropped to the earth and lay still.

Longarm had levered a fresh shell into the Winchester's chamber before the echoes of his first shot faded. Keeping the muzzle trained on Bright and his finger on the trigger, he walked cautiously up to the prone man. He'd seen more than one supposed corpse make a miraculous recovery and jump up shooting.

Bright did not move, and as Longarm reached him and stood over him, looking down, he saw the bright red of fresh blood staining Bright's shirt. He bent down for a closer examination just as Bright began to moan and stir. Longarm pinned the fugitive to the ground by shoving the Winchester's muzzle into his throat with ungentle pressure. Bright opened his eyes and looked up.

"Well," he said, "I guess your aim was better than mine. Or you pulled the trigger quicker."

"Whichever it was don't matter," Longarm replied. "How bad are you hit?"

Bright started to sit up, but Longarm kept the muzzle of his rifle firmly in place.

"My hand," Bright said. "It's bleeding all over me."

Longarm looked at the man more closely. Bright's right hand lay across his chest, and blood was seeping from it.

"You ain't too bad off," Longarm said coldly. "Looks like when my slug knocked your rifle away it took a big slice of meat off your trigger finger."

"Well, are you just going to stand there and let me bleed to death?" Bright demanded. "Do you intend to finish me off, or what?"

His voice as hard and cold as a lump of ice, Longarm answered, "I oughta just pull the trigger and get it over with, but I don't guess it's in me to shoot a man I've worked with in cold blood. I'll let the hangman do the job."

Bending down, Longarm yanked Bright's revolver out of its holster and tucked it into his waistband. He fished out his handcuffs and, in spite of the blood that still oozed from Bright's wound, snapped the cuffs around his wrists. Only then did he help Bright to his feet. He patted his prisoner's hip pockets, feeling for a handkerchief, felt the wad of a bandanna in one, and pulled it out and bound it around the wound.

"That'll keep you from bleeding like a stuck pig until you can get it fixed up proper," he said curtly. "Now, come on. We got to get over to the mainline in time to flag that train."

"I never thought I'd see the day when you'd be taking me in as a prisoner, Longarm," Bright said bitterly. "I think I'd rather you killed me."

"You'd be dead now if my slug hadn't hit your gun." The weapon had fallen a yard or so away from where they stood. Longarm nudged it with the toe of his boot. The rifle's action was dented, the trigger guard bent, the stock shattered. He said, "It ain't worth saving. Besides, you won't be needing it any longer."

"No," Bright replied thoughtfully. "I guess I won't. Even if you didn't kill me, Longarm, I'm a sick man. Chances are I won't live long enough to stand trial."

Longarm did not reply, but took Bright's unwounded arm and led him across the hundred yards of bare earth that separated the chute siding from the Dalhart siding. They stopped when they reached the rails, and Longarm released his prisoner's arm.

"You stay right where you are, Gil," he commanded. "I got a shell in the chamber of this Winchester, and if you try anything, I won't miss you this time."

"I wouldn't say you missed me with your other shot," Bright said through tight lips. "My hand hurts like hell, now that the feeling's coming back to it."

176

"Just grit your teeth and stand it." Longarm's voice showed no emotion. "I got some unfinished business to wind up and some new business to start."

Darkness was almost complete now. The only light was the glow that seeped from the fading crimson of the western horizon. The pair had been waiting by the tracks for only a few minutes when the locomotive's headlight glared into brilliance and with a whistle blast the train began inching toward them.

Even in the short distance from Dalhart to where Longarm waited with his prisoner the train gathered speed. Longarm took off his hat and tried to flag it down, but the engineer did not throttle back until Longarm stepped between the rails and stood firm, still waving his hat. Then the train squealed to a halt.

"What in hell you think you're doing?" the engineer shouted angrily, leaning from the cab. "That's a good way to get yourself killed."

"I stopped you, didn't I?" Longarm asked. "But that ain't here nor there. My name's Long. I'm a deputy United States marshal, and I got a wounded prisoner here that needs a doctor. I'm getting on with him, and I want you to back up to Dalhart, where he can be tended to."

"If you're looking for a doctor there, you're looking in the wrong place," the engineer said. "There's not any."

"How about someplace up ahead where you'll be stopping?"

"I don't stop again till we get to Trinidad, Marshal, and that's the end of the line. This rattler's not scheduled into Denver."

"Trinidad suits me just fine," Longarm told the engineer. "I'll switch to the Denver & Rio Grande there and get my man to the Denver jail by morning."

"If you can square things with the conductor, it's all right with me," the engineer said. "He's in the passenger coach. Or you can ride in the crummy with the brakies, if you'd rather. But if you're going to ride this haul, get on board and don't hold me up any longer. I don't want to have to try to make up time going through the mountains."

Longarm looked along the tracks toward the rear of the train. The caboose was between the freight cars and passenger coaches. "We'll get in the caboose," he told the engineer. "It'll save getting your passengers all stirred up. I'll look up the conductor and fix up with him about the fares."

Within five minutes from the time the train stopped, it was

177

on the mainline and gaining speed. Longarm and Gil Bright were settled in the caboose, Bright in a corner where he could not make a quick dive through one of the windows. Longarm sat beside him, answering the questions of the curious brakemen without giving them any real information other than the fact that Bright was a prisoner he was transporting to Denver.

Bright did not speak, and Longarm welcomed his prisoner's silence. He had no stomach for talking to the renegade lawman. As darkness set in, and the train mounted the long grade leading up the slopes of Mount Capulin, Bright fell into a doze, his head tilted back against the caboose wall.

In the uncertain light of the oil lamps that shed a dim glow from each side wall, Longarm studied the sleeping face of the handcuffed man, trying to reconcile the Gil Bright he'd once known and trusted with the thin, haunted-looking man he now saw.

Guess nobody's ever going to figure out what turns a good lawman into a bad apple, he mused. *Maybe just some kind of twist in their minds is to blame. Whatever it is, it's a sorry thing for a man to have to watch.*

Pulling his hat down over his eyes to let the brakemen think he was sleeping, but in reality watching Bright all the time, he sat silently until the train pulled into Trinidad.

"All right," he told Bright. "It's late, but I guess we can find a doctor to fix up your hand. Only I got two things to do first. One is to find out when the train to Denver comes through. And then I got to send a wire to the St. Louis & Southwestern and tell the trainmaster to send a tender full of water to them poor devils that got stranded out in the middle of noplace, and to send my saddle gear on to me in Denver."

"If it's all the same to you, Longarm, I'd like to have a drink before we hunt up that doctor," Bright said. "When I was trying to stay alive long enough to finish my job, I did what the doctors told me: quit drinking and smoking. But since it don't matter any more, I think I'm entitled to a drink, now."

"We might not see eye to eye on what you're entitled to," Longarm replied. "But maybe a drink would make us both feel a little bit better. We'll find a saloon and have one when I've tended to my chores."

By having the D&RG stationmaster send a message over railroad wires to Fort Worth, Longarm managed to get both his tasks finished with a single stop. He told the stationmaster,

"If you can steer me to a good doctor here in town, I'd be mighty obliged to you. You can see I got to get this man's hand fixed up."

"You'll find one of the best doctors in Colorado at the Baca Hotel right now," the stationmaster replied. "Doc Matthews. He's company doctor for most of the mines in this part of the state, and this just happens to be the week he's in Trinidad."

Walking down the street to the hotel, Longarm told Bright, "We've got four hours to kill before train time, and I don't fancy putting that much time in at one of these miners' saloons answering a lot of questions about why you got handcuffs on."

"You could take the cuffs off," Bright suggested.

"Sure, only I ain't about to. But if we're having a drink in a saloon, there might be some softheaded jackass that'd agree with you about taking off the cuffs. Then I'd be in a ruckus taming him down. No, what I'll do is buy a bottle and get a room in that hotel where the doctor stays. We'll wait in the room till train time. It'll be the best way to be sure we won't miss the doctor, too."

At the Baca Hotel, Longarm found that Dr. Matthews was out but was expected to return soon. He rented a room, asked the clerk to have the doctor stop in, and escorted Bright upstairs.

"I guess that hand of yours is hurting pretty bad by now," Longarm said, locking the door of the room. "You ain't worth me worrying about you, but we been through a few things together. So I'm going to take the cuffs off your hands and shackle one of your ankles to a chair rung. That way I can settle back a little bit, too."

Longarm stood his rifle in a corner, removed the handcuffs from Bright's wrists, and shackled his ankle to the rung of a straight chair in the middle of the room. He took off his hat and coat, putting Bright's pistol on the bureau out of the bad apple's reach, and opened the bottle of second-choice Maryland rye he'd had to settle for. He took the two heavy hotel tumblers that were on the bureau and poured generously. Handing one tumbler to Bright, he put the bottle down, went back to the table, and settled into the remaining chair.

For a moment neither man spoke. Then Bright said, "I guess you're wondering why I went gunning for those men."

"No. I figured out why. You set yourself above 'em."

"Damn it, Longarm, I *was* above them! You knew most of them. You must've seen them, pistol-whipping handcuffed

179

risoners, shooting a man after his gun was empty in a fight, etting up men to try to escape and backshooting them. Things you and I never did!"

"You're right, we never done them things. But that don't mean you got the right to be judge and jury and executioner all in one. You backshot Keller. And I'm betting he wasn't the first. Hell, when you turned bad apple, you got worse than they did!" Longarm fished a cheroot out of his vest pocket. "What I want to know is why." He struck a match and was about to light up when Bright replied.

"They were the bad apples, Longarm. Not me. And when I found out I had TB and was going to die pretty soon anyhow, I figured I might as well clean up things a little bit."

"Don't lie to me. You went out trying to get yourself killed because you wanted to leave your mother well fixed with that insurance money. You might've killed yourself if it hadn't been that the company wouldn't pay if you committed suicide."

Bright's jaw dropped. "You know about that?"

"I found out. Never mind how." The match Longarm was holding scorched his fingers. He dropped it and struck another. Lighting his cigar, he puffed luxuriously.

Unexpectedly, Bright said, "I haven't had a cigar for nearly two years, Longarm. How about lending me one of yours? I'll buy some for you tomorrow."

"Never mind," Longarm said. "I'll give you one."

He gave Bright a cigar and struck a match for him.

Bright inhaled, gave a gasping cough, and reached for the tumbler of whiskey. He drained the liquor at a gulp, but when he'd swallowed it the gasping still did not stop. Holding the glass out to Longarm, Bright motioned to the bottle on the bureau.

"Need another—swallow—quick!" he gasped.

Longarm took the glass to the bureau. He was pouring the liquor when a flicker of motion in the mirror caught his eyes. Bright was bent double in the chair, his head hanging down. Hurriedly putting down the bottle, Longarm turned to go help him just as Bright straightened up and levelled the small nickel-plated revolver he'd taken from his boot.

Bright's move caught Longarm in the middle of his incomplete turn; his feet being off balance slowed him down. By the time Longarm dived behind the bed, Bright had triggered the pistol and was thumbing the hammer back for a second shot. The two reports were spaced only a second or so apart. The first slug missed, shattering the mirror. The second pellet creased Longarm's thigh as he went down, but the wound from the little .32 was a mere scratch. Longarm slid under the bed, anticipating Bright's next move.

Bright had started moving as well, dragging the chair with him, trying to get around the bed to where he could get Longarm in his sights again. Longarm rolled under the bed. As Bright dragged the chair past him, he grabbed one of the chair legs and pulled. Bright fell heavily to the floor, the nickel-plated gun flying from his hand. By the time he'd recovered from the fall, Longarm had his own Colt in his hand and was standing over him.

Lying on the floor, Bright looked up and said coolly, "I never did shoot worth shit with my left hand."

"You were a damn fool to try it," Longarm snapped. "And I was a bigger damn fool for trusting you as far as I did."

"You knew I'd try, Longarm," Bright said calmly, as though they were discussing the weather. "And I knew you'd know I'd try."

Longarm nodded. "I figured you'd hang on to that hideaway whore's gun you used before. I wanted to see how far you'd go in using it on me. We were pretty good friends one time. Now I know just how bad an apple you are."

"Why didn't you kill me?" Bright demanded. "Damn it, I'd rather go quick from a bullet than stand on a trap and wait for the hangman to pull that lever."

"Looks like that's what you'll be doing, though," Longarm said, with no mercy in his voice. "And it can't be too soon."

A sharp knock sounded at the door. Longarm stepped over to open it, his leg reminding him to take it easy. A middle-aged man in a sober black serge suit stood there, a slight frown creasing his brow.

"Marshal Long?" he asked. When Longarm nodded, he said, "I'm Dr. Troy Matthews. The desk clerk said there was a man here needing my professional attention." He looked at Longarm's leg. "I suppose it's you, from the fresh blood on your trousers."

"There's two of us need a look now, I guess, but all I got is a little scratch. Come on in, Doctor."

"I'm not a specialist in this kind of case," Matthews said, putting his small satchel on the table. "Most of my practice is among the coal miners here and in Durango, who are very susceptible to pulmonary diseases, but I've certainly seen enough gunshot wounds to take care of yours."

"Look at him first," Longarm said, jerking his thumb at Bright. "I ain't hurting all that much."

Matthews flexed Bright's forefinger, fingered the flap of flesh torn loose by the rifle's trigger-guard, and said, "A stitch or two will fix the flesh wound, but I'll have to splint your finger, and I'm afraid it'll always be a bit stiff."

Matthews opened his case and with the deftness brought by experience soon had the wound cared for. He made equally short work of the shallow crease in Longarm's thigh, for the glancing slug from the pocket pistol had merely scraped away the skin in a line little more than an inch long and half as wide.

While Matthews was applying a gauze compress with plaster over the small lesion, Bright asked, "Did you say you're a specialist in lung disease, Doctor?"

"That's my chief practice, yes."

"Maybe you can take a look at my chest, then. I'd like to know how much longer I'm going to last," Bright said.

"You're suffering from tuberculosis?" Matthews asked.

Bright nodded. "And pretty far gone, from what other doctors have told me."

"Very well," Matthews said after looking questioningly at Longarm, who nodded assent. "Unbutton your shirt."

"I'm afraid you've not been diagnosed properly," the doctor told Gil Bright. "I'd have to make a sputum test to be absolutely sure, but what you have is a small abscess in your trachea, not your lungs."

"You sure of that, Doctor?" Longarm frowned.

"Quite sure. I studied under Anderson in London and Dubos in Paris, and I've examined hundreds of tubercular miners in the past ten years. Your lungs are quite healthy. The lesion in your trachea creates a mucus discharge that might deceive some doctors who rarely see tuberculosis, but I'm positive my diagnosis is correct."

When neither Bright nor Longarm spoke, Matthews said, "My fee for professional services is ten dollars, Marshal."

Longarm extracted a gold eagle from his trouser pocket and handed it to Matthews. After the doctor had gone, the two men looked at one another with sober faces.

"What a damned fool I've been," Bright said at last. "I listened to a quack doctor and it's ruined my life."

Longarm took a cheroot from his pocket and lighted it before

182

he spoke. His voice was as hard as flint, but an undertone of sadness crept into it.

"I'll say this much, Gil—and then I don't want to talk to you no more," he began, unmindful of the fact that until now he hadn't addressed Bright by his first name. "When lawmen turn into bad apples it ain't because of what somebody done to 'em. It's a rot from inside. And, sooner or later, it's bound to come out. When it starts to show, there ain't only one way to cure it. And that's the cure you're heading for—from a judge and a length of rope.

"Now get yourself ready. We got a train to Denver to catch."

Look for

**LONGARM AND THE
LONE STAR VENGEANCE**

coming in July!

In *Longarm and the Lone Star Legend*,
your favorite western hero met an exciting
new action team! Now don't miss the
thrill-packed second novel starring
Jessie, Ki and Longarm!

Also, watch for

LONGARM AND THE BOUNTY HUNTERS

fifty-seventh novel in the bold
LONGARM series from Jove

coming in August!

LONGARM

Explore the exciting Old West with
one of the men who made it wild!

_____	06576-5	LONGARM #1	$2.25
_____	06807-1	LONGARM ON THE BORDER #2	$2.25
_____	06809-8	LONGARM AND THE WENDIGO #4	$2.25
_____	06810-1	LONGARM IN THE INDIAN NATION #5	$2.25
_____	06950-7	LONGARM IN LINCOLN COUNTY #12	$2.25
_____	06070-4	LONGARM IN LEADVILLE #14	$1.95
_____	06155-7	LONGARM ON THE YELLOWSTONE #18	$1.95
_____	06951-5	LONGARM IN THE FOUR CORNERS #19	$2.25
_____	06627-3	LONGARM AT ROBBER'S ROOST #20	$2.25
_____	06628-1	LONGARM AND THE SHEEPHERDERS #21	$2.25
_____	07141-2	LONGARM AND THE GHOST DANCERS #22	$2.25
_____	07142-0	LONGARM AND THE TOWN TAMER #23	$2.25
_____	07363-6	LONGARM AND THE RAILROADERS #24	$2.25
_____	07066-1	LONGARM ON THE MISSION TRAIL #25	$2.25
_____	06952-3	LONGARM AND THE DRAGON HUNTERS #26	$2.25
_____	07265-6	LONGARM AND THE RURALES #27	$2.25
_____	06629-X	LONGARM ON THE HUMBOLDT #28	$2.25

Available at your local bookstore or return this form to:

JOVE
Book Mailing Service
P.O. Box 690, Rockville Centre, NY 11571

Please send me the titles checked above. I enclose
Include $1.00 for postage and handling if one book is ordered; 50¢ per book for
two or more. California, Illinois, New York and Tennessee residents please add
sales tax.

NAME _____

ADDRESS _____

CITY _____ STATE/ZIP _____

(allow six weeks for delivery)   5

LONGARM

Explore the exciting Old West with one of the men who made it wild!

____ 06580-3	LONGARM IN NORTHFIELD #31	$2.25
____ 06582-X	LONGARM AND THE GOLDEN LADY #32	$2.25
____ 06583-8	LONGARM AND THE LAREDO LOOP #33	$2.25
____ 06584-6	LONGARM AND THE BOOT HILLERS #34	$2.25
____ 06630-3	LONGARM AND THE BLUE NORTHER #35	$2.25
____ 06953-1	LONGARM ON THE SANTA FE #36	$2.25
____ 06954-X	LONGARM AND THE STALKING CORPSE #37	$2.25
____ 07142-0	LONGARM AND THE COMANCHEROS #38	$2.25
____ 07412-8	LONGARM AND THE DEVIL'S RAILROAD #39	$2.50
____ 07413-6	LONGARM IN SILVER CITY #40	$2.50
____ 07070-X	LONGARM ON THE BARBARY COAST #41	$2.25
____ 07127-7	LONGARM AND THE MOONSHINERS #42	$2.25
____ 07091-2	LONGARM IN YUMA #43	$2.25
____ 05600-6	LONGARM IN BOULDER CANYON #44	$2.25
____ 05601-4	LONGARM IN DEADWOOD #45	$2.25
____ 05602-2	LONGARM AND THE GREAT TRAIN ROBBERY #46	$2.25
____ 07418-7	LONGARM IN THE BADLANDS #47	$2.50
____ 07414-4	LONGARM IN THE BIG THICKET #48	$2.50
____ 06250-2	LONGARM AND THE EASTERN DUDES #49	$2.25
____ 06251-0	LONGARM IN THE BIG BEND #50	$2.25
____ 06252-9	LONGARM AND THE SNAKE DANCERS #51	$2.25
____ 06253-7	LONGARM ON THE GREAT DIVIDE #52	$2.25
____ 06254-5	LONGARM AND THE BUCKSKIN ROGUE #53	$2.25
____ 06255-3	LONGARM AND THE CALICO KID #54	$2.25
____ 06256-1	LONGARM AND THE FRENCH ACTRESS #55	$2.25